Unstable Environment

By Marcia Colette

Other works by Marcia Colette
Half Breed
from Double Dragon e-Publishing

Unstable Environment

By Marcia Colette

Parker Publishing LLC

ISIS is an imprint of Parker Publishing LLC.

Copyright © 2008 by Marcia Colette
Published by Parker Publishing LLC
12523 Limonite Ave., Ste. #440-438
Mira Loma, California 91752
www.parker-publishing.com

This book is a work of fiction. Characters, names, locations, events
and incidents (in either a contemporary and/or historical setting) are
products of the author's imagination and are being used in an
imaginative manner as part of this work of fiction. Any resemblance
to actual events, locations, settings, or persons, living or dead, is
entirely coincidental.

ISBN: 978-1-60043-035-0
First Edition

Manufactured in the United States of America

Cover Design by Jaxadora Design

Dedication and Acknowledgements

I'd like to thank my terrific editor Jackie who helped me make this a stronger book. To the fabulous, Lori Perkins for taking a chance with me. My biggest fan and beta reader, RJ, you rock! Kathy, you're a well of inspiration and to that, I owe you my sincerest thanks. The same goes to the Ultimate BiAW crew and Magical Musings. Huge thanks to Edie for her blurb incite. Mark S., Debbie M., and my amazing crit partners, Carol, Gloria, and Tish. I can't thank you enough for your encouragment. A special thanks to Emily Rose for loaning me her shoulder and Jenna Black for introducing me to an amazing group of writers (HCRW). My loving family, you make me want to be a better person. Aunt Helen, you're the best "big sister" I could have. Last, though not least, I think God for getting me here and the incredible journey I have yet to discover.

Chapter 1

The ringing bells and shrill buzzers from the game booth grated on Sinclair Duval's last nerve. Every time someone won or hit a bull's eye, triggering a buzzer, she closed her eyes and prayed for the torture to end. The only good thing about Jungle Kingdom was it made for a nice place to go for indoor fun during the chilly winters.

Sinclair spent the last eight days stuck in the cockpit of a commercial airliner traveling between Raleigh-Durham, Orlando, and DC. It was a small price if she wanted to switch shifts with some of the other pilots to have a few days off at the end of the month. Those days she reserved for her three-year-old niece, Nahla.

"Hey girl." Barb Lowens placed her purse on the picnic table and sat on the bench across from her. She helped her five-year-old unlace his shoes before shooing him off to the Jelly Bean Jumping Tent. "Where's Nahla?"

Sinclair pointed at the tent. "The same place where your son's headed."

Both women met by accident at Jungle Kingdom a few months ago when she needed a Band-Aid for Nahla's skinned knee. She pointed Sinclair in the right direction and they've been friends ever since. Both women made it a point to meet once a month to go through the torture of the crowds, screaming children, and outrageous prices.

Barb shook her head and smiled. "How do you do it? Raising a daughter while flying a big commercial jet. Your sister must be a godsend."

Ha! What a crock.

Sinclair and Nahla pretended to be mother and daughter whenever they came here. She didn't want sympathy for that worthless skeleton stretched out in her closet. She would rather it go away, but it was too hard to get rid of her drunken-pothead sister, Mina.

Nahla's mother was a real piece of work. Whenever Mina disappeared, Sinclair had to shoulder the task of finding Nahla a babysitter while she flew across state lines. Although Mina swore she never tried anything harder than marijuana, Sinclair caught her trying to "loan" her newborn out for a bag of LSD. Since that day, Sinclair refused to leave those two alone if she could help it. With Mina's arrest record, Social Services looked for any reason to take Nahla. Sinclair was the only thing that stood between them. Had their parents been alive, things might have been different. Maybe.

Sinclair glanced at her watch. "You're late, Barb. They're about to let the kids out of the Jumping Bean."

Her friend waved a dismissive hand. "Phil finally got himself another contract. It's not a big job, but at least it'll help. I made him a congratulatory breakfast this morning."

"Mmmm hmmm. Depending upon how his day goes, he might be giving you a big 'thank you' tonight."

"That's what I'm hoping for."

Both women laughed.

From the corner of her eye, Nahla's sweet smile made Sinclair's laughter trickle into a heartfelt smile. She cursed herself for not taking off more time from work to be with her. Her niece grinned with every bounce inside the Jumping Bean tent. Two pigtails bounced on either side of her head as she jumped around on the air-filled trampoline. She never thought a child not birthed from her own womb could fill her with so much happiness.

Sinclair ran her fingers through her short, corkscrew spirals. Both aunt and niece had the same golden brown hue that earned compliments from complete strangers. Sinclair was one of the women fitness gurus hated. She didn't have to work hard to keep her slender figure.

So why couldn't a nice guy see that? All she ever seemed to attract was Mina's raggedy leftovers who looked like just they stepped out of solitary confinement.

"Earth to Sinclair." Barb fanned her hand in front of her. "Girl, are you having a flashback or something?"

She shrugged. "Just thinking about family is all," she lied. "It hurts to see all these families around here and all I've got is me and

Nahla."

Barb folded up her son's coat. "Be grateful you have that. Some women aren't as fortunate. They've either got a fool for a daddy or they're so damn career-minded that they don't have time for a family."

Sinclair flinched. Once upon a time, she was that career-minded woman...until her sister called about the bank taking the house. She cut her international flights, refused two promotions, and took shorter legs just so she could be home with her family. Her paycheck got them out of the red, but three years later she still struggled to keep them in the black. It would help if Mina could hold down a job for more than one month at a time.

She sighed. "Maybe. I wish there was more I could do for Nahla. It's just so hard and..." She let that thought go before Mina's name entered the picture.

"Shoot, girl. You're lucky you found out about her stupid father when you did. A crack head like that has no business being around a child. Just be thankful those drugs didn't mess up your little girl."

"She's too young to tell right now." She hoped to God there wasn't.

Her friend stared at her. "The doctor's didn't say anything?"

Sinclair nodded. "They said Nahla could develop some learning problems later on down the road. Or maybe something like ADD. We just don't know yet."

If that ever happened, Sinclair would beat her sister with a crowbar. She couldn't get her hands on Brian, Nahla's father, because he had disappeared two months after his baby was born.

"Stop beatin' yourself up." Barb unscrewed the cap off her bottled water. "Nahla's fine and there are plenty of men out there. You'll find one. You just have to stick with it. Heck, I'm surprise you haven't run into one of those cute Captains of yours. Do a little pilot to co-pilot."

"Girl, please. Just about all of them are white and I feel funny dating outside of my race. I still want to give a decent brotha a try. You know. Keep hope alive?"

"Good luck. Even the white girls are sinking their claws into our decent men."

"You need to stop."

Barb chuckled. "Don't mind me. Look, I'm sure the right guy is out there, if you opened your mind a little. Now take that sweet piece of Hispanic juju over there in first-aid. Hoooooney, if I could get away with it, I'd make sure my son has an accident all the time."

Sinclair's jaw dropped. "Girl, you need to stop. Here you are a married woman and you're still spying the eye candy."

"Girlfriend, just because I'm married doesn't mean I can't stop looking." She cut her eyes to the first-aid office on the other side of the indoor park.

Sinclair couldn't argue. The guy was as fine as a piece of expensive marble. That rugged, Antonio Banderas look worked for him.

A loud bell rang, signaling the end of the ride. Sinclair and Barb gathered outside the entrance behind the line where the parents claimed their children. As soon as Nahla poked her head through the slit opening, her face beamed in delight.

Sinclair's heart swelled again. Seeing her niece this happy made her happy.

The attendant lifted Nahla out of the attraction. Her little feet scampered across the area rug heading straight off for Auntie.

Sinclair enveloped her niece in a hug. "Did you have fun, baby?"

Nahla pulled away first and lifted up her foot to her aunt. "Mmmm-hmmm. Can I do 'gain?"

Sinclair knelt and began covering up Nahla's dirty sock with a small sneaker. "How about we try some of the other rides first? If there's nothing else, we'll come back here. Deal?"

Nahla nodded, her pigtails jerking about either side of her head. "Deal."

Cedric, Barb's son held up a bloody finger. "Mommy, my finger hurts."

Looking at Sinclair, Barb grinned. "Ask and you shall receive. We've gotta go to first-aid."

"Oh, lord," Sinclair laughed. "You oughta be ashamed of yourself. Using your child like that."

"No shame, girl. My son is in need of medical attention. Wanna come?"

She finished with Nahla's shoes and stood. "I won't be able to keep a straight face."

"That's because your jaw will be droppin' once you spy a piece of that El Niño boo-tay."

"How about we meet you guys somewhere?"

"Ooooo, Aunt--! Uh...I mean...Mommy..." Nahla pointed at the giant jungle gym.

Sinclair's looked up and her stomach tightened.

That jungle-gym maze was three stories tall. Sure it looked like a great place for Hide-N-Seek, but something about those multicolored tubes bothered her. They looked too small and tight. Even though the sign read adults less than 150 pounds could enter it didn't help. Nahla would want Auntie Sin to go with her for sure.

"Looks like you've got your hands full," Barb said. "How about we meet you there?"

She gulped, unable to take her eyes off the monstrosity. "Uh…"

Nahla squeezed her hand and began tugging. "Peeeeeze, Pretty peeeeeze?"

Sinclair rolled her eyes. "All right, baby." Letting her niece lead her away, she looked over her shoulder at her friend again. "We'll meet you over there."

Barb nodded and dragged her son off to the first-aid office.

Nahla stopped twice to tug wedgies from the back of her overalls along the way. Sinclair wasn't in any hurry to feed her light touch of claustrophobia. However, if she could sit for hours inside a small cockpit, then there was no reason why she couldn't do this. Right?

Scooping Nahla in her arms, she marched to the jungle gym, determined to conquer her fears. Before she could kick off her sandals, Nahla's rear wiggled through one of the tubes.

"Hold on." She grabbed her niece's overalls. "We're not going that way. This way." She lifted her up on a rope net. At least that bought her some time before she had to climb through one of those suffocating tubes.

Fifteen minutes of screaming children inside the 3-D maze had worked a headache between Sinclair's temples. She stuck her head out of a tube and almost collided with another adult chasing after their child. When Nahla led her to a rope bridge, Sinclair had serious doubts that the ropes would hold her weight. At least there was a vat of foam blocks below to break her fall.

By the time they made it to the top of the three-story maze, Sinclair halted Nahla so that she could rest on the padded floor.

"Having fun?" She swiped the sweat beading on her forehead.

The little girl nodded. "Can we do round next?"

"Round?"

"Mmmm-hmmm. The one wit' the horsy."

"Oh…you mean Merry-Go-Round. Sure." She'd agree to just about anything to get them out of this place.

Pop! Screeeeeeeeeeeeech!

That didn't sound good. Did the maze sway? Other than the sounds of little kids running and laughing nothing seemed out of the ordinary.

"Sweetie," she said, taking her niece's hand and standing her up. "I think we should go."

"Down?"

"Yeah. I don't think—"

A loud grinding noise cut her off. Then, silence shattered the wild enjoyment below. Other parents and children must have felt it too. This thing wasn't so safe after all.

Screams broke out. Sinclair grabbed Nahla and shoved her through the tube leading down to the next level.

She never had a chance to crawl in behind her.

Plastic tubes and cables rain down around them, tossing and throwing their bodies in different directions. A harsh buckle cracked Nahla's tub in half and sent both of them plummeting three stories to the cement floor. Sinclair screamed.

Chapter 2

Sinclair jerked awake. "Where's my baby? Where is she? *Nahlaaaaaaaaaa!*"

Hands grabbed her. Pain shot through her left shoulder. Sinclair jerked away. Agonizing pain exploding throughout her nervous system. She clutched her arm and fell into the pillows.

"Relax," said a soothing voice with a Spanish accent. "You're okay. Does your shoulder still hurt?"

Gulping, she chanced a quick nod before snapping her eyes open. "Where's my niece? What have you done with her?"

Rio Velasquez fumbled with the sling he was about to use to secure her dislocated shoulder. She woke up so fast the he nearly jumped out of the window. Considering he was a were-cheetah always on his guard, that was a hard thing to do.

Despite Nahla at the forefront of her mind, Sinclair couldn't help noticing the handsome olive man sitting next to her. The thick black waves of his hair caught her eye first. He had the most amazing dark eyes. Haunted almost. Light three o'clock shadow dusted his jaw and cheeks. She knew she saw him somewhere before, but couldn't put her finger on it.

"May I?" he asked, holding up a sling he had spent the last couple of minutes making.

Sinclair forgot about clutching her hand to her chest and an achy shoulder to boot. Another gulp and a quick nod.

Helping her sit up, he eased the sling around her head and tucked her arm inside. He couldn't resist a quick whiff of her hair. The scent of sweet flowers made his mouth water. It was a relief from the antiseptic smell of the hospital.

However, the pained look on her face drew him out of his revelry. The woman in his arms had been through a lot. Thank goodness his medicinal herbs seemed to work on her. Had she and the child died, his were-cheetah King, Dante, would be facing more questions and possible charges. After all, his people owned Jungle Kingdom.

"That should help." Rio sat his hip next to her on the gurney. "My name's Rio Velasquez. I'm a physician's assistant. You were tossing in your sleep and the sling came off. This one might be a little better."

Now, she remembered that face. He was the Aztec God who ran the first-aid station at Jungle Kingdom.

"Where am I?" Sinclair gritted her teeth through the pain. "Where's my niece?"

Rio sighed. "Is there someone we should call?"

Panic tore through her. Had it not been for the pain reminding her to keep still, she would have pounced on the man for answers.

Mina would've been a great person to call if it weren't for her having a track record of unreliability. What good would it do her now when they really needed her? Chances are Mina would be so overwrought with "anguish" that she would drown her sorrows with whiskey and a few joints. Sinclair and Nahla had nobody. "No," she mumbled.

He blinked. "Then it's just you and your niece?"

She fixed her eyes on him, doing her best to look menacing. "I won't ask you again. Where's Nahla?"

He didn't want to be the bearer of bad news. Still, if it were his child he would want to know. "I'll bring you to her." Rio left the room. When he returned, he pushed a wheelchair next to the bed and offered the fragile woman a hand.

Unanswered questions flooded Sinclair's mind. Where was he taking her? Why didn't he just answer her question? Where were they now? What was going on? Instead of voicing them, she took his hand and let him help her sit up.

Never in her life, had she touched a hand so soft. His warmth enveloped her like the cozy heat of a fireplace. She leaned into him and slid off the bed. Weakened knees buckled, collapsing her against his chest. Rio caught her, his eyes taking a moment to meet hers. The warmth heated her insides.

Rio's heart tripped. He had been around strong women for so long having one this helpless in his arms was foreign. For a moment, he forgot what he was supposed to do. A blink brought him back to reality. When he helped her into the wheelchair, something tugged on him. Though it hurt to see her like this, he knew he needed to distance himself from humans. This one in particular.

Less than a minute later, they entered the elevator, up one more level, and exited onto the Pediatric Critical Care Wing.

"Where are we?" Sinclair asked, glimpsing inside the rooms as he wheeled her down the hall.

"You're at Parkside Memorial."

"Why? Isn't Wake closer?"

He couldn't help staring into the rooms as they passed. Rio hated the medicinal smell. He could smell the sickness and death. He wanted to help everyone, but couldn't. Helping these people would mean bringing humans one step closer to their hidden world.

"This is the best hospital in the Triangle area," he replied. "Don't knock it."

"But it's too—"

"Expensive? Don't worry about that. The Martinellis said to spare no expense."

"Who are the Martinellis?"

"The owners of Jungle Kingdom."

"What?" She tried to grab the wheel to stop them, but her fingers slipped off the handles.

Ignoring her efforts to stall, Rio pushed open a door and wheeled her inside.

Nahla lay on the bed wearing animal-print training pants. It was the best way to make room for all the tubes that stemmed from the girl's tiny body. A cast from her toes to her thigh encased her left leg. A large white bandage fitted over her right side with a chest tube running out the center. Suction cups glued to the other side of her chest, wired into beeping monitors at the head of her bed. Another cast was on her right arm, extending it out to side with a rod that propped it away from her body. Her chest rose and fell with the clicks of the ventilator. What used to be one of the prettiest faces in her aunt's world had turned into a swollen mass of cuts and bruises.

Air flooded Sinclair's lungs as she drew her hands up to her agape mouth. Nothing could have prepared her for blow to the gut and twist of her heart. She planted her feet on the floor and pushed off the chair before Rio could move her closer. Everything in her pain-ridden body numbed. She couldn't take her eyes off her baby girl.

Sinclair broke. Leaning on the rail, she clutched the metal until her knuckles turned white. Tears blurred her vision. She hardly noticed Rio lowering the bar. She wanted to touch her baby. Sinclair hoisted her sore body on the bed and pressed kisses to her niece's swelled cheek.

"It's going to be okay," she whispered, clutching her niece's lifeless fingers. "It's okay. Auntie Sin's right here. I'm not going anywhere."

Sinclair swiped the tears off her soaked cheeks. "She's going to need physical therapy. What else? She'll…she'll need round-the-clock nursing too. I'll pay for everything. I'll find a way to…" A thought flashed through her mind. She glared at Rio. "You find that bastard! I want Martinelli. He's going to pay for this. I'll sue the fucking cotton out of his pants!"

Rio touched her shoulder. She shrugged him off. He stepped back. Ms. Duval was upset and had every reason to be, he told himself. After all, this was her flesh and blood. Had their roles been reversed, he would have shaken the hospital from its foundation too.

"Ms. Duval," he said, in a calm voice, "I understand how upset you are, but you have to under—"

"What?" she spat. "Is that bastard trying to shuck his obligations by bringing us to the best hospital *his* money can buy? Look at her! There's not enough money in the world that can fix this."

Rio couldn't believe it. For a woman who seemed so delicate a few minutes ago, Sinclair burned with a fire that made him think raging inferno. He also knew if something bad happened to her niece, it would awaken the wild animal inside her, begging to get out. As much as he lived on the wild side himself, he didn't want to see her go crazy on anyone.

"Ms. Duval," he said, "your niece is dying. Most of her organs were damaged in the accident. It's a good thing you woke when you did." He paused, taking in a deep sigh. "Nahla might not make it through the night."

"Who are you to tell me my niece's going to die? You don't know that. Where's a doctor?"

Again, Rio held his hands up in defense. "I'm also a healer of unorthodox medicine. If you want me to help your niece, I can."

"How?" she spat.

Rio glanced over his shoulder. He could hear people coming down the hall, but couldn't place the steps. They could be anyone.

Should he even risk his neck to tell her this?

In the last twenty-four hours aunt and niece lay unconscious in the hospital, Rio spent most of his time back and forth between their rooms, holding the hand of one then going to the other. He couldn't get the delicate feel of Nahla's fingers curled around his index finger out of his head. She was so small and so innocent. Children had that effect on him or he wouldn't have asked to work part time at the first-aid station. He couldn't flush the horrific image of digging through the rubble to find Nahla's crumpled little body buried underneath a large tube out of his head. After seeing a hand holding the little girl's ankle, he moved more rubble to find Sinclair. Never in his life had he seen anything like that. The hurt went so deep that he wanted to gouge out his own heart out to keep the pain away.

"Like I said, I'm a healer among my people." Rio paused, sucking in a quick breath. "I'm not sure if my herbs can help your niece the way they've helped you."

"Excuse me?"

He hesitated, eyes burrowing into hers. "Your injuries were severe but not like hers. You still need more healing, but right now it's your niece who needs—"

A throat cleared behind him. Rio damned himself for not being faster.

Chapter 3

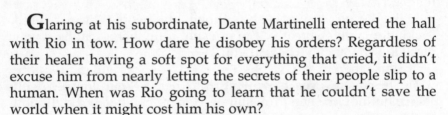

Glaring at his subordinate, Dante Martinelli entered the hall with Rio in tow. How dare he disobey his orders? Regardless of their healer having a soft spot for everything that cried, it didn't excuse him from nearly letting the secrets of their people slip to a human. When was Rio going to learn that he couldn't save the world when it might cost him his own?

Rio knew his King was about to let him have it. Between the baldhead and the black goatee, Dante had a knack for looking dangerous. He couldn't miss it in those narrowed eyes. The way his smoke gray suit fit his linebacker body, the man had enough muscle to reek of intimidation.

They stopped in the hall just outside the door, Rio gulped. "Before you say anything—"

"What the hell do you think you're doing?" Dante clenched his jaw. "I let you use the herbs on the woman. If it's not enough to help her niece, then there's nothing more you can do."

"*Mi Dios, hombre*, do you know she's planning to sue?"

"That's why I have lawyers, Rio. We settle this out of court. Pay the woman off, then she can go and have as many children as she likes."

Rio's jaw dropped. Did he just hear the callousness he thought he had heard? "Dante, that child is all she's got and that's just her niece. There's no mother or father, so God only knows what happened that they're not in the picture. We're talking about her entire world."

A twitch worked beneath Dante's right cheek. "We can't afford the publicity. I just spoke to reporters about the incident. I made a promise that I'd take care of the aunt and niece and that's what I'll do. But we're *not* miracle workers."

Rio shook his head, focus drilling into his King. "You have no idea what's going on. You weren't in there watching her cry at the sight of her niece. You weren't the one who had to look her in the eyes and tell her that her baby was going to die."

"Is this about you or them? You know how fragile these humans are. Or do I need to remind you about Ashley?"

How dare he bring her up? Had he not known that Dante could beat him in a fight, he would have torn the man's throat out.

Ashley was his fiancée. Rio knew it from the day she bumped into him at a party. He had no problem with winning her affections and bedding her in a week's time. She wanted to wait a few months before making it official, but he could have married her that night and spent the rest of his life with her.

His clan picked a lousy time to enter into a territorial dispute with the Charlotte Coalition. Rio distanced himself from Ashley to keep her safe. His people, the Triangle Coalition, ended up putting Charlotte in their place. By the time the war ended, he decided to return to his mate.

He was too late. Someone from Charlotte had raped her and left her unable to bear children. Ashley found out about their secret existence and spent years rocking back and forth at St. Joseph's Hospital for Mental Health. Five years ago, the nurses at St. Joseph's found her hanging from one of the pipes in the day room.

Rio got his revenge. He went after the men who raped her and killed them. He hadn't been the same since. Until eighteen months ago, he stopped practicing medicine and lived as a recluse in the mountains. Dante, one of his best friends, talked him into coming back to work part-time at Jungle Kingdom.

Now his "best friend" stood before him, condemning him for something he wanted to set right. This wasn't Sinclair's fault any more than Ashley's rape wasn't hers. The excuse about being in the wrong place at the wrong time just didn't cut it anymore.

The accident at Jungle Kingdom was a setup. Everyone knew it wasn't spotty craftsmanship. As the primary owner, Billie Martinelli, Dante's mate, was always careful to dot every "*i*" and cross every "*t*" when it came to doing business with humans. Rio knew what the problem was. The Charlotte Coalition refused to walk away without throwing a fit. They would do anything to drive his people into the ground, including financial ruin.

Dante glanced down the hall, wrinkling his nose with a sniff.

Either he loved the smell of antiseptic or something else had his attention.

Nurses excused themselves as they cut between the two shapeshifters. Dante followed them with his eyes before turning his head in the opposite direction. He stepped across the tiled floor, nose sniffing out spots on the wall.

Rio glanced over his shoulder, hoping the medical staff didn't think he had lost his mind. In fact, he had hoped his King wasn't crazy either.

"What are you doing?" he asked, slightly irritated at his leader.

"Sniffing out a scent."

"So?"

Dante lifted his eyes from the railing beside Rio and stared at his beta cat. "You're the only cheetah I've allowed to have contact with the Duvals."

Panic ripped through Rio. If Dante and Billie had forbidden their people from visiting the hospital, then their word was law. Either someone in their clan had broken that law or...someone from another clan paid the Duvals a visit. Even worse, they found the scent right outside little Nahla's room.

"Damn."

Dante's eyes narrowed. "The woman and child are off limits from here on out. If this trail means what I think it does, then Charlotte will use them to get to us."

Rio kept his voice low, eyes cutting left and right. "How can you write them off like that?"

"They're human beings; that's how. Besides, the little girl is beyond hope."

"You certainly didn't lack any hope when you trekked twenty miles into the woods to find me. Not only did you succeed, but you convinced me to come back so that I could help deliver Salome's triplets. Forgive me for not being able to turn my compassion on and off like that."

"The sympathetic man you once knew doesn't have that luxury anymore. I speak for Billie when I say we'll do whatever it takes to ensure our people continue to thrive."

"So how about starting with the obvious first? Like how they got inside the park?"

Dante didn't answer him right away. He placed his palm on the metal handle and shoved the staircase door open. When he stepped onto the landing, he motioned for his friend to follow. It wasn't until after the door closed and Dante leaned over the railing, listening for footsteps, did he answer. "George, our maintenance guy, has disappeared."

"Tell me you at least got a chance to interrogate him before you killed him."

Dante stared at is friend. "I planned on sending the head back to his leader as a warning, but Marianne beat me to it. He fired the first shot, so she slashed his throat in self-defense."

Rio jammed his hands in his pockets. "We're going to war with Charlotte, aren't we?"

"My friend, we were at war with them a long time ago. Like when the police received an anonymous call about serving alcohol without a permit and them finding the crates of cheap whiskey planted in our store room."

"I'll need supplies," Rio replied. "I'll have to go down river to Donna's place to gather ingredients for poultices too. She'll want something...in trade."

He lifted his head upward. Did he hear a crack? In the musty smell of the light gray stairwell, they were the only people there. Or so Rio thought.

He pointed upward and looked at his King for confirmation. Dante gave him a slight nod.

A metal door clanged opened and slammed shut.

Rio sprinted off, taking the stairs four and five at a time due to his cheetah speed. He climbed three and a half floors in a matter of seconds before he stopped and sniffed the air. The were-cheetah's scent stopped too.

Someone had overheard their conversation. If the eavesdropper ran, then it meant they would take their information back to Sloan, the Charlotte Coalition's King.

Rio leapt down to the previous floor and yanked the door open. A startled nurse yelped in surprise while wheeling a crash cart from a patient's room across the hall. He held up a single hand to say he was sorry before hurrying down the hallway and scanning each of the rooms.

By the time he made it to the end of the hall, he had lost the scent. Whoever this mysterious cheetah was, they probably managed to snag the elevator by the time Rio finished hiking up the staircase. Still, he couldn't let them go.

Rio darted back into the stairwell. After glancing over the railing for anyone who might catch what he was about to do, he leapt down to the next floor. He continued like this until he reached the bottom.

The were-cheetah tore open the door and went straight for the elevators. There he stood, waiting for the doors to open. When they did, he turned his head into the crowd of people rushing by him, inhaling as many scents as he could. No good. None of them smelled like a shapeshifter. Half had a medicinal smell while the others reeked of city life.

Where did Dante go? A nod of the man's head let Rio know his King had planned to corner the intruder from another direction. He should've run into his leader in the lobby by now. Something must have happened to him. Rio jabbed his thumb into the elevator button and proceeded to wait for the next car.

When he made it back to Nahla's floor, he couldn't believe the scene. Dante stood on the opposite end of the hall fixing his disheveled tie while sporting a small bruise on his cheekbone. Two orderlies held Sinclair down on the floor while she rifled off obscenities at his King.

"What's going on?" Rio asked, unable to take his eyes off her.

"Your human attacked me," Dante growled. "She confronted me before I could get to the elevators to catch our mysterious interloper."

Nobody in their right mind would think about hitting Dante unless they had suicidal tendencies. Rio glanced at the man's face again. "That's some confrontation."

"You have no idea."

A nurse hurried down the hall with a syringe in hand. She lifted Sinclair's sleeve, exposing her right shoulder. A sharp needle pierced her arm. It took a few seconds for the sedative to take affect.

Something tugged at Rio's gut. He hated seeing her like this. In a way, he wanted to rush to her side and promise her that everything would be okay. He couldn't do that in front of Dante. However, he wasn't about to abandon her like he did Ashley either.

Now that their enemies knew about Nahla and Sinclair, finding a way to get them out of this hospital was imperative.

Chapter 4

Rio worried about leaving Sinclair and Nahla alone. Suppose she woke up while he was gone and went crazy again? Suppose another unwanted visitor decided to use them to make matters worse for his clan? The best Rio could do was to ask the nurses to check in on them a little more than usual or call if either of them woke. Dante had invested enough money in the hospital for the staff to not ask questions.

Rio watched his footing through the thick wooded area miles from his home. The loam invaded his sensitive nostrils, fresh earth thick on the air.

Another half hour of hiking through the forest and a touch of sage sailed on the chilly breeze. He knew he was close to Donna Tucker's hovel.

Half stumbling and hiking down a small incline, his clunky boots splashed in a bubbling brook. A thick fog hovered above the waters. This would be the perfect setting for an ominous version of Little Red Riding Hood. He should be scared. However, in this darkness he was the most dangerous thing out there.

Except for the mysterious Donna.

Cracking sounds in the distance made him glance away from the rippling water to scan his surroundings. It might have been the usual night creatures…or something more, depending upon how far he could stretch his imagination. Rio remained silent, opening his senses to his vicinity.

"That you, cat?"

Donna stepped through the bushes from the opposite side of the stream and smirked at Rio. Her appearance never ceased to amaze him, despite cornering the market on overalls. The root-doctoring mystic claimed it was easier to carry roots back to her place after hiking a distance to harvest them.

Donna wasn't bad looking by any means. She wore her hair in dangling locks that looked more like black pea pods. With the sun having gone down, her dark skin glistened under the indigo sky like dark chocolate, smooth and sensual to the touch. If only she would do something about those ratty overalls that were at least two sizes too big. However, the tight white T-shirt redeemed her because it rounded out her voluptuous breasts. When she stepped down into the ravine to get a better look at Rio, her painted and ringed toes curled around a rock as though she knew it would be there.

Donna refused to leave the backwoods thinking behind and step into the twenty-first century. By most standards Rio was a hermit himself, but his predicament was nothing like hers. At least he occasionally hung out with his clan brothers for a beer after work.

She smirked at him, meeting his eyes. "You need something, don't you?"

He nodded. "It's for a friend. She's injured and in the hospital."

"Hospital?" Donna started in the other direction, walking along the ravine. "You know, I don't do hospitals. If they find my roots in her blood—"

"They won't." Taking the que—she hadn't told him *not* to follow—he hurried across the brook to the other side. "I've been giving her what little I had left and it's helped. Her ribs are healing and she's not paralyzed any more."

"Then what does she need more for?"

He slipped on wet rock, but threw his hand out to a tree to keep from falling. "She re-injured herself when she went after Dante."

Donna stopped and half turned. "She attacked, Dante, eh? A girl after my own heart."

"This isn't about Dante."

"Then what is it *really* about?" Not allowing him to answer, she continued on her way, hiking up her wide pant leg before a protruding branch snagged it.

"She needs help. I need to get both her and her niece healthy enough to leave the hospital. Sloan's already sent one of his people to spy on them. I just don't know if... The little girl is hurt bad. I don't know if anything can help her, to be honest with you."

"You already know what can. It's in your nature, Rio, but it's also a weakness. Right now I need to harvest my moonshade hyssop."

"¿Cómo?"

She stopped and waited for him to catch up. Understanding his words, even though she spoke no Spanish, she replied, "It's hyssop, but I mixed it with a little of this and a little of that. The only problem is I have to collect it before midnight."

"Why?"

She lifted her head, staring at the trees canopying above them. "Midnight is a magical time on the witch's clock. Things happen that tip the scales. Some roots and herbs need to be cultivated before, while others have to be done right on the dot. Some are so sensitive that they're dependent upon the full moon."

Rio smoothed the sweat from his forehead. "I can help harvest if that's what you want, but I still need those herbs."

"But do you have what I need?"

Pulling the huge backpack off his shoulder, he unzipped it and held the opening up for her to see.

Her tastes were simple. Things she couldn't get unless she left the woods, her clients brought to her. In Rio's case, he always brought her the best: packaged meats, canned foods, and linens. He never bought her anything like perfumes or jewelry because he didn't feel right getting that personal with her. When he tried to arrange a visit from the local grocery store at least once a week, Donna scared the delivery guy so bad that the store refused to have anything to do with her. So Rio started leaving boxes of goods near the stream. Dante paid for everything because she did a lot to help Rio help the Coalition.

"Nice," she replied. "Did you bring me some of those wafer cookies this time?"

Turning the backpack around, he unzipped another pocket and exposed six small packs of vanilla, chocolate, and strawberry wafers. He smiled. "Good?"

Her grin said it all even though she turned and continued on her journey.

They walked for some time around the hills until they came to a cliff with a narrow river running below. The valley awaited them and just in the distance was Durham's dotted skyline. Down there were people probably camping out for the night, unaware of the dangers surrounding them. A few miles away, the falls gushed with the recent series of downpours.

Donna crouched near a patch of foliage hidden by what looked like a fern splotched with yellow paint. Reaching through the leaves, she plucked white berries off several patches of overgrown moss. Once she had a bunch of the berries, she cupped her free hand over them, closed her eyes and lifted her chin. Her lips moved, whispering incoherent words.

Rio respected the woman's magic enough not to ask questions. Besides, she didn't like anyone quizzing her on her techniques. He should know because she cursed him with laryngitis for a week when he grilled her on measurements and cleanliness.

When she finished the spell, she opened her eyes and let the berries drop in her oversize front pocket.

Rio crouched beside her. "Is that the moon stuff you were talking about?"

"It's used for urinary tract infections." She repeated the process a second time before pocketing the berries again. "They're also good for poultices, although I haven't experimented enough with them yet."

"Another family recipe?"

She laughed. "Perhaps. Or it could be something I got from my root sisters. They're still trying to get me to buy a computer so that we can e-mail recipes back and forth. That would mean an extra bill I don't have the money for."

Rio straightened and ran his hand through his hair. "You know you could ask Dante for the money. I'll ask him for you if you want me to."

"No!" Donna stood and shoved a pair of clippers in her side pocket. "I only take what is owed to me. Nothing more."

"And you don't think we've taken our fair share of herbs?"

"You have. But that would imply I need something from him. Or that I want something. I won't start down that path."

Just as Rio was about to step back, Donna pushed him aside. Before he could ask, she kicked a pile of dead leaves. Metal jaws clamped together and a chain clanged.

Rio's heart jumped in his chest. It was a bear trap.

Donna walked around the closed metal jaws, unable to take her eyes off it. "I know these parts like my hovel. A pile stacked that well doesn't happen unless a tree decides to drop all of its leaves in one spot.

"Someone put it here."

She nodded. "It's not the first. I've noticed them scattered throughout the woods." She lifted her head to Rio. "You don't need me to tell you to be careful. I've seen your tea leaves. I know someone is hunting your Coalition, cat. I have a feeling that little woman you want to save is somehow caught in the middle."

There were times when Donna creeped him out. Now was one of them, since he had no idea how to classify her. Rio couldn't even get the woman to admit to being a witch.

Instead of questioning her, he simply averted his gaze to avoid her penetrating eyes. "She and her niece were hurt. Bad. It wasn't even their fault."

"Cat, territorial disputes are in your blood." She shook her head. "You want to keep her from suing, not that I blame her. Dante can't afford for his cheetahs to be brought to light. You also realize there's an easier solution, right? I just don't know if you're willing to go that far."

"I'm not going to bite her, if that's what you mean."

She arched an eyebrow. "If you can answer that fast, then you've already thought about it."

"Not that much," he muttered.

"Then perhaps you should think on it further just in case." She started back down the path that brought them to the cliff. "Come. I'll give you what you need, if you think it'll help. But I have to agree with your first thoughts. Biting the woman and little girl will keep your people safe. Whether Dante condemns it or not, you have to think about your species as a whole. Making her one of them will make life easier for all, cruel as it may sound."

Rio pushed a long branch out of his way and ducked his head around it. "I'm not ready for that kind of responsibility."

"As a last resort then?"

"Donna…"

She stopped and faced him. "I said 'perhaps.' I never said it was a cure-all."

Then why had their conversation clung to his brain? He could never bite Sinclair and curse her into this dangerous world with him. The sooner he collected everything he needed from Donna, the sooner he could put the thought out of his head.

Chapter 5

Rio returned to the hospital, collected more supplies for his "clinic", and shipped them to his home via a member of his clan. Had things been different he would have gone with them. However, he didn't want to leave Sinclair's bedside longer than necessary.

She stirred.

Rio woke from a dead sleep. He leapt out of the chair and lowered the railing on her bed. Her moans worried him. Either she struggled to wake or was in pain. Since cheetahs didn't have the best vision at night, he couldn't tell. He switched on the light above her bed.

Sinclair squinted and tried to shield her eyes.

Rio lowered her hand. "Are you in pain?" He watched as she nodded. "I can give you something."

She licked her lips. "Nahla?"

Rio picked up a pouch on her nightstand and sprinkled the contents into an awaiting cup of water. "You've got a strong little girl. She's a fighter like her aunt."

"Nahla." Sinclair's eyes slitted open and she tried to sit up.

Rio helped, but only to offer a sip of Donna's potion. When she got enough down, he nudged her to lie back. The ground herbs were more potent that the last batch, so with a little luck this would keep her quiet.

Steeling himself, he pulled the blanket up to her chest. "Nahla doesn't have much time. There's nothing you can do." He paused, meeting her eyes. "But there might be something I can do."

"Haven't you and your cohorts done enough?"

Rio was taken aback. She made it sound like his people set out to kill them. He closed his eyes and tried again. "I can help your niece, but I need your permission."

"Unless you've got a miracle in your black bag, don't you ever go near her again."

Rio spent the last few hours agonizing over his decision. When he returned from Donna's, he went straight to Nahla's room to check on her. The last shot he had given her didn't make her any better.

Nahla's death would kill something inside him. In the short time he sat with her, he loved fluffing her soft hair and fingering her tiny toes. It hurt that her small finger didn't have the strength to wrap around even one of his digits. If she were his child, it would destroy him to see her hurt and helpless.

What he proposed in the next few minutes would forever change not only Sinclair's and her niece's lives, but his as well. Had there been another way he wouldn't even consider what he was about to do. "I can save your niece," he said, "but I won't do it unless you're ready for what it entails."

"What are you saying?"

Rio paused to gather his thoughts. "Nahla might still die. But if I don't help her, she'll die for sure. The choice is yours. I won't do anything without your approval."

"You're talking experimental drugs, aren't you?"

"Something like that. What you need to understand is that your niece will always be your niece. Perhaps…a little different. It'll take time getting used to, but she'll adapt."

"Listen, buddy." Fatigue began worming its way through her bones. "If you say you can save my baby girl then do it. She's the only thing that keeps me sane."

"Then sleep. Things will be different in the morning. I promise."

As Sinclair's eyelids grew heavy, the last thing she noticed was a shadow moving on the other side of the room. Had she known Billie stood there the whole time she might have spat on her.

Billie's long lines grew as she rose from a chair that was sitting in the shadows and sauntered to Sinclair's bedside. Her beautiful fiery red curls bounced about her narrow shoulders when she moved. A pair of emerald green eyes settled on Rio. When her lips parted in the most ethereal smile, Rio's breath caught in his chest. Even a raggedy sweater with shredded edges and a pair of black leggings couldn't detract from her beauty. It was a good thing Dante snagged her for his mate or someone else would've snatched her up.

"Which herbs are you giving the child?" she asked.

"Some lavender and tarragon." Rio continued looking at Sinclair when he said it. Had his Queen seen the look in his eyes, she might have sensed the lie. "Of course, they're infused with Donna's earth magic. They should help ease Nahla's pain. The only thing is she might have to stay on it for a long time. These are more powerful than anything else I've given her."

"Is that the adjustment you were talking about? That the little girl would have to have the herbs for months? Or years?"

Rio glanced over his shoulder and nodded. "The herbs won't cure her. She'll be on them for…maybe the rest of her life. I'll have to monitor—"

"Whether this child lives or dies, once the aunt is of sound mind, she'll gather an army of lawyers to sue the hell out of us."

"I know."

"We can't afford that kind of publicity, Rio. If she knows—"

"I know!" He never raised his voice to his Queen like that, but he wasn't about to take it back either. Instead, he closed his eyes and sighed, calm washing over him.

She opened her mouth to say something, but closed it.

Her mate had spent the last few hours reminding him to distance himself from the Duvals and concentrate on his job at Jungle Kingdom. It didn't surprise him that she was like-minded. The Martinellis put him in charge of first-aid to keep him busy, but he knew he wasted his skills there. Had it not been for the children's smiling faces, he would've called the Martinellis on giving him a "junk" job. The Duvals not only put his skills to the test, but also made him recall why he had gone into medicine in the first place.

"I'll leave you to it," Billie mumbled, making her way to the door. "We expect to see you at the enclave tomorrow night. I'm sure Sloan will be delivering a message, so we want everyone accounted for. We'll talk about increasing Donna's pay to supply the herbs, later."

Rio watched as she left the room, closing the door behind her. He would be at the enclave tomorrow night…assuming he didn't give his leaders enough reason to hunt him down.

◆ ◆ ◆

Rio pushed a chair under the doorknob to Nahla's room. He clicked on the light above her bed and pulled up a stool. If he could, he would have taken the little girl into his arms so that she could feel a warm body instead of cold bed sheets and wires. He had to settle for slipping a finger under her lifeless hand. Had it not been for the clicking ventilator pump and the beeping of the heart monitor, dead silence would've reigned.

Rio stood and pulled his tee shirt over his head, revealing a hairless chest ripped in muscles. Next, he unbuckled his jeans and took them off. Had anyone walked into that room at that point, he would've been arrested for indecent exposure and attempted rape of a minor. He was too busy being hell-bent about saving Nahla's life to worry about that.

Lowering himself to the floor, he began to change. Bones snapped and cracked. His facial bones broke in several different places to reshape his jaw. Hair spouted up along his skin, over-saturating every pore on his body to leave a soft coat of spotted fur. His ears rounded and expanded until they slid toward the back of his head. What started out as a bump just below his tailbone had elongated into a tail about six inches in diameter. Bones shattered across his contorting back. His hands and feet formed padded paws as his legs cracked into place to create haunches.

Rio's change took all of five minutes to complete.

Seeing the stool where he left it, Rio leapt onto the metal disk and placed his paws on Nahla's bed. Since the cheetah virus was more concentrated in changed form, this was the best way to ensure it took.

Second thoughts hammered his conscience. Suppose it didn't work? Suppose it made her sicker than what she was? People had been known to go insane or die from a single bite. The insane ones usually died later via suicide or another supernatural creature. Nahla had a 50-percent chance. That was a hell of a lot more than what the doctors had given her.

Nevertheless, death was inevitable if he did nothing. He could tell by the amount of sickness clinging to the air and the injuries to her body. Nahla wouldn't make it to daybreak.

Rio lowered his head to the same hand he touched earlier and slipped his front fangs around her smooth skin. Again, he paused. Closing his eyes, he said a quick prayer before clamping down. The coppery taste of blood filled his mouth. Infected saliva watered from his taste buds, coating the wound.

Nahla moaned and squirmed in her bed. Rio let her hand drop. To make sure he got the results he wanted, he licked the teeth marks clean of blood. When the wound kept bleeding, he stopped.

Shit! I bit too hard. Need to change so I can fix this. I might have broken her hand.

Nahla squirmed again. Her face contorted in pain and her heart monitor began to race. He'd forgotten to unplug the machines.

Convulsions racked her small body.

Oh no!

The doorknob turned. When it didn't open, a hand pounded from the other side. A nurse shouted, "Let me in! Whoever's in there open this door!"

Panic tore through Rio. He leapt to the floor and scurried underneath the bed. They would be in the room before he could change back. The last thing he needed was one of them witnessing his brand of "miracle medicine." Still, it would be better for them to get in here and help Nahla because he couldn't do anything for her in cheetah form.

Rio crawled out from underneath the bed and knocked the chair to the floor. The door yanked open, slamming against the doorstop. Rio hurried into the hall.

"What the—?" The nurse didn't finish her statement. The jerking little girl had caught her attention. So did the blood trailing from her fresh wound.

Chapter 6

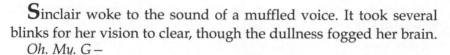

Sinclair woke to the sound of a muffled voice. It took several blinks for her vision to clear, though the dullness fogged her brain.

Oh. My. G—

On the other side of the room was a naked man standing with his back to her. The curve of his rounded buttocks awoke a need in her that clenched her stomach muscles. Add those toned muscles across his back and extending to his arms, and he had decadence written all over him.

She shook her head, bringing herself back to her senses. *A naked man in her hospital room. What kind of freak show was this?*

"What do you think you're doing?" she asked. That would've come off a lot better had she sat up, but one move in the wrong direction and she couldn't be sure if her aching bones would hold together.

"*Le volveré a llamar,*" Rio murmured, and hung up the phone. Turning around, he met her eyes.

It was a good thing Sinclair wasn't attached to a heart monitor or her palpitations would send a Code Blue over the PA system. His perfect length teased the lusting side of her brain.

Focus, Sinclair. Focus.

She coughed and darted her eyes anywhere in the room but there. "Um...you need to take care of that."

Rio blushed. He forgot that humans had a problem with casual nudity, whereas another were-cheetah wouldn't give him a second thought. He hurried to the foot of the bed and began dragging the top blanket towards him.

"Mind if I borrow this?" he asked.

"Yeah," Sinclair replied, snagging hold for a tug of war.

A grin splayed his face for the first time in days. "Then would you prefer I stay like this?"

Her eyebrow arched. Did he really want her to answer that? "Why are you in my room like that to begin with? Does this look like a nudist camp to you? Or do you have a medical fetish that nobody knows about?"

Rio chuckled. With a quick snap, he tore the blanket from Sinclair's hand. "You see? You still have the sheet. If you're cold, I'll have the nurse bring you an extra blanket."

Sinclair smirked. "I'd like to see you try to explain why you're in a toga."

Rio tossed the loose ends over his shoulder. He liked this side of her. For the first time since she had been here, she hadn't thought about tearing someone apart, lawsuits, or dire circumstances. This was a nice change; one he had hoped to see again.

However, now was not the time.

Rio made his way to the side of her bed and sat. He pressed a button on the controls that raised her head high enough for her to see the rest of the room. She winced with each inch. Getting her out of here would take more effort than he first thought.

"I have a friend who's bringing me some clothes," he said. "We need to leave soon."

"Leave? Do I look like I can pee without someone sliding a bedpan under me? And have you forgotten about Nahla? I'm not going anywhere without her."

"I checked on her a little while ago and—"

"Not dressed like that, I hope."

He shook his head, unable to hide the grin and the heat seeping into his cheeks. "No. Not like this. I lost my clothes when I took a shower. I guess someone either thought it would make a great joke or the orderly thought they were rags. I don't know. Anyway, the point is that your niece is...well...she's..."

Her heart stopped. No way in hell would she sit there if something bad had happened to her baby.

She threw the sheet off her legs and scooted to the edge. Rio sat there wasting her time while her baby niece could be dead for all she knew. She wouldn't have it. She wanted answers. If she had to, she'd go through him to get them.

Rio clamped a hand on her uninjured arm and stopped her. "Nahla needs specialized care, but not here."

"She *needs* the best care the Martinellis can buy."

"Do you remember anything that we talked about last night?"
Confusion knitted her brows. "What does that have to do with—"

"I've administered the first in a series of treatments a few hours ago. Unfortunately, the longer she stays here, the more the doctors will get in the way. I need your permission to take you guys out of here."

"Why? I thought you said you were a doctor or something. Don't you have some pull?"

Rio sighed. "I'm a physician's assistant and a healer. I practice modern medicine mixed with some eastern influences."

Studying his face, Sinclair reached back in her brain for answers. "Wait a sec. You said something about herbs. Is that what you are? Some loony herbalist?"

"Lady, if giving your niece a fifty-percent chance to live is crazy, then call me Mr. Loony Tunes."

"Fifty? What kind of a chance is that?"

"More than what the doctors had offered. If you think I'm lying, then you can ask them yourself. You saw her with your own eyes. Even if she does recover, she might not be the same for a long time."

Sinclair snatched her arm away from Rio. "I can't deal with this right now. I need to be with my niece."

Did he really think she'd buck the medical system for some ancient, herbalist horse crap? For all she knew he was probably reading tealeaves and smoking up the room with incense. Her baby girl needed modern medicine. That's all. Nahla would be as good as new the sooner she could take her home and give her some extra special TLC.

Rio didn't go with her this time. He wanted nothing to do with influencing her decision from here on out. Sinclair would have to make up her own mind about what was best for everyone.

With Rio hiding in the bathroom, Sinclair buzzed the nurse to wheel her to Nahla's room. When they entered the child's room, she couldn't see her for all the ice packs surrounding her frail body. More machines appeared since yesterday with louder suction and more beeps. At least the ventilator had disappeared. Was that a good sign or a trade off for the ice packs? Two doctors, stood at the end of her niece's bed talking softly while a nurse dabbed her baby's sweaty forehead.

"What's going on?" She struggled to get the words out.

"Ms. Duval," one of the doctors said, offering his hand. "My name is Dr. Rothchild. I've been attending to your niece since the two of you were brought into the ER."

Sinclair shook his hand without taking her eyes off Nahla. Pushing out of the wheelchair—biting back the horrendous pain in her back and ribs—she grabbed hold of the bed and pulled herself up the rest of the way.

"You're standing?" the second doctor said. Shaking his head, he offered his hand to her too. "My name is Dr. Kenji. I came down here to visit Dr. Rothchild so that I could get an update on your niece. But...you're standing!"

"Why's that a big production?" Sinclair couldn't help feeling crabby whenever she was frightened. The only way she knew how to cope was with anger. Touching her niece's sweaty forehead, fear sliced through her.

"Ms. Duval, you injured your back in the accident. There was swelling around your spinal cord and you didn't have any motor function from the waist down. By all accounts, you should be paralyzed."

Paralyzed? Okay, that piece of information threw Sinclair off kilter. In fact, it was the first time she had taken her eyes off Nahla since arriving. She absentmindedly adjusted her sling. "What about my shoulder?"

"Dislocation. A very bad one at that. Does it hurt?"

"Some," she lied. "But I can handle it."

"Amazing," he murmured, and adjusted his glasses. "I'd like to run some tests, if you don't mind. To make sure that—"

"Doctor, right now the only thing I'm concerned with is Nahla's health. If she doesn't leave this hospital alive, then whatever happens to me isn't worth a damn."

Kenji nodded. "Of course, Ms. Duval. I should have been more considerate."

The other doctor wrote something on a metal chart and handed it to the nurse with further instructions. Sinclair couldn't understand their doctor-speak, but she knew it couldn't be good just by the grim look on both their faces.

"What's wrong with my niece?" she asked. "What's up the ice packs and the bandaged hand? She wasn't like this yesterday."

Dr. Rothchild's sighed. "I don't know how to say this. It's rather embarrassing."

"Just say it!"

Another pause. "We think an animal got into the hospital last night. The nurse caught him running out of Nahla's room. Anyway, it looks like he—it—." He sighed. "A dog bit her."

This can't be happening.

"As if my niece didn't have enough to worry about, how the hell could you let some animal in here? Have you people lost your freakin' minds? What kind of madhouse is this?"

"Ms. Duval—"

"Don't you 'Ms. Duval' me. You people had better have your papers in order because as soon as I leave, Jungle Kingdom won't be the only ones on my hit list for lawsuits."

"I understand how upsetting this must be, but right now, your niece is the main concern."

"Amazing?" Sinclair mocked. "How did you come to that conclusion? I guess all those years in medical school came in handy after all, huh?"

He hesitated, his gaze going to Nahla's prone body. "She's off the ventilator, so the fever is the biggest concern. We ran some tests and we think that the dog carried a new strand of rabies."

"Rabies in a freaking hospital." Sinclair glared at Rothchild. "Is my niece going to die?"

Again, he hesitated. "It's hard to say. In fact, I'm amazed she survived this long."

"Another twenty-four hours then?"

"I don't know. If the worse should happen...then it wouldn't hurt to do an autop—"

"Uh-uh," she exclaimed, waving her hand. "You people aren't doing jack. If Nahla's gonna die, then I don't want it to be here when it happens. You've already mucked up once by letting some damn dog take a chomp out of her. What next? Accidentally toss her in a biohazard container? Hell no."

Dr. Kenji stepped forward. "Ms. Duval, we have to insist—"

She raised two fingers. "I've got two words for you. Law. Suit. Get one, because you're going to need it for your day in court."

Rio stepped into the room fully clothed in a pair of baggy jeans and a light blue tee. His attention went from her to the doctors and back again.

Her mind was made up. "We're getting the hell out of this slaughter house you call a hospital."

"Ms. Duval, I must insist—"

"—that you keep your mouth shut. Or do I need to call my lawyer?"

No one said a word.

Chapter 7

Sinclair was antsy in the rear seat of the minivan. Wherever Rio planned to take them, it was so far from the city that second thoughts needled her.

Whether she knew anything about this man, it didn't matter. The doctors gave Nahla another day at most. If she died, then Sinclair would follow. She was certain of that the moment the doctors gave their prognosis. Looking at the grand scheme of things, it didn't matter where Rio took them. It couldn't be any worse than what they had suffered so far.

Where the heck was Mina? Surely, the hospital tried to contact her about their condition. Then again, the only thing she could manage was lifting a whiskey bottle to her lips. There was a good chance she lay stretched out on her back somewhere. Like either in a jail cell or tossed into detox. Again. After all, it wasn't unusual for her inept sister to disappear for days at a time.

A bead of sweat meandered down her forehead. She brushed it away and readjusted herself against the pillows. With the minivan able to hold seven people, it allowed her plenty of room to stretch out.

Rio sat in the middle row next to Nahla where he could monitor her condition. Up front Kyle — they had a brief introduction in Rio's hast to leave the hospital — sat in the driver's seat.

"You okay," Rio asked.

"No," she said. "I'm..."

"Lay down. It'll be easier on your back. And what happened to the sling I made for you?"

"I lost it somewhere." Good thing too because she wanted to

strangle the doctors with it. How could they let some dog into the hospital to bite her innocent baby?

Snorting, Kyle glanced at the rearview mirror. Rio met his eyes with a glare that could turn a person to stone. Kyle lowered his gaze.

Kyle knew what had happened. In fact, Rio gave him the details last night right before he went into Nahla's room. His friend spent the day getting all the preparations in place. After renting the van, he stocked Rio's cabin with food and supplies, then drove to the hospital to pick them up. Though he tried to talk Rio out of it, his friend had saved his little brother when a storm accidentally washed him down river. It was a small price to pay in return. Kyle would've done anything for the man, including disobeying his King's orders.

Rio turned his attention to Sinclair. "You need to rest as much as Nahla does. Especially since I haven't had a chance to finish your treatment."

Sinclair shifted against the pillows at her back. "Speaking of which, what did you give me?"

"You mean last night?"

"Don't play coy with me. That doctor said I should be paralyzed."

Rio turned his attention back to Nahla. Stalling, he touched the back of his hand to her forehead. "They're herbal remedies. I'll be the first to admit that some of them aren't exactly legal. But when they're mixed with other herbs, the effects can be quite dramatic."

"So other than giving me illegal drugs, why haven't you at least written a paper or worked at a university?"

Rio chuckled. "Because I'm just a PA. My medicine is more on the mystical side. Face it, science and mysticism don't mix. Assuming the medical community would give me five minutes of their precious time, they'd use another five to laugh at me."

"Maybe. All I know is whatever you gave me, I appreciate it. Especially if what the doctors said was true about the paralysis."

Rio smiled. "*Gracias*. But unfortunately, we're not out of the woods. Only a little further along."

She knew what he meant when her attention went to the back of Nahla's fluffy afro. A lump formed in her throat. Before the tears could slip down her cheeks, she turned and gazed out the rear window. She couldn't allow herself this luxury. She had to be strong for Nahla's sake. After all, the little girl had gone through enough.

Please God, tell me I'm doing the right thing. Tell me I'm not prolonging my baby girl's misery.

That was another thought that hadn't come to mind. Suppose this was hurting her instead of helping? Sinclair would rather die before inflicting more pain on Nahla.

A hand touched her arm. Sinclair jerked her head around, meeting Rio's luxuriant eyes. His thumb caressed her forearm through the oversized shirt.

Sinclair touched the back of his hand, caressing the unusual softness of his skin. That was all she'd allow of herself. A momentary weakness to a man she hardly knew.

The van wobbled from side to side on the dirt road, drawing both Rio and Sinclair's attention from each other. Rio unbuckled an unconscious Nahla from her booster seat and hauled her into his arms. She didn't need anymore jostling.

"Hold on guys," Kyle said. "We're almost there."

"Where is 'there' exactly?" Sinclair clamped her jaw tight, biting back the pain prickling her lower back.

"My place," Rio said. "Everything I need is there."

"You sure you have enough room for us?" She studied his face. An internal chuckle quivered up to her lips. "Don't look at me like that. I've seen plenty of bachelor pads. I know how single guys live. That is…unless you're married or have a girlfriend."

"There's plenty of room," he said. "Since I'm a healer, I have to have extra bed space. You never know when you're going to have patients laying around."

He wanted to say "cats" but decided to leave that alone for now. Since the Coalition was like family, they liked hanging out at Rio's place. Using it as a hideout whenever the Martinellis were on the warpath also came in handy. Rio made a great mediator because he hated patching up someone for pissing off Dante or Billie.

Sinclair watched as the line of trees passed them by. "Why are you this far out? You must like the seclusion."

"There's that, but there's also the matter of an herb garden. Plus, I grow cannabis, but it isn't what you think. It has significant medicinal properties that I enhance with other herbs."

Sinclair arched an eyebrow. "As long as you're not dealing it, I can let the weed go."

Kyle barked out a laugh. "That boy scout, a dealer? I'd like to see the day."

Smiling, Rio slapped his friend across the back of the neck. "Mosquito, *hombre*. And watch out for potholes. But to answer the *señora's* question, I have a cute little cottage with two bedrooms and two bathrooms. There's a breakfast nook and a huge counter that separate the kitchen from the dining area. On the other side of that is a large living. But my favorite places are the screened in deck out back and the bonus room that I turned into a lab of sorts. When I'm not working, I'm sitting on the couch with a good comic book."

"Comic book?"

He chuckled. "Yeah. Can't a guy have a hobby?"

"We're here," Kyle said, bringing the van to a halt.

Rio hooked his hand on the handle and popped open the side door. He slid the child from his arms and onto the seat. After stepping out, he reached inside and offered a hand to Sinclair. He'd get to Nahla in a minute, since her delicate body required more tender loving care.

Moving as gingerly as possible, she took his hand and eased from the seat. Bending over to get out almost brought her to her weakened knees. She fell forward.

"Whoa!" Rio exclaimed, eyes widening. He slipped his arms around her back and hoisted her out of the van. "I can't have you falling flat on your face."

"Thanks."

Sinclair met his gaze. Even his full lips looked enticing enough to eat. The urge to just taste them overwhelmed her to the point that it knotted her belly. Sinclair put her arms on his toned chest and gave a nudge.

Rio got the idea and released her, but wouldn't let go of her hand.

Kyle sauntered around the front of the van and thumbed inside at Nahla. "Seeing as you've got your hands full, you want me to take the little one?"

Rio shot him a harsh look. "You're asking to get slapped across the back of the head again."

"I thought you said it was a mosquito."

"It was." He wound his hand back. "Maybe if I backhanded it, it might go away."

Sinclair chuckled.

Smiling, he though she had a beautiful laugh, carefree like a young girl's. He hoped to hear it more often than not. "Can you walk on your own or do you need some help?"

Sinclair shook her head. "I think I can handle it, flyswatter. Just don't rush me."

"Okay," he chuckled. "I'll get Nahla."

She started for the one-story cabin. Between the white trim, light gray exterior, and the bay window on the side, this place reminded her of a storybook fairytale. What kind of single man would live in a house like this?

It didn't matter. She wasn't going to get involved with him no matter how attractive he was. Her life revolved around Nahla and she accepted that without question. She didn't believe in Prince Charming sweeping her off her feet. Guys like Rio didn't fall for women like her. Her last so-called boyfriend was proof of that. Not only was she the stereotypical, career-minded black woman, but she had baggage she wouldn't give up for anyone. Rio probably thought she was on welfare and only wanted a man for his wallet. He was a gorgeous Hispanic guy with exotic good looks. She didn't stand a chance. Chicks probably threw themselves at him and he would be the type of guy who would take advantage of it. Well, she wouldn't be a part of his harem. She had devoted her life to raising Nahla.

Just as Sinclair touched the railing, the front door opened. She choked on a scream and stumbled backward. The sudden movement sent a bolt of pain spiraling up her spine. Her weakened knees gave out underneath her and she landed on her butt. More pain cascaded down her back.

"Sinclair," Rio yelled. He barely got Nahla handed over to Kyle before rushing off to help her. The agony on her tight face and the sweat beading across her brow told him she was in excruciating pain.

Dammit, he should have given her the Theradin before leaving the hospital.

Lifting his attention away from her, he glared at the person standing on the porch. Rio growled at the smug look on Marianne's face, Billie's second-in-command.

Lifting his head to the porch, he muttered, "Thanks a lot. I take it Dante's not too far behind."

The King pushed through the overgrowth just to the right of the house. "Closer than you think."

Chapter 8

Rio had a headache by the time all was said and done. His first challenge dealt with trying to calm Sinclair down long enough to take her medication. Despite her bruised and sore body, she wanted to finish what she started with Dante. Luckily, he had strength and patience on his side. As soon as she finished yelling her peace from behind bedroom doors, she took the Theridan and passed out on the bed.

That wasn't the end of it. His next stop was Dante and that brown-nosing, blond-leech, Marianne. Why his King had to show up with that heifer in tow, he didn't understand. Unfortunately, it wasn't his main concern. The verbal lashing kept him preoccupied.

Dante whirled on him with supernatural speed, clamping his hand around Rio's throat and slamming him against the front of the house. "You bit that child!" Snarling, his face came within inches of his subordinate. "Tell me something, Rio. Did you think I wouldn't find out? I called the hospital to get an update on their condition from Dr. Youst. He told me about the spotted dog, the child's bite, and her fever. Do I look stupid to you?"

Rio said nothing. He knew he had broken Coalition Law by biting a human, so what good would a physical challenge do now? Dante was stronger, faster, and more cunning than anyone he knew. That's why he was a natural-born leader and Rio wasn't.

Marianne cleared her throat. "Um, Dante. I hate to break this up, but we still need him. He's the only healer we have."

Dante seethed. Rio knew he wanted to do so much more, like beat him within an inch of his life. Instead, Dante tossed him aside and stalked away.

"What happens if that child dies?" he growled. "Her aunt will go to any lengths to make sure we're brought to justice. Including, exposing our race."

Rubbing his neck, Rio coughed. "You forgot to ask yourself what happens if the kid survives."

Dante glared at him.

Straightening up a bit, Rio took a deep breath. "If Nahla lives, she'll be a shapeshifter like us. If her aunt goes public, then she'll be condemning her own blood. After the fight she put up I'm sure she'll do anything to protect her baby."

"Oh, please! Don't stand there and tell me you did this to protect us. We were nothing more than an afterthought and you know it."

"Look, all I'm trying to do is a little clean up."

Marianne laughed. "Some cleanup."

Rio eyed her. "Nobody asked you, flunky."

A scowl contorted her pretty face.

Dante stepped between them. "They're your responsibility. If that child dies and her aunt gives us any trouble, she'll follow that kid to the grave. It goes no further. Are we clear?"

Bracing himself, he nodded. Sinclair and Nahla weren't to have any contact with the rest of the Coalition. He'd pretty much locked himself into the care of this...family. If necessary, he might become their executioner too.

◆ ◆ ◆

Rio knew he couldn't keep Sinclair drugged. It wasn't fair to her and she needed time to make sense of this. Were-cheetah or not, her niece will look to her aunt for cues...if she survived. The sooner Sinclair trusted him, the sooner Nahla would too. Both their lives depended on it.

While she slept, Rio tied a poultice to her shoulder. He had just finished making up another one for her lower back when she stirred. Taking care not to wake her, he placed the cloth filled with heated herbs, twigs, and spices at the swell of her back and tied it off to her side.

The thought of flipping her over so that he could get another glimpse of her breasts stirred his libido. They weren't big, but the Hershey's Kisses nipples delighted him nonetheless. Small and pert, just like her waist. Since he wanted to make sure he covered her tailbone with the poultice, he lowered her drawstring pants enough to expose the supple side of her plumber's crack. *What a fine crack it was.* Though she was nice and slender, she had just enough hips to fill out a pair of jeans. If things were different, he'd buy her the tightest jeans he could find so that he could marvel at the way they hugged her thighs and butt.

This wasn't right. He was her caretaker for heaven's sake. He couldn't sit there and ogle his patient while she slept. It was…unethical.

Uh huh. Then why had his index fingers curled around the edge of her drawstring pants, resting the nail against her brown cheek? All he had to do was peel back the rim of her pants. His erection twitched so bad that he shifted on the bed.

He'd give anything to take her from behind like a real wild cat. To have her cuddly, rounded buttocks snuggle up against his—

"Copping a feel?" she mumbled.

Rio yanked his hand away. "Sorry. My hand sort of—well, uh— it sort of just…"

"Fell there." Sinclair looked over her shoulder. Nothing on her face read friendliness. "Where's my niece? And what's that dog crap you put on my back?"

Rio pursed his lips. "That 'dog crap' happens to be what cured your paralysis. I use it in conjunction with the Theridan."

"Theridan?"

"The poultice keeps the swelling down while the Theridan does the healing."

"It smells like horseshit."

"Fine. Would you rather be paralyzed then? Because I'll be more than happy to re—"

"Forget it." She would endure the horseshit as long as it worked on her aching back. "What about Nahla?"

"She's sleeping."

"I want to see her." Sinclair tried pushing off the bed.

Rio pushed her down. "I just put that poultice on. You've got to give it some time to work."

"As if I should trust you. You're the one who had Martinelli waiting here when we arrived. If I had enough sense in the first place, I never would've handed us over to you."

"It's not what you think."

"I can't believe I let myself get caught up…" Again, she tried pushing off the bed.

When Rio touched her shoulder, she slapped his hand away and sat up on the opposite side. With her back to him and legs dangling over the edge, the coolness of the room struck her skin and hardened her nipples.

"You son of…" she spat. "What did you really bring us here for?

So you can rape me?"

As pretty as she was, Rio had had enough of this woman. He stalked to the dresser, yanked a button-front shirt out of the drawer, and tossed it toward her. "If I wanted to rape you, I could've done it by now."

Sinclair yanked the shirt off the bed and covered up. "Make no mistake, Rio. What you're doing for me and my niece doesn't lessen the hell that I'm going to give you. You and your friends are responsible and I'm going to hold all of you to it."

Rio shook his head. Between Dante's rage and Sinclair snarling at him, perhaps putting her out of her misery wouldn't be such a bad idea.

Chapter 9

Nothing could pry Sinclair from her niece. The little girl lay on a twin-size bed with more ice packs covering her tiny body. Frostbite was a possibility, but with Nahla's fever hanging close to 104 degrees, she prayed the packs were enough.

Rio huffed whenever Sinclair got in his way. However, he couldn't deny her from wanting to help. When it came time to change Nahla's dressings, Rio had saved the one hiding the bite on the toddler's tiny hand for last.

Sinclair choked back a sob.

Red, angry veins webbed out from the puncture wounds and it smelled like rotten meat. Even worse, curded puss had developed in and around the pulsing wound.

"Don't sit there and tell me that's normal!" she shouted.

Rio continued cleaning her wound with complete calm. "It's infected, yes, but it'll go away. We just need to keep the wound cleaned and the bandages changed."

"Let me guess, you're going to put a horseshit poultice on her too?"

"Yes."

"Unbelievable." Sinclair grabbed hold of the headboard and used it to stand. At times like this, she paced through her thoughts, though the pain eating away at her back kept her walking to a minimum.

"Maybe this was a mistake," she said more so to herself. "I should've taken her to another hospital. Instead I'm stuck in the middle of nowhere with a Grizzly Adams wannabe who's using some backwoods hocus-pocus to cure my little girl."

"You thought about what was best for her." Rio placed a smaller poultice on Nahla's wound and tied it off. Pushing his medical supplies aside, he left the bed to stand close without crowding her space. "Twenty-four hours. That's what the doctors gave her. I'm telling you, I can give her more than that. In fact, her fever was at 105 when we left the hospital. It's already gone down a degree. Stick with this and I promise you Nahla will be fine."

"Then what? We go back home and pretend like nothing happened?"

"If that's what you want."

"Well I'm sorry if I don't have that kind of tenacity. She has a leg broken in two places a dislocated shoulder that might have lead to nerve damage, and internal injuries. You can't tell me Nahla won't need things like physical therapy. Not to mention, long-lasting effects. She has nobody to take care of her except me. Nobody. To hell with my job. I'm going to be playing nursemaid for God-only-knows how long. You'll be gone, Martinelli will be gone, that hospital will be gone. In the end it'll be just me and Nahla. As usual."

Damn Mina for abandoning them. So many times Sinclair had to pick up the pieces after Mommy Dearest left them high and dry for days on end. Sinclair was there when Nahla woke in the middle of the night, screaming about the "big-bad-mommy monster" who had slapped her for no reason. Barely out of the womb and Nahla knew as much about her mother's drunken foolishness as any member of an AA meeting. A three-year-old shouldn't have to go through something like that.

A tear rolled down her cheek before she could turn away from Rio. She didn't want him to see her like that. She wanted to be strong because she was supposed to be strong.

Rio tossed caution out. Closing the distance between them, he slipped his arms around her shoulders, hugging her close to his chest. She squirmed a bit at first, but once she gave in, she gave in completely.

Her body hurt. She grew tired of fighting. She just wanted to be held. To know that someone cared about *her* for a change. Was that so wrong? Even though Nahla lay sick and dying, was she not allowed to seek comfort during her own time of need? When the tears increased, Sinclair didn't bother wiping them away.

Rio would've done anything to stop her crying. She was an aunt sick with grief over a child. Things had to turn out for the better. They just had to.

The bed squeaked.

Rio turned and noticed Nahla twitching. Swearing under his breath, he raced to her side just as the seizures rattled her small body out of control. Somewhere in the background, he heard Sinclair scream, but he didn't have time to think about it. He needed to restrain Nahla enough to make sure she didn't bump her head or fall off the bed. Sinclair's pleading for him to do something didn't help.

Now was not the time for this.

◆ ◆ ◆

Sinclair did her best to stay awake, but sleep took her down hard.

Rio planned all along to let her sleep in his king size bed, but she decided to take the other twin bed in Nahla's room. However, after two more seizures during the middle of the night, Rio knew she wouldn't get any sleep. To make her more comfortable, he carried Nahla, then Sinclair into his bedroom where both aunt and niece slept more comfortably. He wanted to curl up behind Sinclair so bad. It hurt to see them like that, alone in bed just as they had been in life.

Come morning, Rio woke from the rocking chair and checked on his charges. Both were still asleep, so he decided to get breakfast started. With everything going on last night, he only managed to snag a sandwich. Sinclair hadn't had anything since she left the hospital and she needed to eat.

When he finished, he carried a plate of waffles, bacon, and eggs into the bedroom. He was surprised to see Sinclair lying on her side and stroking her niece's sweaty brow.

"You need to eat," he said, placing the food on the nightstand.

She said nothing, only continued to study Nahla's face. "The swelling and the bruises are almost gone. Yesterday they were..."

"I know." He left briefly and returned with glasses of milk and orange juice. He wanted to make sure he covered the basics. "It means she's healing."

"But this fast?" Sinclair couldn't believe it. Whatever he had stashed away in his medicine cabinet certainly did a number on her niece. Nahla almost appeared normal. In fact, Sinclair thought about trying to get a comb through her baby's curly afro before she woke up and started complaining about having her hair pulled.

Rio sat behind Sinclair, smoothing his hand across her back. She jolted at his foreign touch, but relaxed just as quickly. That touch alone sent spasms across her skin.

"How's your back?" he asked. "Any pain?"

"A little," she lied. "I can't believe she's healing like this."

"I'm glad you approve. And as long as I caught you in a good mood, I'd like to take a look at you before you dive into your breakfast."

"Me?" Hardly needing his help, Sinclair sat up and stared at him. "Don't you think you should be checking on Nahla first?"

He smiled. "I did before I made breakfast. Now how about I see how you're progressing?"

Actually, Sinclair wanted to know the same thing herself. Although the pain in her back and shoulder were still there, it had tapered off. Nodding, she began unbuttoning her shirt.

Rio bit his bottom lip. Man, how he wished he was the one undressing her right then. He wouldn't stop at her shirt either. He wanted to peel her clothes off slow and easy like peeling a banana. His tingling balls agreed.

Before she could undo another button, Rio slipped his hand through the slit in the front and brought the sleeve down far enough to expose the poultice on her shoulder. He gulped through the thick clot in his throat. As he untied the knot, he couldn't help letting his finger brush across her smooth, butter-brown skin. When he peeled back the poultice, the smell never touched his nose. He had his mind on the beautiful shoulder blade that connected to her delicate neck.

He cleared his throat and shifted so that he could sit closer. "I need to see your back too. To make sure…that …everything is in the clear and all. You know."

"Mmmm-hmmm," Sinclair hummed, her tone not buying it. With the way his hands moved across her skin, it left her begging to be touched some more.

Rio could smell the arousal saturating the air. She was just as turned on by him as he was her.

He finished peeling off the leftover twigs and flower petals and smoothing in the mint salve along her shoulder blade. There was still some bruising left, but the swelling had gone down. He made a mental note to thank Donna for the potent herbs the next time he ventured to her place.

Smoothing his fingers underneath her arm, she giggled and pulled way from him.

He laughed. "Ticklish, I take it?"

"Stay back, you. Yes, I'm ticklish. So now you know my dark secret."

"Hmmm. I'll have to remember that next time."

"Next time?"

"The next time you dislocate your shoulder. But, I need you to lift your arm up so I can check your range of motion."

Sinclair got it to the level of her shoulder blade when she winched in pain. Rio helped her ease it back down.

Kneading her joint with his thumbs, he leaned in close. "Does that feel better?"

"Mmmm-hmmm." Closing her eyes, she tipped her head for him without even thinking. This man had warm fingers of the gods.

Her short, curly hair brushed his nose, wakening him like a fresh shower. He saw her action as an invitation. Oh, man was he going to enjoy this!

The phone rang.

Damn!

"Be back in a sec," he muttered. After getting off the bed, he disappeared into the other room.

Sinclair was glad. She must have lost her mind, letting this man fondle her while her injured niece lay unconscious less than a foot from her. Despite snapping back to her high moral standards, she couldn't shed the residual warmth of his hands on her.

Next time there wouldn't be a phone to save her. What would she do then? After easing off the bed, she started for the door.

"Go to hell!"

Something smashed against the wall from the other room.

Sinclair jerked to a halt just outside the door. On second thought, perhaps she should leave him alone for a few minutes.

"Auntie."

That tiny voice froze Sinclair. She jerked her head over her shoulder and whispered, "Nahla? Baby?"

Chapter 10

Nahla opened her heavy eyelids and blinked at her aunt. Sinclair dropped onto the comforter and pressed kisses into her niece's soft cheek. Other than watching her be birthed into the world, she had never felt a more joyous moment in her life. Her heart drowned in love for her niece.

She was about to slip her hand under Nahla and lift her when Rio appeared out of nowhere and stopped her. He snatched the stethoscope from the nightstand next to the bed and placed it in his ears. He touched the other end to Nahla's chest and listened to her heartbeat.

"How are you feeling, sweetie?" His voice was much calmer than what she had heard just a few minutes ago. "You still hurt anywhere?"

Tears bled out of the corners of Nahla's doe eyes as she nodded. "Every-ting hurt. Leg itchy too."

Sinclair's heart broke in half. She'd do anything to take the agony away from her. "Can you give her something? Like the same stuff that you gave me?"

He nodded. Pulling the stethoscope out of his ears and setting it aside, he began pressing on her abdomen to see if he could get a reaction. Everywhere he pressed Nahla whimpered and pushed his hand away. Partly because she hurt, but also because she didn't know him. Nahla turned on her side, burying her face in her aunt's thigh, leaving her traction arm rising straight up at her side. Sinclair's tears resurfaced as she combed her fingers through her niece's silky afro.

For some reason her hair seemed silkier than normal. Strange.

Putting that aside, she carefully lifted her feverish niece into her arms and held her close. She had to be careful of the dangling casts and making sure Nahla didn't put too much weight on her injuries.

"Is she going to be okay?" she asked Rio.

"It's going to take time." Crawling backwards off the bed, he left the bedroom.

Cradling Nahla in her arms, she followed him into an office just off the living room and stopped in the doorway.

This wasn't an office. One side was a wall of glass cabinets filled with jars of different sizes and shapes, each of them labeled. Rows of books ranged from human physiology to plant biology to dinosaurs lined another wall. An island sat in the center of the room with a bunch of glass tubes and beakers set up to look like a seventh grade chemistry class. Near the bay window, a desk with a computer and yellow sunrays beaming across stacks of papers and several open books. It was good to know she wasn't the only egghead around.

"This is some setup," she commented, patting her niece's bottom. "I take it you don't keep medicine in your medicine cabinet."

"Actually, I keep my razors in there." Rio sat a jar of yellow powder on the counter and filled up two glasses of water from the sink.

"What's that?"

"It's the Theradin." He motioned her towards the island. "Have a seat. Nahla's not going to like this, so you'll have to hold her still."

Sinclair pulled out the stool. She sat, ignoring her own pain when her bottom settled on the metal surface. She cradled Nahla on her lap and pressed a soft kiss on her head. When Rio approached, he held two small glasses filled with something that looked like pineapple juice mixed with bits of grain and black pepper.

"Who's the other glass for?" she asked.

He placed it on the counter in front of her. "You."

"But I'm feeling—"

"You keep taking it no matter how well you feel because there's always the chance of a relapse. Besides…you were lying about how you felt just so that you could be awake when Nahla woke. Well, she's awake. Time for you to start taking care of yourself again."

Sinclair cut her eyes at him, trying to keep a scowl from blossoming. So what he had pegged her. Wouldn't he have done the same thing?

She looked at the glass with a raised eyebrow. "What's in it?"

"Herbs and spices. The one I gave you in the hospital was more potent because you needed it."

"So how did you give it to her?" she said, shifting Nahla on her lap.

"An injection. And I hate to say this, but it would help if you didn't handle her so much."

"But—"

"Sit with her, but don't rock her. In this state, it might make her sicker."

Sinclair frowned at that thought.

Feeding Nahla the serum turned into a fifteen-minute ordeal. As sick and feverish as she was, Nahla pushed and cried, burying her face between her aunt's chest. Anything to keep from drinking the bitter liquid. The last thing the little girl probably wanted was someone forcing some nasty juice down her throat.

It didn't help that Sinclair couldn't get hers down either. She must have been one sick puppy to drink that stuff in the hospital. It tasted like vinegar mixed with a touch of scotch. No one in their right mind could set a good example with that crap.

"You had better give her to me," Rio said, holding his arms out.

Sinclair finished off the last of her vinegar-scotch concoction and slapped the glass down on the counter. "I just want to hold her a little longer."

He shook his head. "The Theradin has a narcotic effect. Even though I gave you less than her, you'll still feel a bit woozy. I'd rather you not drop Nahla on your way to bed."

The moment Sinclair hopped off her chair, the room swayed. No more arguments. She quickly handed her sleepy niece over to Rio and used the counter to support her wobbly legs. Another wave of dizziness hit her just as she had made it to the bedroom.

Rio held Nahla with one arm while slipping the other one around Sinclair's narrow waist. He couldn't help running his fingers across the little girl's thigh. Her skin was so soft that it reminded him of newborn-baby skin. Biting his bottom lip, he fought not to snuggle his nose against her fuzzy hair and inhale her scent.

"Smell funny," Nahla mumbled, scrunching up her nose in her sleep. "You smell funny."

"Nahla," Sinclair scolded. "You shouldn't talk about people like that."

"But Auntie." A huge yawn. "He smell funny. But...he smell

more like me now."

Nervous laughter left Rio's mouth. "It's just the effects of the Theradin. She's a little ti—"

Sinclair didn't hear a thing. She dropped on the floor like a sack of flour.

Rio sighed. Thank goodness Nahla was awake because these next coming days might be a challenge. The Charlotte Coalition had gotten bolder in their threats. To protect the coalition, Dante and Billie had declared a lockdown.

Chapter 11

An old woman crossed the holy trinity over her chest. She kissed the rosary in hand before placing her other hand on the bench in front of her and eased into the pew.

Rio slipped his arm underneath her elbow and helped her to her feet. He offered a smile before mumbling a blessing of his own.

The old woman shook her head. White, wispy hair fanned her face. For a were-cheetah of 112 years old, she hardly looked a day over seventy-five. As was the case with many of their kind. They aged slowly.

"You mind your Catholic manners." Hazel playfully punched him in the chest before squeezing his cheek. "What brings you here? Please tell me it wasn't my worrisome great granddaughter, Marianne."

After finding a bloody handprint on the clan's territory, Dante and Billie agreed to open up their mansion to anyone who sought protection. Marianne jumped on it. Since she couldn't convince her stubborn great grandmother to leave, she called in reinforcements. Rio was the primary candidate because her grandmother respected him.

The request should've come directly from his Queen. Right after Marianne had asked her the favor, she had the gall to ask if Nahla was dead yet. If not, then perhaps he could bring her to the enclave so the rest of the clan could meet the miracle cub before they buried her. Marianne had better be lucky she hadn't asked him face to face or she would be missing hers by now.

That was days ago. It took him just that long to get over his resentment and help Marianne with her great grandmother. He knew the bitch's brashness wasn't Hazel's fault, so why take it out on the old woman?

"Everyone is worried about you." He placed his arm across the back of the pew behind her bony shoulders. "Billie wouldn't have sent me here unless it was important."

Keeping her gaze on the large crucifix at the front of the church, she lifted her chin. Hazel tipped closer toward him, peeking over the scattered heads throughout the congregation. "You're here because of the lockdown on the clan."

"It's for everyone's safety."

"If that were the case, then why is it you're shacking up with some human and infecting her niece? Shouldn't you be in hiding, too?" She whipped her face to him and grinned.

Rio patted the back of her hand. "No, *Madre* Hazel." He stared at the kneeling bench just in front of him. "You know about what happened at Jungle Kingdom, right?"

"Yes."

"Then you should know I bit the child to keep us safe."

"You love this woman? Bite the child to keep her?"

He lifted his head to her and smiled. Being the oldest were-cheetah among their kind and a former Queen automatically granted her a certain amount of respect. He couldn't be mad at her even if she was Marianne's kin. Rio had the patience to stand his ground around Hazel, so only he could get her to give in to anyone's wishes.

"What's that supposed to mean?" he asked.

She patted his knee. "No harm, dear heart. I assume Dante wants her off the property, yes?"

Anger seized him.

Dante called with a million questions shortly after Rio slammed the cordless phone against the wall. Good thing he hadn't broken his cell.

A newspaper article came out about the incident at Jungle Kingdom. Everyone wanted to know where Sinclair was. Dante needed to know she stayed in contact with people so it didn't look like some sort of cover up. Luckily, Rio was a step ahead of him. He had Sinclair call her job, her family, and her friends. Her manager put her on short-term disability once he found out about Nahla.

Rio unloaded his own trump card on Dante. Nahla had survived the last few days when she should've been dead by now. Perhaps that thing with children being able to bounce back better than adults held true when it came to were-cheetah bites.

The lines had blurred. It was no longer a simple matter of tossing both aunt and niece to the curb. The child needed the kind of guidance her aunt couldn't give her. Coalition children didn't reach their first change until after puberty. With this being a toddler, Nahla had just trumped her chance at a normal upbringing. As much as he wanted to, Rio knew his King wouldn't turn his back on Nahla. No King in their right mind would. Her knowledge alone would surpass that of any cheetah by the time she reached eighteen.

Rio sighed. "Sloan is lurking around our territory, which is why Marianne and Billy want me to bring you to the enclave where you'll be safe."

"Don't change the subject." Hazel smirked. "That woman and her child have garnered enough publicity. If their bodies turn up anywhere on Coalition property, we can kiss our secrecy good bye. That's what Dante is trying to protect."

He couldn't blame him either. Still, heaviness about the subject weighed him down. "He's given me until tonight. Tomorrow, they have to go."

"Mmmm hmmm."

A face ducked behind a pillar. He couldn't be sure, but he swore whoever it was had set their sights on them. His fingers sharpened, scratching the wood on the back of the pew.

Rio leaned close, patting his hand on Hazel's shoulder while keeping his attention on the marble pillar. "We should go," he said in a low voice.

"Why?" She looked around.

"I think we've got company."

A man moved in the shadows, gliding sideways like he wore a pair of a rollerblades. Humans didn't move like that.

A growl registered from his throat. Before he could stop it, several irritated heads turned in his and Hazel's direction. The last thing they needed was attention.

"Let's go," he whispered. Clutching her shoulders, he helped her to stand. When she started toward the pillar at the end of the pew, Rio stopped her. "Not that way. Someone's there."

"I might be an old woman, but I'm certainly not feeble."

He didn't argue about that. After all, she could lift about twice her own weight. Still, that only meant whoever watched them could lift more.

"This is a church," he said. "We can't start a fight in here."

"Wanna bet?"

Before he could stop her, she tore off toward the pillar. So much for trying to stay trouble-free.

Hazel stepped into the aisle on the side with Rio on her heels. More oatmeal marble adorned the walls and the row of pillars on their right. Toward the front, hordes of flickering candles and melted wax filled a table.

Rio turned his head trying to pick up a piece of a scent. He found nothing.

His cell phone rang. Frantic, he yanked it off the clip and flipped it open. Marianne's number lit up the screen. Looping his arm around Hazel, he answered the phone while guiding them toward the back of the church.

"Did you find her?" Marianne didn't bother with any formal greetings.

"*Si*," he said, slightly irritated. "We're on our way now."

Silence came over the phone. "You might want to hold off. Better yet, bring her straight to the enclave."

"No. I'll bring her home. Marianne, she's a grown woman. As much as I love her, I can't force her to — "

Sobs cut him off. Something was wrong. In all the years he had known Marianne, the selfish bitch never used her tears to get something she wanted. Yes, her great grandmother's safety meant a lot to her, but she didn't seem like to type to cry over it. Bitching and threatening was more her speed.

Rio held the door open for Hazel. They slipped into the breeze, but he stopped at the top of the steps. A single finger went up and so did a smile, asking the elderly woman to wait while he stepped away to take the call.

"What's going on?" He kept his voice low and his back slightly turned.

Another sob came over the phone before she answered. "It's the house, Rio. Someone torched her house."

Did he hear her right?

"My god, I can smell it." She sniffled. "There's gasoline everywhere. Not only that, when I got the call, I thought she might have been inside.

Rio shook his head. He wanted to reach through the phone and calm her down, but the most he could do was close his eyes in silent prayer. "She's safe, Marianne." Then, he remembered the person watching them.

"Those Charlotte bastards are going to pay for this. How dare they go after my family?" She paused. "You have to tell her, Rio. Please. I don't want her…"

He didn't want to shoulder that kind of responsibility either, but at the same time, he was responsible for the old woman's health. The last thing he wanted was Hazel learning the news the hard way and keeling over due to a heart attack. Gulping, he turned his attention to her. Already, he could see the worry filling her glassy eyes.

"Let me talk to her," he conceded. "I'll call you back when we're on the road."

Not waiting for her to answer, he hung up, and took Hazel's hands in his.

Her head tilted. "Child…? What on earth is wrong?"

"It's your house, *dulce Madre*. Someone…burnt it down."

Hazel's eyes went wide and she gulped. Slipping an arm across her bony shoulders, Rio pulled her close and guided her down the steps.

Before he could make it to her beat-up Honda Civic, he noticed it leaned to one side. A few steps closer and he saw the reason just beyond the shadow of the overhead lamppost. Both the tires on the driver's side were flat. Someone had stalked the old woman.

Sloan's people meant to kill. It was in their nature to go for the weakest of the clan first. If they new about Nahla, she'd be next.

Rio cursed under his breath before hurrying to the other side of the parking lot. Luckily, nobody had messed with his SUV. He steadied the woman and opened the passenger door.

Hazel touched his arm. She took several deep breaths before she steeled herself. "I want to go home."

"*Madre*, there's nothing left by now."

"Don't you tell me to—!" She took another deep breath. "I'm sorry. But this is my home we're talking about. It's been my home for thirty years. I have a right to see it."

Nodding, he understood. Although he worried about how she'd take it, he couldn't refuse her.

Those Charlotte bastards would pay for this. He'd make sure of it.

Chapter 12

Rio spent the rest of the evening running off his anger in the woods. It wasn't enough that Dante wanted him to toss Sinclair and Nahla to the wind like they were nothing more than an afterthought. Now, he wanted a piece of Charlotte for what they did to Hazel's home. As a former Queen herself, they made a mockery of her legacy. Rio wasn't the only one who wanted blood for this. All of the Triangle Coalition did.

He tore through the woods at half cheetah speed. There were too many obstacles like trees and rocks in the way to allow for a full run. If nothing else, it provided great coverage for an animal that wasn't "indigenous" to the region.

Twigs and branches brushed across his spotted fur. When it came to water, he splashed across the streams and brooks before tearing through the ravines. Unlike some big cats, he liked water. Too bad he was too upset to allow himself a quick splash. He just wanted to run until his lungs burned and he collapsed.

Less than an hour later, he did just that.

Resting on his side on the edge of his home, he willed his body back to human form. Bones broke and reshaped, skin stretched and pulled, shaping him back to his bipedal form. By the time the transformation finished, he could hardly stand, so he took a few more minutes to rest.

Staring up at the stars through the canopy of trees, he couldn't get Sinclair out of his mind. He wanted her, but how would she react? Would his advances put her off? The change had left his hormones running wild, so it didn't surprise him that he felt like this.

Rolling onto his stomach, his long legs and rounded buttocks gleamed under the moonlight. Blades of grass and dew coated his skin. Pushing himself into a crawl position, the hunger in his crotch had radiated throughout his entire body. Snatching the pants he left beside a large rock, he had one leg in when the door opened on the screened-in deck.

Sinclair stood there holding her dislocated shoulder. A twinge bit into his abdomen. He hoped she wasn't in pain because she refused to wear her sling. Although she'd been taking her medicine these last few days, whenever asked, she claimed she felt fine.

The way the moon lit up the backyard and danced on her skin, she looked like silk chocolate, too expensive for eating. *Well...* He smiled at the thought of tasting her. She wore one of his button-front shirts and no pants, adding to her sexiness. When she sat on the porch steps and the moonlight hit her short, curly hair, his manhood tightened. Damn was she beautiful.

It was now or never.

Rio finished sliding into his pants and slipped his tee over his head before he stepped out of the woods. With his burning lust leading him to the woman on the porch, he didn't care that his fly remained unbuttoned.

Patterned scuffs caught Sinclair's attention. Perhaps birds or something turning in for the night. The increasing sounds made her jerk her head to the left.

She shrieked. Rio had stalked up on her. He exuded sexiness in those tight jeans and T-shirt. Although she thought it strange that he didn't have any shoes on, she put things in prospective and realized it didn't matter. His olive skin and shoulder-length black hair made her hot.

He seemed a tad disheartened since helping a friend with an elderly grandmother. Even though he seemed truly touched that Sinclair went out of her way to make him a meal for a change, he hardly touched his food. Normally, his appetite had no end. When she suggested they watch a movie, he wanted to go for a walk first. Perhaps she had done something to push him away. Guys usually got funny when she started getting a little territorial. That wasn't her intention. She just wanted to thank him. Perhaps her good intentions had spooked him.

Rio slowed. Although his predatory lust remained on high, she looked frightened for some reason. Had he done something wrong? More than anything in the world, he didn't want to scare her.

He forced a harmless smile to his face. "Enjoying the view?"

"Oh yeahhhh." She flinched at the desire in voice and cleared her throat. "I mean—yes. Yes, I am."

"It's a little cold out here, you know."

"That's usually the case around the fall. But it's okay. I don't mind."

They said each other's name in unison. Both of them had grown tired of the small talk. They wanted to go the serious route, but that little foible left them chuckling.

Rio took a seat next to her and started first. "Do you think about that kiss the other day? Because I can't get it out of my head."

She dipped her head low. "I do."

"Good. I think." This was harder than he had thought. He just wanted to taste her again and wasn't sure how to ask or if he should. Supposed she was the type who liked aggressiveness and surprises. "Well, I think you're beautiful. Sad to say, the longer you stay here, the more we're gonna get in trouble."

Was that supposed to be a come on? Sinclair's quivering lips bowed into a half smile. "Would that be so bad?"

Heaven help him, he didn't want to hear those words. Not while his throbbing cock remained sequestered in his pants. He was so excited that he could have taken her right there.

Taking a chance, he placed his arm on the planks behind her and leaned close. It was time to test the waters.

Sliding a finger across her shoulder, he leaned close and whispered in her ear, "I'd like to pick up where we left off. If that's okay."

Okay? Shooooot. He didn't have to ask her twice. She turned her head into his face, closed her eyes, and smoothed the tip of her nose around his. "Forgive me for the Eskimo style, but it turns me on."

He'd try anything for a first time, so he smoothed the tip of his nose with hers. "I see what you mean," he lied. However, it enflamed his raging libido, which would make the wait more worth it.

"*Usted es hermoso,*" he whispered, lips dangerously close to hers.

She grinned. "That sounds sexy. What does it mean?"

"You're beautiful."

Not another word. Their lips connected and Sinclair practically melted against his heated body. Her hand touched his chest.

Rio slid his arm around her back and brought her closer. He wanted to touch her, taste her, smell her. His tongue caressed her mouth, tingling parts of her that he hadn't touched yet.

Burning to touch his naked body, she pulled out of the kiss first. "We can't do this here. My niece is on the other side of that wall."

Say no more. Rio scooped Sinclair off the steps, kicked open the door, and carried her into the living room where the sofa bed remained pulled out from last night. He planned to collapse there after his run with a bottle of gin to help drown his sorrows. The last couple of nights had made it impossible for him to sleep there anyway. At some point during the night, he'd wake up, ease into the master bedroom where Sinclair and Nahla slept, and spend the night in the rocking chair beside them.

Tonight would be different.

Before he could lower her onto the mattress, he covered her mouth with his and devoured her with another kiss. Without breaking the kiss, he shed his jeans and freed his aching manhood. He pulled away long enough to yank his tee over his head and toss it aside.

Sinclair stopped a moment to take in the luscious man in front of her. Pain be damned, she hadn't felt this kind of desire in so long that she had forgotten what it was like.

"You sure about this?" Rio asked. He knew what he wanted, but he also wanted to make sure she wouldn't have any later regrets.

"I want you," she replied, fingernails scraping across his stomach.

That was good enough for him. Gripping the front of her shirt, he tore the rest of the buttons off and marveled at her beautiful breasts. Without a word, he took one of her Hershey's Kisses, nipples in his mouth suckling so hard that he would have drawn milk if she had any.

Sinclair moaned. When he made his way to the other breast, she used the time to learn how to breathe again.

Rio's hand slipped down to her panties. Like the shirt, he tore them away and began inching his fingers through her nested curls. Sinclair threw her head back, panting. Her body thrust forward, searching for his heated touch. Rio massaged her folds to make sure she was nice and wet.

Sinclair moaned and her hips thrust again. "Oh god! Oh…!"

Rio laughed and lifted his head from her breast. "Not yet, *amor.* I want to enjoy you."

With that, he slid down her front and planted his body between her thighs. Nobody had done that for Sinclair before. When she realized what was about to happen, she almost clamped her thighs together.

Rio pushed her thighs apart and held them down. Lowering his head, he went to town.

Sinclair relaxed into oblivion. Moaning, she slumped back on the bed, helpless to stop him. Her insides bore down harder with every flick of his tongue. She wanted him so bad that she thought she'd explode.

Seconds later, that was what happened. Her stomach knotted with pleasure, sending her into a mind-blowing orgasm. Her head twisted from side to side to keep from screaming. Head twisting against the pillows, she pounded her fists into the mattress. When the tightness subsided within her womb, she relaxed long enough to note the twinkling lights in her sights.

"Now that I've got you where I want you, I'll be right back." Rio bounded off the sofa bed and went into the office. When he returned, he had a condom in place and was ready to go.

Grinning, Sinclair's head fell against the pillows. "Give me a few minutes. I'm not sure I can—"

He knelt in front of her with the condom in place and pressed his penis against her entrance. "Still having second thoughts?" he chuckled.

He was cast-iron hard and thick. Good lord, what had she gotten herself into? Not that she was complaining. "You won't hurt me with that, will you?" she asked.

Rio leaned over her body, being careful not to put his full weight on her. "This is a love machine. Not a spear. The last thing I want is you too sore to make love to me again."

Chuckling, Sinclair reached between their bodies and found his manhood. She began scraping her fingernails along his length, stroking gentle enough to leave him sputtering. Pleasure radiated across his face. Yeah, she had him right where she wanted him.

Rio gasped, struggling not to fall on top on her. He regained his composure long enough to learn how to breath again. "You're a little minx, you know that?"

"Rowwwww," she purred.

That's it. He couldn't take any more. Pressing hard against her slit, his mushroomed head burst through her tight seam.

"You're stunning," he breathed, then kissed her neck.

Sinclair held her breath as he burrowed inch by inch, filling her womb. She clamped her teeth together and lifted her ankles around his waist to give him better access.

Slipping his hands underneath her shoulder blade for support, he began lifting his hips, sliding inside of her. Sinclair pulled back too, trying to figure out the pace he set. When he thrust forward again so did she. However, he wanted to feel every inch of her, so he lowered his mouth to hers for a scorching kiss.

When Sinclair's orgasm hit, her legs tightened around his waist, vaginal muscles milked him.

Rio threw his head back as strain marred his face. He released deep inside her womb. He pushed his climax until there was nothing left to push.

When he finished, he slipped his arm around her waist and rolled them both over so he could collapse on his back while she rested on his front. He remained buried deep inside her warm body. If he had his way about it, he'd never leave.

Chapter 13

Sinclair had been sequestered in Rio's cottage for the last few days. Cabin fever had bit her so hard that she almost decided to leave Nahla alone while she scoped out her surroundings. Each day Rio left her and Nahla for a few hours, claiming he needed to see a friend about more herbs from her secret garden. He said something about the land and soil being just right. As much as she appreciated his hospitality—the sex too—she thought more than once about taking Nahla to see a real doctor. Having a fever that wavered between 101 and 104 degrees for this long just wasn't right.

The phone rang.

Sinclair lifted her attention away from the TV and the comb she had worked through Nahla's tangled hair. She had hoped it was Rio, since she had sent him to Wal-mart for a jar of hair grease, too. He did a good job with the items on her last list, so she had sent him out again.

Planting a kiss on Nahla's warm forehead, she tucked the little girl on the couch after scooting out from underneath her. A quick jaunt around the dining room table, and she picked up the phone.

"Rio?"

"Rio? Who the hell is that?"

Sinclair closed her eyes. She knew that voice. "So you finally decided to call, Mina. Congratulations."

"And you're with my daughter while shacking up with some man. I guess I'm rubbing off on you." Mocking laughter filled her ear.

If only Sinclair could punch her through the mouthpiece. "I'm here with Nahla, yes. But I'm not shacking up with anyone. I left the number on the answering machine in case you cared enough to call."

"I called."

"Days after the accident." Sinclair closed her eyes. Now was not the time for this. "Nahla's under Rio's care. Whatever he's brewing in his lab, it's worked better than anything the doctors had given her."

"I need to know when you two are coming home."

"Why? You need me to make a crack run for you?"

"Scotch is more like it."

She could do nothing except roll her eyes. Lifting her head over her shoulder to check on Nahla, Sinclair stepped into the kitchen and took a seat at the breakfast nook. "I don't know when we're coming home because Nahla's still running a fever and—"

"You need to bring my chile home now, dammit! Especially if your ass called Child Services on me."

"What?"

"Don't act like you didn't hear me! Some asshole came up to my door—my door!—asking me about Nahla. When I told him she was out with you, that bastard gave me forty-eight hours to produce my baby or they'd take me into custody for obstruction of justice."

"Obstruction of justice?"

"I don't know; something like that. Look, who cares what they said? All I know is that my behind is gonna be in a heap o'trouble if you don't get my chile back here. I ain't about to go to jail for nobody. You hear me?"

Loud and clear as usual. "Mina, just calm down. Now what did they say exactly and who were they really? Did they show you a badge? Did you call the lawyer?"

"Fuck that! They said my ass was goin' to jail. Bring my kid back, Cindy, or we'll be sharing a fucking cell."

Click.

She stared at the phone. "That's Sinclair, you stupid junkie."

Nothing surprised her anymore. Mina could be a violent drunk if the moment called for it.

More important, why would she think that Sinclair had anything to do with calling Social Services on her? Mina knew Sinclair wouldn't hesitate to take custody of her niece if she could, but that didn't mean she'd actually sabotage her sister's relationship, or lack thereof, with her daughter. How dare that woman accuse her of such a thing? As usual, Mina remained so entrenched in her own problems that she didn't give a damn about her daughter's prognosis.

If it hadn't been for Sinclair having a conscience and not wanting to see Nahla become a product of the system, she would've told her sister to snort it up her nose. This wouldn't be the first time someone reported Mina to child welfare. Luckily, Sinclair saved her from that debacle. If she planned to save her from this one, she had better start now.

Scrambling around the cottage, she finished a note for Rio before grabbing his spare set of keys off the wall. Although Rio didn't want her leaving the cottage without letting him know, she had to think of Nahla first. Besides, she wasn't ready to immerse him neck deep in her troubles.

"Come on baby," she said, fitting her niece into her new pink and yellow striped jacket. "Auntie Sin's taking you to the hospital."

Nahla wouldn't understand the whole Child Welfare concept, so she told a slight fib about where they were going. It wasn't exactly a fib because two seconds after coming up with it, it sounded like a good idea. Just to be on the safe side, of course.

"Don't wanna go," Nahla mumbled. Heavy eyelids half-covered her eyes and her cast-less limbs worked sluggishly.

"Well, we have to go. I want to get you some real medicine."

"But Wee-oh got weal med-cine."

Sinclair slipped on her sneakers and tied the laces. "I know he does, baby, but a real doctor might make *me* feel better. Don't you want Auntie Sin to feel better?"

"But I like Wee-oh better than weal doc-tor."

Trying to make sense to this child was like hammering a nail with a whiteboard eraser. Although, it pleased her that she liked Rio since she liked him too.

Sinclair hoisted her baby girl into her arms and grabbed her purse on the bed. She did a quick check of the cottage before heading out the door to Rio's Pathfinder. He kept it parked on the side of the house but rarely used it since he had a motorcycle, too.

She got down the front stairs when Nahla started squirming in her arms. It was a good thing the little girl's casts were gone or Sinclair would end up with bruises. Moaning and groaning, she kicked her legs until Sinclair put her down. Nahla ran toward a nearby bush and hunched over. Retching sounds ensued. Getting her niece to a hospital would be impossible at this rate. Maybe she should settle for a doc-in-the-box clinic, which was probably closer. Anything had to be better than watching her go through this.

Sinclair crouched next to Nahla and soothed her back, whispering soft words while her niece threw up white curds. What she wouldn't do to take this burden off her baby.

"What the hell?" a voice said.

Sinclair leapt to her feet and whirled around.

A man stood at the end of the Pathfinder with gray hair that was buzzed flat on his head. His chin poked out and the insidious grin didn't help. Either age, experience, or both had hardened his face.

"What do you want?" Sinclair asked. Small hands clutched her thigh, so she reached down and forced her niece behind her.

Sinclair didn't need anyone to tell her that this man wasn't the next-door neighbor. The way his eyes traveled across her body and lingered on Nahla, she would've pegged him for the neighborhood child molester.

"A better look," he answered, eyes glued to her niece. "Man, I can smell her cub skin from a mile away. Kinda young, isn't she?"

"Back off, man. You come near us and I'll kick you ass from here to the curb."

He bellowed. "Lady, in case you haven't noticed, there aren't any curbs. There's just a back road, a bunch of woods, and no witnesses."

This wasn't going good for her at all. Sinclair hoisted Nahla on her hip and headed to the driver's side door of the Pathfinder. Keeping her eyes on him, she fumbled the keys.

A growl broke out behind her.

Sinclair whirled around to see another man, stepping out of the bushes. Between the long shaggy black hair and his mean smile, she knew the situation had worsened.

Sinclair yanked the driver's side door open and put Nahla inside. Before she could get herself out of harm's way, the heavy-metal man grabbed her by the arm and threw her on the ground.

Smirking, he reached inside the SUV and snagged Nahla's jacket. "Come here, little darling. Nobody's going to hurt you."

When Sinclair heard her little girl screaming and saw her small fists flailing at the man, something snapped inside her. "Get the hell away from my baby!"

She went straight for his face. Even though her fingers were clawed and ready to gouge out his eyes, it was the ignition key that skewered his eyeball.

The man howled in pain and dropped Nahla on the gravel driveway. As he fell on the ground, clutching his face, Sinclair grabbed her niece and shoved her under the SUV.

Chapter 14

The buzz-cut man dragged Sinclair off the ground by her hair. Pain slashed through her scalp. He slammed her back into the SUV and shoved his face within inches of hers.

"You stupid bitch!" he shouted. "What the hell do you think you're doing?"

"Trying to keep your filthy hands off my niece!"

"I ought to—"

His eyes went wide as Sinclair drove her knee into his soft crotch. Veins and muscles strained his reddening face as he grabbed his groin and sank to the ground. When he dropped to his knees, Sinclair kicked him in the throat.

Reaching under the SUV, she felt for Nahla's small hand. She didn't give her niece any time to climb out before tugging her across the gravel. She could live with causing a few scrapes and bruises. However, she couldn't live with herself if something worse happened to her little girl because she couldn't protect her.

Hoisting Nahla onto her hip, Sinclair started for the cottage…and stopped. Another sordid man came around the side of the house. He would cut her off before she could reach the steps. Judging from the scowl on his face as she looked between her and the eye-less man squirming on the ground in agony, he would have torn her apart to get some answers.

Sinclair darted into the woods. Keeping Nahla's feverish head clutched to her shoulder, she burst through the underbrush. Twigs and low branches slashed at her legs and arms.

Her heart stopped as she slowed. Sinclair couldn't take her eyes off the scene unfolding in front of her.

In a clearing, a quivering animal pushed off the ground to stand, its back legs snapping into haunches. On the far right, another that looked more like a bipedal cheetah. It looked humanoid with thick spotted hair carpeting its body. Bending at the knees, cracking bones urged the man-beast down until it was level with the other, fingers pulling back into the palms to form paws.

Sinclair blinked. Those...*things*...had turned into men or...turned into cheetahs. Were-cheetahs? No way! *American Were-Cheetah in London comes to life?* Impossible. Dear God, what next? Vampires? Mermaids? Zombies? All that stuff she saw in the movies couldn't happen in real life. It just wasn't possible.

In her heart of hearts, she knew the scene in front of her was as real as the pounding heartbeat in her chest.

"I scared," Nahla whimpered, clutching her aunt's neck while staring at the mutating bodies before them.

Sinclair turned her niece's head away from the frightening scene and darted in the opposite direction. Given the choice, facing those men back at the cottage seemed like the lesser of two evils. At least there was a getaway vehicle waiting for her and Nahla.

When the cottage came in sight through a tangle of trees Sinclair slowed. Tires screeched across the graveled driveway and a roaring motorcycle engine became quiet. Doors opened and the engine turned off. She tried to wrap her hearing around several mumbling voices but couldn't make out a word.

"Sinclair?"

It was as though time stopped around her. She knew that voice.

"Sinclair?" he repeated.

"Rio," she whispered.

"Wee-ohhhh!" Nahla shouted.

Pummeling footfalls pounded around them. Sinclair clutched Nahla and hunkered down behind a tree.

Several cheetahs stampeded through the underbrush, heading straight for the cottage. Sinclair's heart sank as one led the way, followed by two more on its heels.

When the cheetahs passed within a few feet of them, Sinclair leapt out of her hiding place and shouted, "Rio! Runnnnnnn!"

Growls lit up the area in front of them as they crashed through the forest, paws skidding across the gravel driveway.

She couldn't stay there knowing Rio was in danger, nor could she leave her niece alone in the woods. Who knew what other horrors lurked out there? Hoisting Nahla onto her hip, she forged ahead, prepared to live with the cost of her decision.

Sinclair burst through the woods on the side of the cottage, a few feet from the Pathfinder's open door. It waited for her like a free offering. After fleeing to the SUV, she shoved Nahla in the passenger seat and got in behind her. Unlike the women in the movies, she had no problem with slamming the key into the ignition and starting the engine.

"Sinclair!" Rio shouted.

She lifted her head. Rio and Kyle left the heavy-metal man curled into the fetal position on the ground and came to the driver's side. It dawned on her for the first time that the buzz-cut man and the cheetahs had disappeared. Could they have been the ones in the woods?

Sinclair triggered her window. Before she could say a word, Rio reached inside and pulled her in for a kiss.

"Are you two okay?" he asked, glancing at a frightened Nahla in the other seat.

Breathing hard, she replied, "We're fine. But they're out there, Rio. There are real monsters out there. I'm talking men turning into cheetahs!"

"I know," he said, scanning the area and wrinkling his nose with a whiff. "I want you and Nahla to stay inside until I say it's safe, understand?"

He knows? Sinclair couldn't answer him. How did he know about the monsters lurking around the house? Did he know they would be paying him a visit? Funny, how he showed up at just the right time too.

Sinclair watched her niece as she sat on her knees and rocked back and forth in the seat. It was the smile and the way Nahla looked at Rio that bothered her. "What are you smiling at? Aren't you scared of the monsters?"

She shook her head. "No. Wee-oh like 'em. But he's diff-went. He help us. Not hurt us. Uncle Kyle too."

"What do you mean like them?" She glanced at Rio who pointed toward two cheetahs who began stalking the front of the cottage. Where did they come from?

"Both kitties too. But they friendly kitties. I smell it, Auntie Sin. Can't you?"

Nahla didn't have to say another word. When growling rumbled just outside her window, at first she thought there was a cheetah behind Rio about to pounce on him. Not the case. The growling belonged to Rio. A snarl quivered across Kyle's human lips as he glared at another cheetah coming from behind the SUV. Sinclair had lost count of who was who except for Rio and Kyle being the only people left standing.

Rio nudged Kyle toward the front of the vehicle, pointing at the cheetahs and mapping out a plan for the oncoming attack. He wanted to keep them busy so that they wouldn't give Sinclair and Nahla the time of day.

Out of nowhere, another cheetah leapt for her open window. The big cat got its entire head and the part of its upper body into the metal frame, claws scratching the white paint as it tried to force its way inside.

Nahla screamed and Sinclair ducked across the driver's seat, barely getting out of the monster's way. Heated breath filled the interior with each hissing growl. Sitting with her upper half in Nahla's seat and her lower half under the steering wheel, Sinclair shoved her niece behind her for protection.

"Get away from them!" Rio snarled, grabbing the animal by the nape of the neck and yanking her out of the window. He slammed the cheetah into a nearby tree, cracking it bones in the process.

A fight ensued. More cheetahs launched themselves at the two men. As soon as they got rid of one, another took its place. When Kyle threw one on the ground in front of the SUV, Sinclair scooted back into the driver's seat and shoved the gear into drive. A loud yelp ensued when she bumped the vehicle over the animal's body.

Another SUV skidded across the gravel to a stop. Marianne jumped out of the passenger's side. The engine shut off and another man leapt out from the driver's side.

For every were-cheetah, there was a "human" to fight them off. Sinclair would have put her money on the cheetahs because of their size and the fact that they had teeth and claws going for them. However, the "humans" did a good job at holding their own.

By the time the dirt settled, two cheetahs lay on the ground with broken necks, one dead by the tree, and the one Sinclair used as a speed bump. The man she stabbed in the eye lay unmoving too. Four cheetahs and one of their human counterparts in all. As for the Rio and his friends, they mostly suffered from deep cuts and bites with the worse being an arm that the last man to join the fight was holding in such an odd way that Sinclair wondered if it was fractured.

"We can get out now," Nahla said, reaching for the door.

Sinclair placed a hand on her niece's arm and stopped her. Keeping her eyes on the others, she said, "Put your seat belt on."

"But—"

"Put it on!"

Her tone caught Rio's attention. He turned to face them.

"Sinclair," he warned, meeting her eyes, "what are you doing?"

"We're getting out of here," she muttered as she slid the gear into reverse.

"That's not a good idea. We need to talk about this."

She blinked. Did he hear her? Granted the window was broken out. Still, it couldn't have been more than a mumble under her breath. "Can you hear me?" she whispered.

Rio sighed, lowering his eyes a moment. Dammit, she knew something was going on. He couldn't hide it any longer.

Lifting his head to meet her stare, he replied, "Yeah...I can hear you."

"That's all I need to know."

Sinclair slammed her foot on the accelerator. Gravel and smoke spewed from the back tires as the SUV took off.

Rio let out a curse as he watched his SUV and the angry woman behind the wheel speed backwards down the driveway. He charged after them. Ten percent of his anger had to do with Sinclair leaving like that. The other ninety percent was at himself for not being straight with her in the first place.

Sinclair couldn't believe how fast he could run. Thank goodness, the driveway was relatively straight with a slight curve at the end. When they bounced onto the main dirt road, Rio collided with the side of the SUV and yanked on Nahla's door. Between her sobbing and Rio's anger, Sinclair could hardly think straight enough to slam the gear into drive and peel off down the road.

Rio ran full force behind the Pathfinder, determined more than ever to keep up. As the vehicle drew farther away, his footfalls slowed. His loved ones had slipped from his reach.

Chapter 15

Sinclair didn't know what to do. She hated having to listen to Nahlas's sobs and repeatedly explain why they had to leave. Her little girl had grown so close to Rio during the last few days, and even went so far as to take her medicine like a champ. Now it was time to bring Nahla to a real doctor for real answers.

Nahla hadn't said anything in the last half hour. Sinclair reached across the seat and stroked her niece's silken pigtails. The toddler had curled up in the seat and slipped into quiet mode.

"You okay?" Sinclair asked, breaking the silence.

Nahla shook her head.

Sinclair placed the back of her hand on her niece's brow. "You feel hot. Is your tummy sick again?"

She nodded.

Dammit. If it weren't for her getting lost trying to get out of the woods, she would've had Nahla to a doctor by now. "If you feel sick, then go ahead and throw up on the floor. I'm sure Rio won't mind." A smirk crossed her face. After the hell he put them through, he earned that piece of backlash.

As if she needed another reminder of what she had just been through. Those people had turned into animals. They became monsters right before hers and her niece's eyes. How was that possible? Did she see it right?

She shook her head. Of course, she saw it. She heard the growls coming from Rio and he didn't deny knowing anything about those monsters. Was Nahla right about him being one himself? A...cheetah?

Dear God, she had slept with him. She had sex with a monster.

Tears welled in her eyes. How could she have been so stupid?

"Auntie Sin," Nahla cried, "I gonna...I gonna..."

She never made it. Nahla puked all over her lap and the seat. She didn't have time to do it on the floor like her aunt instructed.

Sinclair pulled the SUV to the side of the road and put the gear in park. Before she could undo her seatbelt, large raindrops plopped on the front windshield. Things couldn't get any worse...until Nahla started crying.

Sinclair cooed, unzipping her jacket. "Don't cry. Everything will be okay."

"Wanna see Wee-oh," she cried.

"Not now, Nahla." Sinclair wasn't in the mood. She just wanted to get her niece out of those filthy clothes.

"But Wee-oh—"

"Stop it, Nahla! He's not here, okay? I can't bring him to you on a silver platter."

Tears drowned Nahla's eyes right before she turned away from her aunt.

Dear God, what possessed her to say that? There wasn't a rock big enough for her to climb under. Sinclair closed her eyes and took a deep breath. She wanted to give herself the luxury of crying too, but that old "be strong for Nahla" voice had popped in her head. That didn't make her any less of a heel for yelling at her when Nahla did nothing to deserve that kind of wrath. God help her, she sounded like Mina.

Sinclair tossed the smelly coat on the floor. "I'm sorry, baby. Auntie Sin shouldn't have yelled at you. I'm just...I want you to get better is all. Rio is gone now. Maybe we'll get a chance to see him some other time. Just...not now. He'd want you to get better, too. That's all I'm trying to do."

"Wanna go home," she whimpered.

"Sweetheart, we can't—" Sinclair stopped.

There wasn't any reason why they couldn't unless someone was looking for them. Who would be, other than Social Services? They beat that wrap before because Sinclair was in the house. They could do it again.

Maybe for once Sinclair would start thinking about what her niece wanted. Besides, it was late and the chances of finding a clinic open would be nil. "Do you miss your mommy?"

Nahla shrugged. "I guess so."

In reality, Sinclair had a feeling that neither one of them missed Mina because she hardly noticed they were gone. Still, no matter how much Sinclair loved her niece, at the end of the day she belonged to Mina. She had no right to keep them apart.

Sinclair nodded. "We'll hangout with Mommy for a while and see how it goes. Okay?"

"Okay," Nahla mumbled.

◆ ◆ ◆

"I can't believe you didn't call me," Mina sniped, dumping a handful of pajamas next to the bathroom sink. "Hell, it was enough that nobody told me what hospital you guys were at. Why would they cover up something like that?"

Sinclair cut a glare at her lazy-eyed sister. The smell of alcohol rolled off Mina's skin invading her nostrils. Heaven only knew what she dabbled in if she couldn't stand without swaying from side to side. Did she forget that they came home because of the visit from Social Services?

"Mina, I left you enough messages for an audio book." Sitting next to the tub, she smoothed her wet hands along Nahla's feverish back. "If you had listened to them, you would've known where we were. Thank God you remembered to call when it mattered."

"I called three or five times. I got a woman who's pissed at me, a number no longer in service, and some teen who said he's gonna rock my world. Ain't none of 'em ever heard of you."

Yeah, she was drunk. If her sentence structure was that bad, then she was definitely tipsy.

Mina plopped down on the closed toilet lid. She slung her medium-length black hair over her shoulder. Dark bags hung under her foggy eyes and her skin was ashen and sickly. A pair of dark brown eyes penetrated Sinclair. "Where the hell were you?"

"You knew which hospital we were at." Sinclair dipped the sponge in the tub and squeezed the water across Nahla's back. "The doctors tried to call you. They left a bunch of messages, Mina. Couldn't you at least call back or something? Your little girl was dying."

Mina waved her hand. "Yeah right. Those doctors probably got her mixed up with someone else. Besides…look at her. She looks so good I bet she can run a marathon."

"Then why did you try to rush her off to a toilet when she had to throw up? Look at her! Can't you see that she's sick?"

"Sick is different from dying. And, if she's that sick, you wouldn't be camping out in the woods."

Sinclair fought not to dunk her sleepy sister in the bathtub to straighten her out. "You know what? I'm tired. Nahla's tired, too.

How about I finish this up so I can get her to bed?"

Mina blinked through her drunken state and smiled. "Uh-uh. I know what you're tryin' to do. You spent all dis time with Nahla and now you want to spend the last few hours with her, too. Girl, had I known your time off from work would be a week and a half vacation, I'd have packed my bags and gone with you. But since um her mother, it's my turn."

Leaning over the tub, Mina yanked her daughter out of the water by her upper arms. Nahla let out a squeal that ricocheted throughout the house. How dare that drunken heifer grab that poor child like that? Didn't Mina hear a word she said about their injuries and being in the hospital?

When her sister ignored the child's wails and plopped her against her hip, Sinclair's jaw clenched. This was nothing more than Mina's day-late-and-a-dollar-short attempt at playing mom and her niece would suffer at the hands of the inebriated bitch.

"What the hell, Mina!" Sinclair leapt on her sister and tore Nahla from her arms to cradle her in hers. "Shit! What's wrong with you? I told you that she was still recuperating. You can't sling her around like a rag doll."

Mina placed a hand on her hip and pursed her lips at her sister. "Don't tell me how to hold my chile! She's my daughter, Sinclair. Don't you ever forget that."

"How can I? You never let me."

"And don't tell me how to treat my chile!" she repeated.

"I won't when you start treating her like one. She's not a trophy, Mina. She's a child who has a heart and feelings just like anyone else. Maybe if your sorry behind weren't so blitzed out on Hennessey and crack, you'd see that!"

"I ain't no fucking crack head! I gave that shit up months ago and you know it!" Mina stormed out of the bathroom and down the hall. "I don't have to take this. Next time you take my chile away without my permission I'll send the cops after your ass and have you charged with kidnapping. How's that for child care?"

Before she could answer her back, the door slammed.

As always Mina had to have the final say no matter how stupid it was. To think Sinclair gave up her condo for this.

With Nahla nestled in her arms, she sat down on the toilet, cooing and rocking her. The tears in her baby girl's eyes burned a hole in her heart. Perhaps coming home wasn't such a good idea after all.

Chapter 16

Sinclair thought about packing up Nahla and taking her to Barb's house. Unfortunately, Barb would have more questions than she had answers. She went out of her way staying in contact with her friend, so if anyone accused her of anything, she'd have Barb to vouch for her. Plus, Nahla had spent too much time away from home already. She needed familiar surroundings.

In the short time she had been alive, Nahla had seen more than her share of dysfunction. Sinclair prayed for the day Mina would come to her senses and give her custody of Nahla.

Sinclair could give her such a better life than this joke of an existence that Mina offered. She made a great living as a co-pilot. Even though when she'd received a promotion to a larger craft, she turned it down in order to be close to home when Nahla needed her. If she could trust Mina to do what a mother was supposed to do, then she wouldn't have to worry all the time.

Once she got Nahla to bed, Sinclair padded down to her room to have a moment to herself. Lying on the bed, she stared at the ceiling.

She couldn't get Rio out of her head. The thought of his warm hands all over her body and caressing her places where she couldn't reach made her ache. Then the thoughts of him turning into one of those crazy cheetah people made her slap a hand across her forehead. Tomorrow, she'd take Nahla to the doctor. For that matter, it wouldn't hurt for her to have a checkup, too. The last thing she needed was to bring some mutant baby into the world.

◆ ◆ ◆

Since Sinclair couldn't sleep she decided to make a call. She needed to make sure that she wasn't in any trouble with the law for acting as Nahla's guardian to sign her out of the hospital. Seeing as an animal bit her while in their care, Mr. Jacob Torrance, her lawyer, didn't see why they couldn't work out a deal to drop the potential charges. After all, they stood to lose a lot more. As for the police, the most they would want was a statement about the accident. Before worrying herself sick, Mr. Torrance promised to look into everything, including a lawsuit against Jungle Kingdom. He even agreed to call Social Services on her behalf.

By the time Sinclair hung up the phone, doubts began plaguing her mind. Rio would hate her for doubting his expertise, but she had to protect Nahla. If Social Services planned to make another visit to their house, then she wanted to be ready for them with a note from Nahla's pediatrician.

The toddler hated going to the doctor. From the moment they arrived, Nahla pitched a fit. She hated everything from the sterile smell to the white coats they wore. The stench from the other sick kids didn't help. They smelled like flu, phlegm, and head colds. Even the blood from the little redheaded boy made her gag. He'd cut his arm on something and it had left a gash that needed stitches.

Dr. Norris led Sinclair and Nahla into his office and asked them to have a seat. The older man finished writing a prescription and handed it to her. "There's one other thing I'm concerned with," he said, sliding his glasses up on his bulbous nose. "The lab ran Nahla's blood. Twice. I asked for a copy of her records when you called this morning for an appointment. Anyway, there's something odd I'd like to talk to you about."

"Odd?" Sinclair said, shifting Nahla's limp body in her lap.

"Yes. I'm going to send you over to the Children's Hospital for more tests. Right now, in fact. I think she might have some form of mutated rabies."

Sinclair wouldn't make that trip. The bad news would only deepen the hurt. Besides, wouldn't her niece have turned into a cheetah cub by now?

"I'm also recommending that we do a full range of tests," he said. "If she's been suffering from seizures, then I want to make sure we know what we're dealing with."

"Uh-huh."

Why couldn't someone else help her sort through this? Dammit, this had Mina's name written all over it. She wanted to break from making the decisions, but at the rate things were going, it would be a while. As long as Nahla depended upon her, she couldn't let her baby girl down. Her so-called mother already did that every time she wrapped her lips around a bottle or a crack pipe. As long she was damming people, damn Brian for being such a cowardice dick and leaving her to take on the parental role. Damn Rio for seducing her and biting her niece. Damn everyone to hell!

"Sinclair?" the doctor repeated, his balding head tilting.

"Yeah?" she replied, tripping out of her thoughts.

"I said this is something that needs to be taken care of. Today. I have a colleague who's working at the hospital. He will be the one attending Nahla when you arrive."

"Now?" She couldn't think past the numbness in her head.

Dr. Norris cleared his throat and sat back in his chair. His blunt fingers drummed on top of the smooth wood surface. "I know all about Jungle Kingdom."

A tremor ripped through Sinclair. He had her full attention now.

Norris continued. "You carry Nahla's medical information in your wallet. The hospital called my office for her medical history. That's how I learned about the accident. The newspapers only confirmed it." He pulled his glasses off and pinched the bridge of his nose. "I'm stunned that she's even this healthy. Last time I spoke to the doctors, they had pretty much written her off. When I called again to check on her, they said you had signed her out of the hospital against doctor's orders."

Sinclair stiffened, tugging Nahla closer. "And here we are, sitting in your office without a mark on either of us. Bet you're wondering what sort of miracle drugs the hospital is pushing these days, huh."

"Something like that." Norris stood and came around the desk. He hiked a hip up on the corner and sat, taking a moment to study both the Duvals. "What happened, Sinclair? The only reason why I ask is because others will do the same. In fact, they already have."

She lifted Nahla off her lap and began putting her coat on to keep from facing that man. He hadn't asked anything she didn't expect and already there were too many questions. She had enough problems that needed sorting out. She didn't need more weighing her down.

"I've gotta go," she declared.

"Sinclair, please. I only want to help. All I'm saying is that whatever happened to you and Nahla isn't normal. Let's see what—"

She straightened and met his eyes. "There's nothing to see. Nahla and I are fine. Better than we were before."

He slid off the desk and waved his plump hands defensively.

"And that's wonderful. However, I think that we should get the two of you in the hospital where we can properly monitor your condition for any residual effects."

Residual effects. Boy, if he only knew. Sinclair shoved the prescription in her pocket before cradling Nahla in her arms. "We have to go. I've got a million things to do."

As she made her way to the door, Norris, touched her on the arm to stop her. "Please, Sinclair, be reasonable."

"Or what?" she yelled, whirling on him. "You'll call Social Services? I've taken good care of this child and I'll keep doing it no matter what you or anyone else says."

"I'm not calling you a bad person. I—"

"Good. Because right now, I'm better for this child than her own freakin' mother." Sinclair took a cleansing breath and lowered her voice. Lifting her chin she said, "Thank you for your help. I appreciate you finding room in your busy schedule for us. Now please…let me take care of my baby girl. If she gets worse, I'll call."

"Please do."

◆ ◆ ◆

As if the visit to the doctor wasn't a shock, when she went to the bank to get money for Nahla's prescription, she discovered more than two hundred grand deposited in her checking account. Only one person had that kind of money. Dante Martinelli. If he knew where she banked, then he knew other things about her like where she shopped, went to church, and even had her hair done. Mina's place didn't feel so safe anymore.

"Tired." Nahla dragged her weary body through the front door and stared at her aunt with large, doe eyes. "Wanna seep."

"I know, baby." Sinclair touched a hand to her niece's head. Oh, boy. Her temperature had risen since coming from the doctor's office. All that running around town didn't help either. Sinclair eased her niece onto the couch and placed a pillow under her head. "Lay down for a sec, okay? Aunt Sin needs to pack a few things for the road."

"What 'bout Mommy?"

Sinclair forced a smile to her face. Mina wouldn't care, let alone go with them. "Aunt Sin loves your momma, so she's not going anywhere without telling her. We'll give her a call. Either that or we can stop by the diner and pick her up from there."

"Then where we go?"

She smoothed a hand against her niece's warm cheek. "On a trip. You know how much you like going on trips."

"Don't wanna go. Wanna stay here where Dolly is."

"Suppose I buy you a new doll?" Bribing a three year old sucked, but it was the quickest way to get the ball rolling.

"Don't want one," Nahla said, crossing her arms and poking out her bottom lip.

Sinclair sighed. Had Nahla not been sick, she would've reprimanded the toddler for being so insolent. That girl had better be glad she didn't feel well.

There wasn't much to pack. Sinclair snagged her overnight bag from the closet and began packing some clothes for both her and Nahla. Next, she went to Mina's bedroom and gathered up clothes in another suitcase. She didn't want to have Mina griping about not having anything to wear. If the chick didn't want to go with them, then she'd leave the suitcase for her at the diner. Under no circumstances would she come back to this house unless it was in handcuffs and there was a warrant out for her arrest.

Grunting from the other room got Sinclair's attention. She had grabbed a rag doll she had found in Nahla's room and headed into the living room.

The scene chilled her.

Convulsing, Nahla's small body jerked back and forth on the couch until she tipped over onto the floor.

Sinclair screamed, dashed across the room, and pulled her niece onto her lap. Her heart hammered against her chest, igniting the silent panic that had tortured her for days. Tears streaked her eyes as spasms tore through the little girl's body.

"Shhhh," she cooed, trying to protect Nahla from further injury. "It's okay. It'll be okay. I promise."

Why in the world was she putting them through this? She needed help, dammit! A good aunt would never do anything like this to her niece. She should've listened to Dr. Norris and brought Nahla to the hospital. Damn her for being so stupid.

A knock at the front door, jarred her from her niece's plight.

Vomit spewed out of Nahla's mouth. Could this day get any worse?

"Open the door," a voice commanded. "It's the police."

She had to ask.

Chapter 17

"Just a sec," she shouted.

They didn't wait. The door burst open, splintering pieces of wood across the foyer. Two cops dressed in black uniforms marched into the house and found her on the living room floor with her niece jerking in her arms and the smell of putrid vomit flooding the air.

The female cop lifted her hat off, letting a long braid drop down the length of her back. "Oh my god! You smell that?"

Her male partner nodded and crouched next to Sinclair.

He lifted his hand to Nahla, letting it hover over her head. "She's changing."

Sinclair yanked her niece away from him. What the hell did he mean by "she's changing?" As Nahla's convulsions slowed, Sinclair snatched a blanket off the couch and began cleaning up her niece. No matter how bad it looked, she wanted these people to leave them alone.

"There's nothing wrong with her," she snapped. "She's just a little sick."

The male cop stood, his height towering over them. "I'm afraid she's more than just sick. I'm surprise you didn't take her to the hospital when you had that chance."

Here we go again. If she heard another unfit-parent story, she would be the next one breaking something. She was so good to Nahla that the little girl slipped and called her "Mommy" several times. They had no right to come here and take her baby away. Sinclair's jaw clenched. She wouldn't give them a fight, but she sure as hell wouldn't make it easy either. Already her brain began ticking through her wallet to find the card with Mr. Torrance's phone number on it.

"If you're going to cuff me then don't do it with my niece around. You take me outside where she can't see."

"Cuff you?" the female asked. "For what?"

"For…" Sinclair opted to keep her mouth shut.

These so-called police officers made her uneasy, but she didn't want to incriminate herself on top of everything else. All they needed was her to crack under the pressure and start spouting stories about were-cheetahs living in the woods. They would lock her up until Nahla was ready for college.

The male cop shook his head. He motioned to his partner to back off.

"Ms. Duval," the man said, regaining Sinclair's attention. "Dr. Norris called me because I asked him to. My name is Killian Sloan and this is Penny."

Sinclair pulled Nahla's sweaty body close to her breast. What did Norris have to do with this? Surely, he wouldn't have called the cops on her because she skipped out on going to the Children's Hospital. Even worse, what else would the cops want with her if it wasn't about leaving the hospital and taking a child under false pretenses? Other than these two acting strange, none of it made sense. However, she wanted some space between her and Sloan.

Scooping Nahla into her arms, she hurried into the bathroom. It gave her a chance to clean off her niece and prove she could take care of her too.

Sloan followed. "I can help. I've seen many like her before. Just…never in one so young. Too young, in fact."

Sinclair had Nahla in her lap and was stripping off her sweaty, stinky clothes. She didn't want to hear anything these people had to say unless they were Miranda Rights. "Are you going to arrest me? That's all I want to know."

"No. But we're here to—"

"How did you know about Dr. Norris? Did you follow me from his office?"

Sighing, Sloan leaned with his back against the counter. "I've been monitoring the Triangle Coalition for a while now. When I heard about you and your niece, I did a background check that led me to Dr. Norris. One phone call and a visit with the right credentials was all it took. I had him watching out for you. I had to see if the rumors were true."

"Then you're not here to take her away?"

"No." He paused a moment to shift his weight to his other foot. "I've seen things like this before, Sinclair. Either you're unwilling to admit that or nobody's told you." Another pause as he crossed his arms over his chest. "Who bit her?"

Her mouth opened to ask how he knew, but she closed it. Slipping Nahla's tee over her head, her hand brushed Nahla's bandaged palm. It drew her attention, bringing back memories of their visit to the doctor's office.

Norris talked about giving her the first in a series of rabies shots while changing the bandages and listening to the story behind it. It smelled so much like rotted limburger cheese that his face paled and he had to step away for a quick cough. He prescribed a strong antibiotic along with the other medications that Nahla was on. If he had his way about it, he would have had her admitted the second they showed up at the hospital.

Sinclair's lip stiffened. She didn't want to talk about this anymore. Her baby would be fine and that was the end of it. "I don't know. All I know is that the hospital let some animal in. A nurse claimed it was a spotted dog." Crouching on the floor, she stood Nahla's exhausted body between her knees so that she could get her out of her remaining clothes.

"Then one of the crazy bastards from the Triangle Coalition bit her." Even as it came out, Sloan realized he had voiced her thoughts aloud. "Ms. Duval, your niece's going to—"

"What do you mean by 'Coalition'?" Sinclair narrowed her eyes on him. She lifted her naked toddler into her arms, letting her baby's head slip under her chin.

Another sigh as the Charlotte King lost momentary eye contact with her. "I'm talking about were-cheetahs. Like werewolves call their kind Packs, we call ours Coalitions. It's the same term the cheetahs in the wild use."

"Dear God." She gulped. "How many of these *Coalitions* are there?" As Sinclair adjusted her niece's limp body, she thanked God the convulsions had stopped.

Sloan shook his head. "I don't know. Our numbers are usually less than werewolves, so I'd guess at least a thousand throughout the world."

Sinclair's stomach knotted. The whole idea of there being more than were-cheetahs out there had scared her. Nonetheless, she continued. "Then you must know of someone or some way to stop this. I don't care if they're werewolf, were-cheetah, or were-guppy."

His gaze lowered. "Once someone is bitten, their chances for survival are fifty-fifty. The only thing you can do at this point is manage the convulsions and hope that she becomes one of us."

"Otherwise, she dies. Is that what you're trying to say?"

"Ms. Duval—"

"I want to speak to your superior. There has to be something you're not telling me."

"I *am* the superior. I'm the leader of the Charlotte Coalition."

"Then get me someone higher."

"There isn't anyone. Each coalition is pretty much like a family where the King and the Queen are the heads of the household and as high as you go."

Her jaw clenched. "You've got some nerve coming up in here and telling me there's no chance for my niece. You monsters got her into this, so you need to get her out of it. I don't care if you have to consult a were-cheetah witchdoctor, but this is your kind's fault." Sinclair stormed past him and out of the bathroom.

He grabbed her arm. "You have to listen to me."

"What for? You just said there was no hope." She yanked her arm free and started for the front door, bare child in her arms and all.

Penny darted from the couch, cutting her off. "You have to listen to us."

"In case you missed that conversation, here's a recap. What for!"

As she tried marching around her, Penny grabbed Sinclair's arms and forced her backwards.

Never in her life had she expected that kind of strength from such a short, stout woman like that. Sinclair pushed her so hard that even Nahla began screaming, terrified that the woman might hurt them.

"That's enough!" Sloan yelled, breaking between the two of them.

Sinclair couldn't fight. Not with her niece scared half to death and sick with fever. A deep inkling inside her knew what they had to say, but that didn't make it any easier to hear.

She backed away from both of them and went into the kitchen. Frightened, Sinclair put the breakfast counter between her and the uninvited houseguests. At least it offered more protection than open space. She even stepped closer to the knives in case she needed to defend herself with more than just words.

"Whether you like it or not, your niece is changing," Sloan said. "You have to come with us. To protect her from the crazy bastard who bit her."

"Bull," she spat. "I'm pretty sure you're not the best thing for us either."

Sloan shook his head as though that would help filter out some of his frustrations. "Listen to me. What happened to your niece is against our Laws. We're..." — he glanced at Penny — "were-cheetahs, too, but I'm guessing you already know that. The point is this should've never happened. Biting one so young... Your child needs the closeness of a Coalition if she's going to survive."

"But Rio—"

"Please." Penny rolled her eyes. "It figures. I bet that pussy never told you any of this. He and his clan are nothing more than a bunch of—"

"Shut. Up." Sloan fixed her with a glare.

She snorted. "Dammit, she's got a right to know! With half the Coalition acting like a bunch of maniacs, they'll kill them. Assuming they haven't tried already."

"Don't you think I know that?"

"Know what?" Sinclair still didn't trust them, but at the same time if they meant her any harm, they could've done it by now. Seeing as she and her niece were attacked by those crazed monsters at Rio's place, she had to hear the rest. After all, Rio had happened to show up at just the right time. How ironic was that?

Sloan sighed. Stepping close so that he could lean on the counter, opposite of Sinclair, the King met her eyes. "A few years ago, Rio fell in love with a woman named Ashley Cavanaugh. From what I understand, he fell so hard for her that he bit her to keep his leader from sending her away. The bite didn't take the way he had planned, so she ended up going insane. She killed herself a few months later. Rio went after our people, thinking we had something to do with it."

"The rape, you mean?"

"No. *That* my people are responsible for. They got what they deserved. However, biting her was all Rio's doing. He's possessive enough to do anything to have a mate. Sound familiar?"

As much as she didn't want to believe it, Sinclair couldn't keep the huge seed of doubt from planting in her mind. God willing, she hoped it didn't take root.

Unfortunately, it made sense. Would Rio have bitten her niece to keep her from going to the police? In reality, she didn't know how far he'd go to please his boss. For all she knew, sleeping with her could have been part of the deal.

"There's more," Sloan continued.

She sighed and shook her head.

"Dante Martinelli has stirred a sense of paranoia among his people, making them think that our Coalition is out to kill them and take their territory. I won't deny that. If that's what it takes to make them stop the madness, then so be it."

"Stop what exactly?" she asked.

"Stop them from turning innocent people like your niece," Penny growled. "Like Ashley. Dante's whole Coalition is nuts. His people have sabotaged our grocery store shipments and even tried to burn down one of our markets a few weeks ago."

"Look, Sinclair, all I want to do is get you and Nahla away from them. Our world is not the place for the two of you. Nahla will need the kind of stability that the Triangle can't give her. Rio is their healer, but even his mystical medicines couldn't save his beloved. If anything, the side effects have probably made your niece's condition worse."

"Don't you get it, lady?" Penny stormed forward and slapped her palms on the counter. "They bit your niece and kidnapped both of you to keep you quiet. You give them up, and you give up your niece too. Does that sound like the MO of a sane man?"

Sinclair didn't want to think about this right now. However, deep in her subconscious she knew it made sense. As if her problems weren't compounded enough, this was nothing more than another weight added to the pile.

"We're not out to push you into anything," Sloan announced. "We can't reverse the effects on your niece either, but we know that we can make it easier for her. The choice is yours."

"I-I-I need some time," she stammered. She clutched an exhausted Nahla to her front. "Please leave. I can't think with you hovering over me like this."

Sloan nodded. He knew he could only do and say so much. The Triangle Coalition had already sunk their claws into her and gained a good foothold. The best he could do was get her thinking about other alternatives.

Reaching inside his back pocket, he pulled out a card and slid it across the counter. "If you need anything...call me."

Nudging his partner, they left through the busted door.

Chapter 18

"**I** can't believe we're just sitting here," Kyle said. "Those bastards went inside and—"

"They didn't leave with her," Rio finished. "If they had, we wouldn't be sitting here. Besides, they're playing games; I'm sure of it."

"Yeah, with your woman." Kyle leaned back and crossed his arms over his chest. He shook his head and stared at the two Charlotte members as they got in their Crown Victoria and sped away. "So what do you want to do?"

Rio knew what he wanted to do. He wanted to run in there and pull both Sinclair and Nahla into his arms and comfort them. That was after he scolded Sinclair for running off like that. Sure, she'd probably put up a fight and push him away. She had every right, but that didn't lessen his need to be with them. He couldn't reveal that to the man sitting next to him no matter how much they felt like brothers.

"We'll wait," he said, slouching in the seat.

He and Kyle had parked the van down the street and out of sight. They knew where she lived. Rio knew Sinclair would go home to her sister's because she had a child who wasn't hers. Since her sister hardly made a peep about her daughter throughout the whole ordeal, it made sense Sinclair would check to make sure Mina was still alive. The question was how long would she stay here? Sinclair was a smart woman. Now that her sister's place had been compromised, she wouldn't stay much longer. They'd have to wait it out.

The thought of that left a bitter taste in the back of Rio's throat.

He hated being robbed of the chance to sit down and tell her the truth. Chances were those Charlotte bastards probably beat him to the punch. Sinclair would never give him the time of day. She'd clobber him with a caste iron skillet and keep pummeling just to make sure he stayed down. If only he had acted faster, he could have gotten to her before their enemies.

"You waitin' for the kid's mother to come home?" Kyle asked. "What happens if the little girl starts changing? It's going to freak everyone out, man."

"Don't you think I know that?" he snapped. "But we can't go charging in there right now. Depending on what those bastards told her, we're the last people she wants to see."

"So I guess that means we're just sitting."

"Exactly."

◆ ◆ ◆

Sinclair didn't know what to do, so she kept herself busy by taking care of her personal affairs via phone and computer. The cordless phone made it easier for her to camp out in the spare bedroom where Nahla slept while she conducted shapeshifter research on the Internet.

She also got a call from Mr. Torrance who wanted to set up an appointment for her to come down to the office, so they could get started with filing the lawsuit against Jungle Kingdom. As it turned out, inspectors had already started giving the Martinellis grief regarding the safety of their attractions. Mr. Torrance also received some good news about the hospital not pressing charges. Just as he'd thought, the threat of a countersuit made them back down. Then there was the issue of her job and whether or not she still had one despite being on disability leave. Lucky for her, her boss finished the paperwork and sent it to HR for further processing.

"What the hell?" Mina shouted from downstairs.

Time to face the proverbial music. Sinclair hauled herself away from the computer and headed downstairs where Mina and Jermaine stared at the handyman working on the new door. He'd just shown up. All he said was that someone came to his office with a thousand dollars in cash and an address.

Sinclair would've preferred someone else—someone Sloan hadn't chosen. Unfortunately, Mina was on her way home and they needed a safe place to sleep for the night. Until Nahla's seizures stopped, carting her around anywhere was a risk she refused to take.

"What's up," Sinclair croaked, tremors working into her fingers.

She clutched the banister to hide it.

Mina waited at the bottom of the stairs as Sinclair descended. Before she could open her mouth, Jermaine, Mina's boyfriend, spoke for her.

"What the hell happened?" he asked, glaring at Sinclair. "And why is there some guy installing a new door?"

Sinclair bit her lip in contempt. She hated his ass. He was lucky she wasn't the one bit by a were-cheetah or she'd gouge burrows all up and down his ass. In the short time she had known him, she knew he was in this house for one reason. Her sister was an easy lay.

Jermaine stood there wearing a red Chicago Bulls jersey and a cap hanging half off his head. His jeans hung so low that the torn hems scraped the floor. The man looked to be in his mid forties, so he was too damn old to be dressing like some street punk. The gold tooth he wore on his right canine didn't help. Neither had the fifteen-year age difference between him and Mina.

Mina stepped in front of him and placed a hand on his chest. "Let me handle this. I'm sure Sinclair has a good explanation."

He snorted. "Yeah right. I've got a good solution. How about you kick her and the bad-ass kid behinds to the streets?"

Sinclair tightened her jaw to keep from making matters worse. Oh, how she wanted to tell her sister about the one time the worthless jackass copped a feel and she retaliated with a slap across the chops.

He was a piece of scum just like the others who had come through Mina's revolving bedroom door. Why cause a ruckus when Sinclair already knew her sister wouldn't believe her? Besides, eventually Mina would get bored and toss him aside. Better yet, she could end the whole thing sooner by telling Jermaine that Nahla was actually Mina's child and not hers. Last night when they showed up, Mina asked her sister to play it off so that her having a child wouldn't scare Jermaine away. Well, perhaps that was the best way to handle a jerk like him.

Had it not been for this house belonging to Mina and her unable to keep the bills paid on her waitress salary, Sinclair would have junked this joint and went back to her condo. She didn't need this foolishness.

"Can I talk to you upstairs?" Sinclair seethed. "Alone."

Jermaine opened his mouth to protest, but Mina shoved her grocery bags in his arms. That shut him up. Ignoring his sputtering protests, Mina followed Sinclair upstairs and into the second bedroom where Nahla slept.

Mina planted her hands on her hips and yelled, "What the hell happened? I can't leave you alone for five minutes and already you're tearing my house down. You're gonna pay for that fucking door."

Sinclair remained calm to her surprise. She narrowed her eyes on her sister. "The door is already paid for. And if you're worried enough to care, there was a break-in while we were here. Nahla and I—"

"Ohmygod! Was it Chuck? That bastard's been looking—" She closed her mouth and turned her attention to her little girl. "My God. She looks sick, Sinclair. Didn't you take her to the doctor?"

Yes, you idiot. I did your job.

Sinclair didn't want to know. It wouldn't be the first time one of Mina's hoodlum boyfriends had broken into the house. "I did." Sinclair pulled the blanket up to her niece's shoulders and kissed her feverish cheek. "Dr. Norris gave me some antibiotics. He gave her a shot too."

"This isn't normal. I'll tell you what. I'll have Jermaine start dinner while we run down to the Clinic-1. I'm sure a second opinion won't hurt."

"Gimme a break, Mina. Don't start acting like you care."

"She's my baby, Sinclair. I care about what happens to her."

"Then why is it that you nursed the bottle more than you did your baby?"

"Don't talk to me about how to raise my own damn child."

Sinclair had had it. When Mina leaned forward to touch her baby, Sinclair jerked her away from Nahla and thrust a finger in her face. "Don't you stand there and tell me that I'm a bad parent when I'm not supposed to be one at all. Where do you think you'd be if it hadn't been for me moving into this hole? You spread your stank legs for Brian and he left you with the burden of raising his child *and* keeping a roof over your head. I didn't ask to come here. You begged me! Now your baby's got clothes on her back, bills paid, and healthy food in the refrigerator. All because of me."

"Don't you stand there and tell me I'm—"

"Your idea of daycare was putting Nahla on the floor with the Disney channel and a box of crackers. I'm the one who came home from work to find your one-year-old baby sitting in a dirty diaper, wrapped in a bunch of cords, and a flipped over chair that nearly crushed her fingers. So don't you damn-well stand there and act like I haven't done a thing to contribute to his household. I'm the one who keeps it running when you've got nothing better to do than run a piece of dick between your legs."

Mina narrowed her eyes on her sister and stabbed a finger in her chest. "Who the hell do you think you are to tell me anything? I never asked for this shit! I never asked to have a kid or her father to run out on me. With everything I've been through, I've got a right to be fucking happy any way I see fit."

Sinclair slapped her hand away and stalked around the bed. "Here we go again. The same pity party that we've all come to know and love."

"Fuck you, Sinclair! Get the hell out of my house!"

"Not without Nahla I don't! You ready to sign her over to me so that we can both get the hell out of your hair? Because we'd all be a lot better off."

"You've lost yo' damn mind. I wouldn't give my baby to you—"

"Let's get something straight. The day you take Nahla away from me is the day I call Social Services. We'll see what they say about your parenting techniques. I'm sure they would love to hear about the revolving pimp door you call a bedroom."

"Go to hell!"

"I'm already there. You got something better?"

Sinclair opened her mouth and was about to yell at her sister again when a knock on the bedroom door stopped her. The contractor from downstairs stood there with a clipboard, staring between the two women.

"Sorry," he said. "Didn't mean to interrupt. The guy downstairs told me to come up and—"

"What the hell do you want?" Mina yelled.

Sighing, he held the clipboard out to them. "I need someone to sign off on the work."

Mina shot her sister one last scowl before she charged for the door. Whacking the clipboard on her way, she yelled, "Handle it!"

Even the repairman looked stunned.

Sinclair shook her head as she approached him. "Sorry about that. My sister gets a little testy at times. Now where do you need me to sign?"

He pointed at a solid line on the bottom. "Don't worry about it. You wouldn't believe how many doors I've fixed because of family squabbles."

Mina could go to hell. Sinclair would make a good mother to Nahla. In fact, she already had. Then again, if she was any kind of guardian, she would have done more to keep her niece from being bitten by a were-cheetah. For that, she'd never forgive herself.

Chapter 19

Rio waited as Eddie, the were-cheetah repairman left. Rio was unable to tear his attention away from the house. Even when the lights went off with the exception of one bedroom, he kept his focus on the window where he knew Sinclair and Nahla slept. He wanted them back so bad that he mourned their leaving as though it were Ashley's passing all over again.

He checked his watch. Nudging Kyle awake signaled it was the time to get his woman back whether she came quietly or not.

The key Eddie gave him slipped into the lock and the deadbolt on the new door. They hadn't had time to get a chain lock or anything else, so if he wanted to make contact with Sinclair, he had to do it tonight.

Both men eased inside the house with hardly a sound from their footfalls. Rio motioned for Kyle to remain downstairs and keep watch while he hurried silently up the carpeted stairs.

When he reached the second floor, he heard the sounds of heated sex. Just as he started down the hall, a shriek brought him to a stop. Rio stopped and lifted his head over his shoulder. A growl rumbled from his throat. That didn't sound like pleasure. A second one followed from Mina's room. Rio paused. A war raged inside him on whether or not to go to his loved ones or to help someone he didn't know.

Ignoring his cheetah instincts, he followed his human ones by hurrying down the hall toward the scream. He stopped just before breaking inside and opened his ears to the sounds.

"Let me go, you bastard!" Mina shouted. "You're strangling me!"

"Just wait a sec, baby," a male voice shouted. "They say choking makes it better."

"No!" she shouted. "Let go, negro! This shit ain't in the program. Stop it! Stop it! Sinclair!"

Rio busted through the door as the man unsheathed himself.

Anger tore through the stranger's face. He wound his hand back and smacked Mina so hard across the cheek that she rolled to the other side of the king-size bed.

Rio concentrated feverishly to fight the change waging war inside him. This man was more of a monster than he was and the jerk planned to prove it with Mina's corpse.

The stranger lifted his head to the Rio. "Who the hell are you, man? You can't be coming up in here when I'm tryin' to do my business."

Rio snarled as he stormed across the room. His hand went around the man's neck, lifting him up and slamming him hard onto the floor. He wanted to crush the man's windpipe to dust. How dare he mistreat a woman like that? Even in his own animalistic sex-capades with the felines in his Coalition, a male would never bring violence to his lover. This man was worse than an animal. He was a piece of sewer scum.

"Stop it!" Sinclair yelled. She gripped his muscular shoulders. "Stop it, Rio! You'll kill him!"

When did she get here? How long had she been in the room? Nonetheless, Rio poured all of his hatred on the man.

"The world would be better off!" He watched Jermaine's lips go pale. Try as he might to throw Rio off, the cheetah knew the human was no match for his strength.

"Not if you're locked up for murder." She tugged on his arm; both her hands going around his thick bicep. She eased her face closer, pleading next to his ear. "Please…let him go. He's not worth it."

With all the anger and rage burning inside him, somehow her voice snagged hold of the beast stirring who egged him to kill Jermaine. He noticed Sinclair's delicate fingers for the first time. She had touched him with those soft hands of hers. How he wanted to feel her golden brown skin against his again, but not like this.

A final snarl and Rio released him. He refused to take his eyes off the hoodlum. "A woman saved your life tonight, you sick piece of shit. Remember that the next time your sorry ass decides to mistreat another one. Kyle, get this piece of shit out of my sight before I neuter him."

If Sinclair had come into the room without him noticing it, then he didn't need to search his loyal friend out. He knew Kyle wouldn't be too far from the commotion either.

"With pleasure." Kyle yanked the man up so fast that his head bobbed between his shoulders. He snatched a pair of pants and a shirt off the floor then pushed him out the door and down the hall. Several thumps later, the front door opened and slammed shut.

Rio glanced at Sinclair. He wasn't sure what to think about her just yet. His instincts told him to tend to Mina first, so he did. Plus, it gave him time to think.

Mina pulled a pillow across her nakedness and scurried to the headboard. Quakes racked her entire body as she hung onto the wood for dear life. Black, flat hair was glued to her forehead and cheeks and there was swelling around her left eye.

Sinclair couldn't help noticing Rio standing at the end of Mina's bed with concern etching his face. Not only was he both hers and Nahla's savior, but now her sister's too.

Sinclair hurried to the bed and sat with Mina. Her skittish sister whimpered and shied away. That hurt Sinclair to no end. Maybe she should've let Rio kill the bastard for what he did to her. Despite her sister being a worthless drunk, that didn't give anyone the right to abuse her. What would've happened had she not been there? Had Rio not been there?

"It's alright," Sinclair assured her. "He's gone now. He won't come back."

"I made sure he won't," Kyle said, appearing in the doorway.

Rio shook his head. "How about we go downstairs and make some coffee? I'm sure everyone could use some right about now."

Sinclair lifted her head to him. "Nahla —"

He waved a hand. "I'll check on her. See to your sister."

Sinclair had a few questions to ask him. Like how he was so sure that she'd come home. How did he know which room she stayed in? How did he get inside the house? Yeah, she had some questions and she damn well was going to get some answers.

"Sinclair," Mina squeaked.

"I'm here," she said, stroking her sister's hair.

Mina said nothing. Instead, she collapsed in the comfort of her sister's arms and cried.

Chapter 20

Rio placed a poultice over Mina's swollen eye and instructed her to keep it there. Luckily, he showed up planning to administer first-aid to Nahla or he might have left his sack of herbs and powders behind.

"It smells." Mina clasped the sheet to her chest.

Sinclair smoothed a tuff of black hair from Mina's honey brown face. "Keep it there. That's what helped put Nahla and me back together."

"It smells like dog shit."

Sinclair laughed. Boy, did that bring back fond memories.

"Herbs." Rio double-checked its placing to make sure it covered all of her bruising. "But it was boiled in brandy, milk, and some other stuff. That's what the smell is."

"That ain't all," Sinclair mumbled, arching an eyebrow at him.

Mina snorted. "Speaking of which, I could sure use a drink right now."

"Like hell you can!" Sinclair interrupted. After everything she had been through, drinking should be the last thing on her mind.

Neither of them brought up Jermaine. It had crossed her mind several times to call the cops, but it was a call Mina had to make. The best she could do was be a good sister to her.

"No alcohol," Rio said. "Not until the poultice comes off. That means either warm milk or hot cocoa."

"How about some aspirin? My ass is..." She trailed off, her good eye lowering in shame. A tear squeeze between her eyelids and slid down her cheek.

"Maybe Sinclair can guide me around the medicine cabinet," Rio replied. He motioned his head for her to follow him into the hall. He closed the door behind them and said in a low voice, "She's bleeding inside. I can smell the blood."

"Bleeding?" Sinclair rushed passed him about to barrel into the room.

He grabbed her arm and stopped her. "I've got something that can help but...it's..." Good lord, how could he say this? He certainly didn't relish the idea of administering it to her. Not with Sinclair hovering over him. "It has to be inserted inside her."

A sputtered sigh left Sinclair's lips. "I could be wrong, but I doubt she's in the mood to have a finger up her ass right now."

"I agree, but it's either that or she should go to a hospital."

The doctors would report Mina's sex play as rape to the police and force Mina to turn Jermaine in. Who knows what he'd do to retaliate? He might turn around and point a finger at Rio with the bruises on his neck as proof. The cops could lock Rio up for attempted murder. Were-cheetah or not, Sinclair couldn't let that happen to the guy who'd save her sister.

"What about that Theradin stuff?" she asked.

He shook his head. "What little I have isn't enough. The medicine will hurt no matter how it's done, but at least she'll feel like a new woman come morning. It's part aphrodisiac."

Sinclair couldn't help the small smile. "Why haven't we tried it?"

Her grin faltered. She shook her head, wishing she could take it back. This wasn't the time to dredge up old memories. However, when a smirk curled the corner of his mouth, she *really* wished she could've taken it back.

"When there's time, we need to talk about us." He met her eyes as his hand reached for the back of hers.

Her stomach clenched. "I have to check on Nahla."

"She's with Kyle. She'll be fine. What I want to do right now is get your permission to help Mina. Otherwise, she'll have to go to the hospital. There's no telling what kind of dirty laundry she'll air in the process."

"But you can't—"

"That's my weakness, in case you haven't noticed. I can't *not* help those in pain. Right now, Mina's hurt. I can't do much about her psychological or emotional state, but I can do something about her physical one."

Sinclair sighed. "Just...let me talk to her first."

Rio nodded. "Then I'll go make Mina some hot cocoa. Just in case we need it."

"Hot cocoa? What's that going to do?"

"It's the something extra that I can put in it to make her more comfortable."

Sinclair didn't want to know what he meant by that.

◆ ◆ ◆

It took a lot of convincing, but Mina agreed to take her chances with Rio's weird medicines. After what he did for her, she wouldn't risk having him spend one night in jail. However, when she realized the salve had to be inserted inside her, she almost reneged. Boy was that embarrassing. Then again, Mina didn't come off as the type to be easily embarrassed. Rio handed her a salve that looked more like cucumber melon lotion and let her tackle the rest. Mina couldn't help eyeballing him before she shuffled her sore body into the bathroom and closed the door.

Three minutes later, an orgasmic cry rifled from the other side.

Rubbing her hands on her pajama bottoms, Sinclair raced for the bedroom door. "I've gotta go. To check on Nahla or something."

Rio grabbed her arm as she hurried past him. "Can we talk?"

Rekindling her anger, she yanked herself free. "What are you doing here? How did you find me? What the—"

He placed a finger on her lips. *God, those lips. So tender and moist.* His manhood stirred to the occasion, packing the front of his jeans. Turning her around, he guided her toward the door and out into the hall. He would've been happier to take her now and answer questions later, but he knew Sinclair wasn't up for that. Not with the amount of fury edging her voice.

"Let me go," she said, jerking away from him.

Rio closed the bedroom door. "You stole my truck. You're lucky I didn't have it reported. God only knows what would've happened to Nahla."

"Since when do you give a damn about my niece?"

"Because she's belongs to me too!"

Sinclair wasn't the only one who had cornered the market on hostility. Sure, she had a right to it, but so did he. After all, she drove off without giving him a chance to explain. For all he knew, she took what they shared and threw it out of the window. He planned to go a lot further than a romp between the sheets, but she never gave him a chance to prove that he was better than that.

"What the heck are you talking about?" she seethed. "My sister is the one who carried her for thirty-eight weeks and I was there when Nahla was born. Not. You."

"Yeah, and I'm pretty sure by now you've heard everyone else's story except for the one that comes from the horse's mouth."

"All right then, jackass, talk!"

He paused a moment to rein in his anger. "You know what I am, so I'm not about to glamorize it for you. So there's the first piece of information. You want the second piece? Nahla would be dead right now had I not bitten her. What she's going through is the transmutation fever."

"One that she could die from anyway, no thanks to you."

"If she were going to die, it should've happened by now."

"Should've? So in other words, you don't know."

He gutted her with a glare. "Would you rather she be back in the hospital? Would that have made this easier on you?"

"Don't you turn this on me. It's not about—"

"It's about keeping your niece alive."

"Did you use that same reasoning when you bit Ashley?"

"What?"

"You heard me. I talked to Sloan. He told me what you did."

He couldn't believe what he just heard. What in the world had the parasite put in her head? "I never bit Ashley."

"Not even to heal her?"

"Hell no! She had already been brutalized. Why would I brutalize the love of my life a second time by biting her? By the time I got to the hospital, the doctors had already performed the surgery to save her life. Biting her would only heal her faster. It wouldn't have given her back her uterus."

He had a point. Although she hated his guts right now, he didn't strike her as the type to make things worse. Perhaps Sloan had lied to her after all.

Sinclair shook her head as though that would stop the tears from welling in her eyes. How did she know he didn't do it to keep her quiet too?

Maybe this was partly her fault because she agreed to let Rio help. *Dammit, couldn't he have told her about the side effects?* This wasn't like a headache or nausea. This was a lifelong affliction that would limit Nahla from having a regular childhood. She never really had much of one, but to steal it from her before she had the experience wasn't fair. What kind of world would her niece grow up in knowing she'd sprout spotted fur and a tail?

Rio held out his outstretched arms to her. She batted them away and backed against the opposite wall.

"There had to be other options." She swiped at her single tear.

"I explored every one of them with the doctors."

"She's just a baby, Rio! How could you do that to her and not tell me? I'm her flesh and blood, dammit! I'm alone in this! You may have given me a choice, but at the same time you left me in the dark." She couldn't plead anymore for his understanding. Perhaps her tears would get through to him.

"That's what I'm trying to tell you now. You're not alone. I'm the one who sired her, so she's my responsibility too. She has my cheetah DNA. That makes her my daughter."

"Bullshit! What do you know about being a father? You think that making a baby—were-cheetah or not—makes you a daddy, then you've got a lot to learn."

"You think I bit Nahla for the fun of it? I knew it would change my life too. Whether you want me as a part of your family or not, raising her is my responsibility."

"I'd like to see how you're going to break the news to Mina."

"She had better get over it."

"She will…as long as you're willing to slip her some skin."

Rio rolled his eyes. "If I wanted her, then I'd be here for her. So whatever hang-ups you've got with guys screwing then leaving, get rid of 'em. I'm not going anywhere."

Sinclair opened her mouth about to rifle a few choice words back, when movement to her left caught both their attentions.

Kyle stood in the hall with Nahla convulsing in his arms.

"Oh no," she whispered, and raced down the hall.

Rio came up fast behind her and took Nahla from Kyle. "Is there another bathroom?"

She waved for them to follow her. She hurried down the hall, sheer panic infested her mind. Her baby girl was in the middle of another seizure that wanted to tear her apart. How much longer would she have to go through this?

Not saying a word, Kyle went around Rio and plugged up the bathtub. He turned the cold tap on as high as it would go while Rio got rid of her nightgown and training pants.

"What are you going to do?" Sinclair cried, feeling completely helpless.

"She needs an ice bath," Rio said. "We've got to get her fever down. Is this the first time today that she's had a seizure?"

Sinclair shook her head. "No. She had one when those fake cops broke into the house and…dear God. She rolled off the couch and then the vomiting started."

"Did she hit her head?"

"I don't…I don't know. Maybe. Why? She's been asleep most of the day."

He didn't answer her. The moment he lowered Nahla into the frigid water, her eyes opened and she screamed. Rio pinned her arms to her sides and held her flailing body until the water came up to her shoulders. When she almost slipped out of his hands, he hoisted her halfway out.

"This isn't going to work," he yelled, above her screaming.

"Let me have her." Sinclair reached for her niece.

"You've got to get in the water with her. She won't stay put and I don't want her to thrash about.."

"Shit!" Sinclair plunged a foot in the cold water, soaking the hem of her pajamas.

"Kyle," Rio said, "we might need some ice. There's a convenience store open a few blocks down on the right."

"Sure." He started out the bathroom, and stopped. "You two okay being left here alone? I don't want to come back and find his eyes clawed out. We sort of need him, Sinclair."

"Get your ass out of here!" Rio shouted.

Grinning, Kyle held his hands up and hurried out of the bathroom. By the time Rio turned around, Sinclair was sitting in the water cradling her whimpering niece.

Holding the toddler close, Sinclair crooned to her. Once again, Nahla kicked and struggled in her aunt's arms, fighting to get out of the frigid water. Normally her baby girl wouldn't put up such a fight. Nahla might huddle to the edge of the tub with water this cold, but she fought with all her might, more powerful than a child twice her age.

Turning Nahla around, Sinclair pinned her arms to her sides and held her niece in place with the water coming just below her chin. Her tiny feet began pounding the porcelain bathtub. Sinclair could only do so much to keep Nahla still. She didn't want her baby hurt anymore than what she was. Rio reached into the chilled water and grabbed her ankles.

"H-h-how l-long?" Sinclair asked, bottom lip quivering.

"At least until her fever breaks," he said, gaze meeting hers. "You doing okay?"

Sinclair shook her head. "C-c-cold."

Rio pressed his hand to Nahla's forehead. "A little while longer, that's all."

"It hurts!" Nahla cried. "Burns! Wanna get out!"

"I know your blood is burning, but it'll be okay. I promise. Everything will be all right."

"No it won't! You hate me!"

A hot spear sticking through his side would've hurt far less than those words. He didn't want Nahla or Sinclair hating him for what he did. After all, they were his family now.

Chapter 21

Sinclair woke surrounded by warmth. Someone had tucked her in bed with a thick comforter and a heating pad that stretched the length of her body. No, wait a minute. The way it conformed to her naked—naked?—body, sculpting her thighs, buttocks and legs, this was more than a heating pad. An arm rested on her waist, the hand limp against her belly. Talk about being possessive.

Sinclair turned her head toward her shoulder. A fuzzy cheek scraped her face. Rio's light breaths steamed up her ear.

"Body heat works much better," he mumbled. "Don't you agree?"

"Where are my clothes?"

"Who cares? I want to feel your skin on mine." Tender kisses pressed against the nape of her neck, moving close to her ear until his tongue sucked the lobe.

"Where's...?" Tightness between her legs made that come out a little breathy. Let's try again. "Where's Nahla?"

"She's sleeping in her bedroom. Don't worry. Kyle is with her."

Rio suckled her ear harder this time. Her legs trembled and her toes curled on the top of his feet. It was nice to know he had that effect on her. A grin curved his mouth before moving his lips to the nape of her neck.

"Nahla's...okay?" she breathed.

"Yes."

"What about Mina?"

"She didn't complain," he breathed. "Then again, the Milodern pretty much kept her sated for the night."

"Milo...?"

"Milodern. It's the aphrodisiac."

"Damn." That had a two-fold meaning. Not only were his kisses pushing her close to the edge, but… "When do I get to try some?"

"Curious?" Rio purred. He cupped his hand on her hip and turned her onto her back. Reaching just over his shoulder, he produced a jar of salve. "How about now?"

Sinclair licked her lips and swallowed. "Well…as long as you have some on hand. Besides, I'm sure it'll make me even warmer. Not only that, you still have some apologizing to do."

She couldn't be sure when she forgave him, but being here last night to help with Nahla's seizure had certainly helped. He only wanted to save her life. In a way, she did the same by taking on the motherly role that Mina has passed on.

"Oh…you have no idea how much I want to make it up to you." He juggled his eyebrows.

Pushing back the comforter, he exposed his erection. Unscrewing the cap, he swiped his finger in the salve.

Sinclair ran her fingers along his, smearing the creamy aphrodisiac on her hand. "Allow me."

Before he could replace the cap and put the ointment back on the nightstand, Sinclair captured him. Rio's hips jerked forward. His head fell back in the pillows, a silly smile plastering his face.

Sinclair had been dying to get her hands on him. Gliding her hand along his shaft, she worked from base to tip, massaging him. Judging by the smell of his other remedies, she didn't want that stuff anywhere around her mouth, so she'd have to save the taste test for next time. For now, her hand would have to suffice.

Rio didn't seem to care one way or the other. His chest rose and fell with a huge sigh, body quaking in her hands. His head tipped backward, eyes shut tight. When her hand slipped down to his sack fingernails raked his sensitive skin. Again, his hips shot forward.

"Shit, woman! You're going to be the death of me."

A deep chuckle rumbled from her throat. She enjoyed having him at her mercy. Before he could slip into complete ecstasy, she pressed her mouth to his and tasted his lips. She couldn't help running her free hand through his soft, silken hair. One of his hands sneaked between them. His rough thumb pad scraped across her nipple, she jerked and her hand pumped him harder and faster.

"Stop!" he shouted. "Enough, woman!"

He sat up and grabbed the Milodern off the nightstand. Lopping his hands under her arms, he dragged her across his front. Ramming his swollen lips into hers, he flipped her over on her back and forced his legs between her thighs. He pulled out of the devouring kiss and watched her giggle.

"You think that's funny? I'll show you something funnier." He smeared his fingers with the Milodern and massaged her vaginal lips.

"Oh my God," she shouted, pulling away from him. "What the...?"

Now she understood why Mina's climax hit her so hard and fast. Rio rubbed something ten times the potency of Ben-Gay inside her. Momentary heat bled into her vaginal muscles before turning into icy coolness to relax them. Rio hooked his arm around her thigh to keep her still. Every inch his fingers explored, it incited the heat. When he pulled them away, the coolness rushed in. It took a moment of getting used to, but when she did, her hips bucked against him. Sinclair thought she'd tear her hair out in complete ecstasy.

"Oh man," she breathed. "Apology accepted."

"Not so fast," he said, continuing to play with her.

Sinclair wriggled in his grip. The hot/cold sensation had her creaming between her legs. The tightness welled inside her until she exploded in a blinding orgasm. She came straight into his hand and went through several spasms before her body had spent itself.

"Oh man," she breathed. "It was so..."

"I take it you like the Milodern," he chuckled.

"You didn't say that it sends you spiraling through orgasms. Notice the plural."

"Oh? In that case, you'll love this."

His finger entered her again.

Her taut thighs clamped down on his exploring hand as another orgasm began building inside her. "Dammit! You're going to kill me."

"Not yet. I'm having too much fun."

He removed his finger and slipped his hands over her hip so that his could guide himself inside her.

Sinclair's head fell backwards into the pillows. There was nothing she could do or say that would sound coherent at that point. Too much heat and all of it went to her head.

Rio couldn't help himself either. Between the hot and the cold, he needed her so bad that he ached. He began pumping inside her, stroking her, building the heat between them. The hotter it got, the more he massaged her. Sweat slicked their bodies. He lowered his head and claimed her breast. He suckled, nipped, and teased her nipple while cupping the mound of her sweet buttocks.

Sinclair wrapped her ankles around his thighs, forcing him deeper inside her core. He filled her completely, pumping her into decadent oblivion. She could feel him pulsing inside her, heard the suctioning sounds as he milked her to dripping wetness.

Sinclair came so fast and hard that it took her by surprise. Her hips rocked back and forth in time to his movements, slamming hard against him as if to suck him dry. When he hit his climax, another orgasm erupted inside her.

Several orgasms later, they calmed down long enough for Rio to turn sideways to keep from collapsing on top of her. Although her thigh remained trapped between his and the bed, he was too tired to move. He gathered her up in his arms. "Damn," he breathed, "you're so beautiful. Oigo campanas de la bo—"

"Shut up, lover," she mumbled. "You're ruining the afterglow."

He chuckled and kissed her on the head. It was a good thing she had stopped him because she might have mistaken his "I hear wedding bells in our future" for a proposal when he meant it to be a compliment. He wasn't ready for that kind of a commitment. Not yet, anyway.

A knock on the door incited a groan from both of them. Rio reached over and covered their spent bodies with the comforter. He snuggled Sinclair in his arms and kissed her forehead. Sinclair never opened her eyes. Despite the soft smile pressing into her cheeks, she would've gladly slept through the intrusion.

"Come in," Rio grumbled.

"Can't...can't get it," a tiny voice replied.

Both of them separated and bolted upright. Rio threw back the blanket and ran across the floor, scoping up a pair of boxers and his pants. He finished slipping them on then looked back at Sinclair. She had leapt out of bed and rummaged through a chest of drawers until she came to an oversized T-shirt and a pair of jeans. She finished dressing just as Rio opened the door. Nahla stumbled forward against his legs, her eyes half closed.

He scooped the little girl into his arms, planted a kiss on her cheek, and carried her to the bed.

"Hand her to me," Sinclair demanded.

Rio chuckled before planting a kiss on the toddler's soft cheek.

"Wanna seep with you guys," Nahla mumbled. "With Auntie Sin and Wee-oh."

Sinclair smiled. She loved the way her little girl mispronounced his name. So cute and innocent.

He didn't hand her over. Instead, Rio cuddled her warm, little body against his chest .She was a part of him now and nothing could change that. Planting his nose into the depths of her silken afro curls, he inhaled her were-cheetah scent. She was now his daughter.

He cursed himself repeatedly for never taking the time to notice her while she played at Jungle Kingdom. He'd give anything to see her laughing and playing in the backyard of his cottage. One of the first things he'd do when she got well was buy her the best swing set that money could buy. She'd won him over so much that he'd go through hell to see her happy.

Sinclair remained propped on her elbow, staring at him.

Rio sighed. "I know you can't get enough of me, but unless we plan on doing the deed in front of *our* niece, there's no reason to send her out of the room."

Of all the – ! Giggling, she clobbered him with her pillow. "You've got some nerve. And what's this talk about 'our' niece?"

"Please," he yawned, waving a hand. "I'm in no mood to fight. Just tell me one thing. Are we going to have...you-know-what again or not? Because if we are, let me know so I can bring her back to Kyle. Otherwise, snuggle in and go to bed."

Nahla reached for her aunt's cheek. "Auntie Sin seepy too. Git warm wit us."

Aw shit! She didn't want to throw Nahla out in the cold. Looking at the love on Rio's face, she couldn't bear to take her child away from him. If her baby girl managed to sneak out of her room after a horrible seizure and stumble her way down the hall to theirs, then it wouldn't be right to send her back.

Sighing, Sinclair hunkered down, sliding her arm over her niece and Rio's waist.

He, in turned, hugged both of them close. Whether Sinclair liked it or not, they were his family now. If anyone so much as laid a finger on them, he'd tear them apart and bask in their blood. Even if that "anyone" turned out to be his own people.

Chapter 22

Mina watched and sipped her coffee from the doorway as Sinclair played lovingly with her niece. Multicolored building blocks lay scattered on the bed while they snapped the pieces together to form animals. Nahla was still feverish, but this was the most active she had been in the last few days.

Mina longed to have the bond those two had. She knew she messed up big time. Sinclair was more than just an aunt to her little girl. She was a surrogate mother who was always there for Nahla. Mina knew she wasn't ready for motherhood, so she never embraced it. Her big sister had. Whenever she needed to go out, Sinclair never flinched at the thought of having to baby-sit her daughter. She found out that her sister would proudly lift her head and tell anyone who asked that Nahla was her daughter. She truly loved her little one as though she were her own.

"Why didn't you tell me about Rio?" she asked, and tipped her cup to her smiling lips.

Sinclair snapped a plastic head on a giraffe. "He works at the first-aid station at Jungle Kingdom. He may only be a physician's assistant, but he's done a world of good for Nahla."

"Wait a minute. Are you telling me that bastard works for the people responsible for hurting my child?"

Sinclair rolled her eyes. "Please. Don't act like you care after the fact. He's in your house, he saved your sorry behind from being strangled, and I happen to be sleeping with him. There. Now you know everything."

"But that motherfuck—"

Sinclair clamped her hands over Nahla's ears and scowled at her sister. "Would you shut your trap? There's a child here, for heaven's sake."

Mina snorted before sipping her coffee again. "Still, I don't like him downstairs calling himself fixin' lunch for us."

Sinclair rolled her eyes. "Lord, give me strength not to hurt this woman."

Sighing, Mina sat on the bed. "Well, whatever he is, he likes you."

"No—ya think?"

"I'm serious, sister-friend. If you weren't so absorbed with Nahla, you'd see that."

"Don't turn this into her fault."

Mina held up a hand. "Look, I'm not saying that devoting all your attention to Nahla isn't in your best interests. All I'm saying is that you need to pay attention to what's right in front of your face too. I may not like the bastard because he owns Jungle Kingdom—"

"His employer does."

"Whatever." She stared into space. "Shit. I lost my train of thought."

"Drugs will do that to you."

"Would you shut up and let me say my peace? Then you can rag me all day about my alcohol and drug problems."

She snorted. "Nice to know you're not in denial."

Mina's jaw clenched. "If he's planning to be a part of this family, then I think I've got the right to say whatever I damn well please."

Okay, did she miss something? She knew Mina went downstairs for a cup of coffee, but she didn't stay long enough to carry on a conversation with Rio. In fact, she went out of her way to avoid him today. Whenever he entered the room, she'd blush and hurry out.

"You mind telling me what you're talking about?" Sinclair asked.

"Look, I know about these things."

Sinclair snorted. "Really?"

"Would you just listen to me? He's got the hots for you. He's not like these knuckleheads I bring home. I think he's good for you even if we're going to sue his boss."

Sinclair didn't know how to respond to her senseless logic. Sure, she still wanted to sue Dante, but sleeping with Rio presented a slight problem because…well…she wasn't sure why. The thought of how much it might hurt him made her stomach clench. She didn't want to sue, but at the same time, it seemed like the right thing to do. As if that made any sense. Everything had gotten so confusing in the last couple of days.

"Can we drop this?" Sinclair asked, handing a green block to her niece. "Really, Mina. You're not qualified for heart-to-heart conversations."

"Look, just because I missed the boat on a few things in life, doesn't mean the same thing has to happen to you. Okay? All I'm saying is you need to loosen up."

"Enough, Mina." She watched as Nahla took a moment to flex her small fingers then went back to playing with her blocks.

Shrugging, her sister continued. "I still think he's a keeper. My big sister done good with finding a fabuliscious hunk like that. But we're still suing him."

"Mina! Don't you dare say stuff like that around him."

She waved her hand. "It doesn't matter. All I'm saying is I think he's good for you. That maybe it wouldn't hurt to give him a chance. I'm sure there's more to him than what you think."

She had no idea how true that was. However, she wasn't ready to break the news about him being a were-cheetah and her daughter joining their ranks. Things like this just don't happen in the real world. Now with this mess thing going on, she certainly wasn't about to spill the were-cheetah news to her. Just like she never told Mina about her daughter slipping and calling her "Momma".

"The sex must have been good for him to break into a house to come claim his woman," Mina said.

"We don't have a relationship."

The deflated tone of her voice made it obvious she hoped that wasn't true. Sinclair wasn't looking for a relationship with anyone, but it wouldn't hurt to have someone who cared about her for a change. With every passing moment it felt as she were holding the weight of the world on her shoulders. Nahla was her world, but the weight of her sister's drinking, outrageous boyfriends, constant disappearances made her want to walk away so many times. Unfortunately, that would be like taking it out on Nahla. Why should her niece have to pay for her mother's mistakes?

Sinclair watched as her sister tugged the emerald green robe to her chest. "You should be in bed. Nahla and I would be more than happy to take these toys to your room and keep you entertained."

She laughed. "Yeah, right."

Nahla yelped and dropped her blocks. She shook her hands and begin scratching them as though someone had stuck them in a vat of itching powder. Then she began ripping at her clothes.

Sinclair and Mina watched in shocked.

Crack!

Sinclair's focus went to the bulging bone sticking out under Nahla's nightgown. When worm-like muscles began slithering under her skin, her eyes bulged out of her head. The last time she saw something like this was in the woods at Rio's place when the people changed into monsters.

"Ohmygod!" Sinclair shrieked.

"What the hell?" Mina was on her feet, staring at her daughter.

"Make it stop, Auntie Sin! Make it stop!" Nahla leapt to her feet, but another bone cracked in her back and dropped her down on all fours. "Auntieeeeeeee!"

Sinclair wrapped her arms around her niece and pulled her close. "Go get Rio! Now!"

Mina charged down the hall, screaming Rio's name.

Seconds later Rio rounded the corner with Kyle in tow and charged into the bedroom. He'd heard the screams.

Nahla's wreathing body trembled as a bone broke behind her face. Tears slipped down her protruding cheeks. Claws extended out of her pawed hands, digging into Sinclair's sleeve and tearing slits in her shirt. Horror masked both of their faces.

Pushing Kyle and Mina into the hall, Rio slammed the door and locked it. Kyle would have to keep Mina from barging through the door.

"Put her down," Rio shouted at Sinclair.

"But she's—"

"She's changing. You have to loosen up on her, Sinclair. She's new to this and scared. You don't know what she's capable of."

"Then she needs me more than ever!"

"Honey, if she bites you in this state, then I'll have two cheetahs going through the transmutation fever. I've only got time to walk one of you through it."

Damn him for being right. Sinclair loosened her grip and let Nahla slide into her lap. The little girl's shifting malformed skin caused a fresh batch of tears to break free. Her baby's body wreathed and pulled, bones were breaking like twigs. Even if Nahla lived through this kind of torture, she wasn't so sure that she would.

"Why aren't you doing anything?" she yelled, glaring at Rio.

He dropped besides Nahla's twitching and mutated body. Rio stroked his large hand across the mantle fur on her back. That alone amazed him because he had only seen the downy, Mohawk on cheetahs in the wild. Since his kind didn't change until they've reached puberty, very few cheetahs had the mantle and if they did, it was nowhere near as soft and luxurious as hers.

"*Allí allí, sweetie*," he said. "Just relax and let it go. Don't fight it. Close your eyes and sleep."

"Sleep? Is that all you can do is tell her to sleep? What good is that? Help her dammit! Can't you see she's in pain?"

"Sinclair, it doesn't hurt. Uncomfortable, yes, but there's nothing I can do at this point. She's at the end of her transmutation. That's why she's changing."

Sinclair wanted to beat him upside the head. She wanted to punch him into the floor, snatch her niece, and run out that house to find a *real* doctor. The small form mutating on the bed howled like a kitten, begging for mercy. The upper part of her body was feline more than the lower part. Her small legs barely had noticeable spots at this point. That did nothing for Sinclair's sanity.

"I can't watch this," she said, hopping off the bed and standing with her back to the window. "I can't sit here and do nothing while my niece is turning into a monster."

Rio's eyes hooded. "Is that what you think we are? Monsters?"

"Do you have a better description? I know what I saw in the woods, Rio. Those people — and I use the term loosely — attacked us."

After what had happened to her, she had every right to distrust him.

Nahla stopped writhing. Her body made it halfway through the change before the thickened spotted hair rescinded through her pores. The fangs protruding from her jaw had pulled back into the gums. Bones snapped in place, pulling her tiny body back into a humanoid shape. By the time she finished changing, she lay in a deep sleep, curled up in Rio's lap.

"She's okay," he said, placing a hand against her forehead. "Still a little feverish, but she should stabilize in another day or so."

"What happens then?" Her voice came across so weak that Sinclair hardly recognized it.

"She'll go through the whole change next time. From start to finish."

The room tipped sideways. Sinclair felt herself falling. The last thing she heard was Rio yelling her name.

Chapter 23

Rio finished tucking Sinclair in, then he eased the door closed. She only fainted. Considering everything that happened to this point, she needed the rest.

He opened the door at the end of the hall on the opposite side and looked in on Nahla. She remained sleeping with her pink blanket wrapped around her.

The half-change left her probably ten times more exhausted than Sinclair, but at least she'd recover faster. At some point, he'd have to call Dante and fill him in, something he dreaded.

It bothered him that he didn't know what had happened. Even worse, he prayed she'd go through an entire change the next time. If Nahla didn't, she'd look like a mutant. Cheetahs tend to shy away from their kind if they sense some sort of defect in them. Although he'd never dismiss Nahla like that, he couldn't say the same for his people.

Shaking his head, he erased that thought from his mind. *First things first. Let's make sure Nahla can change.* Seeing as her fever had returned, there was a good chance that her body was in the middle of working out the kinks in her metamorphosis.

He heard voices. Kyle hurried up the stairs and down the hall. Before Rio could open his mouth, his friend beat him to it.

"The guy from Social Services is downstairs," he said, thumbing over his shoulder. "You better get down there. Right before you disappeared, I caught Sinclair's nut ball sister in the kitchen throwing back a bottle of coconut rum. I got her in the kitchen drowning in coffee, but I doubt it'll be enough."

"Damn."

Rio darted around Kyle. He raced down the hall and took the steps four and five at a time. Two leaps across the foyer practically landed him on the stranger's toes. Rio braced himself with a huge smile and offered his hand.

Mr. Gallagher was the average, skinny social worker who looked more like a schoolteacher. He wore a brown sports coat with a pair of jeans. The clipboard he held said he was serious.

Gallagher looked him up and down after shaking hands. "I came here to speak to both Mina and Sinclair Duval. Are they around?"

"Sure." Rio showed the social worker to the living room. "Sinclair is resting upstairs. Still recovering from that unfortunate mishap at Jungle Kingdom. You've heard about it, *si*?"

"I have. " Gallagher began flipping through pages on his clipboard. He triggered his pen and stared at Rio. "Can I get your name? For the record, of course."

Confused, Rio gave the social worker his name and a number where he could be reached. He turned his head to look over his shoulder. Where was everyone? Why was the house so quiet? Shouldn't Mina be here to field this?

Nervous laughter left Rio. "I'm sure Mina's coming."

Gallagher snorted. "She's probably in the kitchen still working off her tirade."

"Tirade?"

"Yes, Mr. Velasquez. Just after slamming the door in my face, your fiancée threw a fit and had to be herded off into the kitchen by your cousin."

Fiancée? Cousin? Rio struggled to ramain impassive.

"By the way..." Gallagher stopped scribbling long enough to stare at Rio. "You're not planning to beat my face into the ground, are you? Of course, 'face' was not the term your lovely bride-to-be used."

Oh. My. God. What in the world did this crazy drunk get him into?

Feigning a bright smile, Rio excused himself from the living room. His hand slammed into the kitchen door so hard that it crashed into the wall.

Mina stood by the sink guzzling coffee. She eyed Rio right before he snatched the cup out of her hands and shoved her down a small hall leading toward the backyard.

"You'd better get your hands off me!" she shouted.

He wanted to pitch her through the window, but that would certainly give Gallagher the report of the year. He settled for shoving her against the wall.

"What the hell is wrong with you?" he snarled. "Whatever game you're playing with this man, I don't want any part of it!"

Drunken laughter tumbled out of her. Instead of anger, she fell against him and began smoothing her hand along the inside of his thigh. She came dangerously close to his penis.

Other than his curling fists and a scowl masking his face, Rio remained completely still. Taking on the entire Charlotte Coalition was preferable to this.

"Come on, baby." She rested her chin on his chest. "I thought you liked playing games."

He snatched up her wrists. "Not with you."

She laughed, alcoholic breath steaming from her mouth. "Then how about this kinda game? I know how much you like my sister and my little girl. You want to keep them happy, you'll play along."

"And if I don't?"

"Not a problem. But if my kid ends up in foster care, your entire company, including your boss, will end up on the chopping block. *If* you get my meaning."

Rio shoved her aside.

Shaken, Mina managed to keep her sniveling smile in place. "What are so mad about? All we have to do is play it up like lovebirds. That bastard will go away and that will be the end of it. All that man's looking for is a stable environment anyway. What can be more stable than having a man in the house?"

He glared at her. "How about an honest man in the house? But then again, we've both seen your track record." He swiped a hand across her bruised eye as a reminder.

She slapped him away. "Fine. I'll go in there and tell him the truth then. I'll tell him my last boyfriend tried to strangle me, but you two came along and nearly killed him, so now my kid is super sick and my sister can't take care of us anymore. Satisfied?"

Just as she started to leave, Rio snatched her back in place. Oh, how he wanted to snap her neck and just wash his hands of this mess.

He released her. A smirk that had more to do with vehement thoughts curved his lips. "Lead the way, *perra repugnante*."

Mina jabbed a finger in his face. "That better have been something nice you said about me."

He continued glaring. She might have issues with being called a nasty bitch.

Mina let it go and led the way into the kitchen. Before she could open the door to the living room, Rio snagged her by the arm and pulled her back to the coffeemaker. He forced another cup of black coffee into her hands before returning to the living room.

Gallagher stood on the other side of the room with the phone up to his ear. With his back to them, Rio sneaked closer to the couch where the man left his clipboard. He peeked at his notes. Most of the sheet had check boxes checked and chicken-scratch notes where there was room for more information. Gallagher turned and Rio yanked back in place.

Mina wasn't as discreet.

Before Gallagher could pick up the clipboard, Mina yanked it off the couch and stared at it.

"What's all this shit?" she asked. "You tellin' lies about me and my man?"

She chucked the clipboard onto the couch and slunk back over to Rio's side. When her arm looped through his, he closed his eyes and paled.

He snatched the clipboard and tucked it under his arm. "Everything I've said is the truth, Ms. Duval. Now if you don't mind, where's your sister and daughter? I need to see them."

"Sinclair's resting," Rio said. "She and Nahla are still recovering from their wounds."

"So I've heard. You mind telling me about this hospital up in Virginia?"

Rio's mouth opened, but nothing came out. Instead, he swiveled his head and glared at Mina. She was lucky she was Sinclair's sister or he would've shoved her head in the microwave for sixty seconds.

"It's not a hospital," he said. "It's more like a retreat or a hospice. Where both she and Nahla could rest up. Away from all the publicity."

"Name, please." He triggered his pen and pressed it on a piece of paper. "I won't ask you again."

"Who the fuck do you think you're threatening?" Mina stuck out her chest and started to charge the man. Rio yanked her back. Still, that wasn't enough to break her violent glare. "You can't be comin' up in my house actin' like you're the boss of me."

Rio yanked her harder, nearly throwing her off her feet. He feigned a sincere smile. "You want to see Sinclair and Nahla, right? To make sure they're okay?"

Gallagher stared blandly at him. "Yes."

"Then how about—" He pointed to Kyle. "My cousin. He'll

show you to Sinclair and Nahla's rooms, but I have to ask that you be quiet. They're resting and Nahla isn't feeling particularly well."

"Has she seen a doctor since she's been back?"

"Yeah," Mina snarled.

Rio dragged her off toward the kitchen. He shoved her through the door before turning back to Mr. Gallagher again. "Kyle, could you bring our guest upstairs while I have a word with my…fiancée?"

He didn't wait for an answer. Instead, he pushed the door open and proceeded to curse Mina out in low, snarling voice.

Oh, how simple it would be to walk away. Fortunately, he cared about the woman upstairs. Not to mention, there was Nahla. Foster care wasn't the place for a child on the cusp of her first full-body change. Nobody knew when it would happen or how. He just knew it would. Foster parents waking up to see their little ward morphing into some cat creature would be enough to garner worldwide media attention. Heaven only knows what next.

Footsteps descended just as Rio got in the last word. He exited the kitchen all smiles while Mina wore a scowl.

"I don't know who you think you're fooling," Gallagher said. "I was on the phone with our lawyer. He's working to get the court date moved up."

"Moved up?" Mina shouted. "What for?"

He met her fiery eyes. "For you, Ms. Duval. Two people in need of care shouldn't be relying on a drunk for that. If you can't clean up your act, that trial will be the last time you see Nahla again."

"You son of a bitch," she hissed. "You can't—"

"But I can and I have. You can replay this fiasco in front of a judge."

Mina sputtered, but nothing came out.

Rio hurried across the living room and guided Gallagher outside before Mina could do any more damage.

Chapter 24

A white blur shaped into a ceiling fan. The blade stilled like the rest of the room. Planting her elbows into the mattress, Sinclair pushed up and took in her surroundings. Master bed with a white rocking chair in the corner and a sliding glass door that emptied onto a screened-in deck. A king-size bed rested against sky blue walls except for the dressing area with the extra sink. The pale, mustard yellow walls extended into the bathroom where the large bathtub with separate shower lay.

She was back at Rio's cottage.

The door opened. Smiling, Rio stepped into the room with Nahla perched against his hip. Though she seemed a bit tired and pale, the little girl lifted her head and managed a tiny smile for her auntie. Dangling a brown Raggedy Ann doll in one hand, she reached for her. Sinclair smiled. The last time she'd smiled like that was when she'd caught a glimpse of Nahla in the Jumping Bean tent. When Rio sat next to her, letting his "niece" sink into her awaiting arms, she beamed as much as Nahla. Sinclair kissed her baby girl's face and snuggled into the little girl's unusual warmth.

"How's my baby?" she asked, nestling her nose against Nahla's cheek.

"Tired of bein' sick," she replied. "Can I seep wit you?"

Sinclair glanced outside the large window and noticed the twinkling stars high above the tree tops. "Auntie Sin's got enough sleep for one day. Maybe we could—"

"No." Rio snuggled closer to feel her warmth. "You're staying right here. You and Nahla together. You scared the crap out of me, fainting like that."

"I'm fine, and I don't faint."

"Yeah right. So that acrobatic movement you did was actually a swan dive for the floor."

She couldn't deny the fatigue deep in her bones. Her sleep had been chaotic at best over the last few days. Spending the rest of the night in bed wasn't a bad idea as long as someone else provided the pampering. Based on the glint in Rio's eyes, he seemed perfectly content with the job.

"Where's Mina?" she asked, stroking Nahla's baby-soft hair.

"Who cares?" he shouted.

She couldn't help snickering at his frustrations. Mina must have given him hell before they left the house.

He smiled. "Let me fill you in on a few details."

He told her everything, right down to threatening Mina with a branding iron to the butt for acting like a jackass.

Given the choice, he'd rather take this burden from her, but in the human world, he had no rights. He had to stand by and watch like a parent in the stands. One way or another, he'd have to help them find a way out of this. Not only was Nahla's life at stake, but his Coalition was too.

"How did you get us out of the house?" she asked.

He inched closer to her on the bed, looping his arm across her shoulders. "After Gallagher left, Mina finished off a bottle of rum and passed out on the living room floor. Kyle and I put her on the couch, left a note, and left with you guys tucked in the back of the SUV. Which reminds me. You might want to give her a call before she has the police at our door."

"Our door?" Nahla's doll waved up in the air, blocking her view of Rio. She clamped her fingers on its head and drove it down to her niece's lap. "Since when is this—"

"Our door," he repeated. Rio cupped her cheek, leaned in for a kiss, and pulled back to marvel at her. "You're stuck with me, too, whether you like it or not. Even that awful woman you call your sister. Now I'll be more than happy to give up my cottage and live with you guys, but I'll have to come back to the woods occasionally for a run. And to commune with my clan, but not that often. The older Nahla gets, the more she'll feel the need to be around her other sisters and aunties too."

Not only that, the females grew restless about meeting the new cub. Their natural instinct would drive them to take Nahla under their wing. Tragedy would definitely ensue if they tried to take her niece and it wasn't so much Sinclair he worried about.

She arched an eyebrow. "Sisters? Aunties? You care to explain?"

"We're not like human families."

"No kidding."

He laughed and pinched her side. "Would you let me finish? As I was saying, we don't flock together under one roof unless we have to. The men will mingle long before the females will."

"What about married couples? How do they cope?"

Rio blinked. For the first time, she actually showed a little bit of an interest in his people. He smiled. "Everyone has their own place scattered throughout the Triangle area. The same with the married couples. It isn't unusual for male to disappear days on end because he's hanging out with his brothers."

"Or another woman," she mumbled.

He leaned close and nuzzled his nose against her cheek. "We don't stray. The scent alone would be enough to give us away. Since our women are our equals in every way, they could tear us apart. But being cheetahs means we're also quite loyal to our mates."

Sinclair giggled. "So everyone is like this."

"In a way. There are times when someone will put together a group for a movie night or dinner, but that's about it. If we come across each other in passing, it's like we're old friends. Everyone knows everyone's scent, so we know if they're a part of our Coalition or not. If a new cheetah comes to our land, they're better off going to Dante and Billie and asking for permission to stay. Otherwise, we're within our rights to tear them apart."

Rio's hand rested on her shoulder. He glanced at Nahla who looked between the two of them with her eyes wide open, an innocence so precious that it ached his heart. He hated the idea of bringing someone so young into his world, but it was either that or death. Death was inconceivable.

"I was bitten about twelve years ago," he said. "At the time I was on a ride-along with an ambulance company."

"Twelve years? But that would make you about...?"

"Forty-seven." He chuckled.

Sinclair half smiled. "Well damn. You look good for a guy your age. I had you placed around early thirties like me."

Her thoughts went straight to Jermaine and her sister. That jerk was about same age as Rio. It wasn't so much as his age, perhaps the way he carried himself that made her sick to her stomach.

"We don't age as fast as humans." Rio snuggled against her cheek again, smacking her soft skin with a kiss. "Our oldest is 112 years old."

Deep in the sewers under the city, he and his crew picked up a homeless woman who had two broken legs and a shattered pelvis. They thought she'd die before they could get her back to the ambulance.

While carrying her in the litter, they noticed that she kept twitching under the blanket. It got so bad they had to stop and put her on the ground. When Rio pulled back the sheet, this huge cheetah head came out of nowhere and bit him on the arm. One of the paramedics found a stick and started beating the animal until she let go. The cheetah was so mad that she tore off the straps trying to get them. The paramedics killed her and Rio ended up being the patient.

The fever came on fast and hard just like it did with Nahla. Someone had leaked information about his condition around the medical channels. Before dawn the next day, Dante showed up in Rio's room and began unhooking him from the machines. His King and his Coalition brothers took him to Dante's house and nursed him back to health.

"How did the woman get down in the tunnel in the first place? Dante didn't just cast her aside, did he?"

He shook his head. "No. The Triangle Coalition was looking for a rogue who was preying on the homeless. The woman who had bitten me was the Coalition's last healer. She knew she was dying by the time we got to her. Crazy as her logic sounds, she needed someone with medical knowledge to take her place. Someone who believed in more than just herbal remedies and potions. When she fell down a shaft, she called 911 without Dante's permission."

"She did it on purpose, so she wouldn't leave your people high and dry."

He nodded.

Sinclair straightened up enough to pull away from him slightly. Adjusting Nahla on her lap, she asked, "If she knew all this stuff about herbs and potions, how the hell did she teach it to you if she was dead?"

Rio turned on his side so that he lounged like a giant cat. "I hated the b-i-t-c-h for what she did to me. Dante didn't have any expectations. After they finished training me, he let me go."

"Just like that?"

He chuckled. "Not exactly. He stayed in constant contact all the time."

"Because they thought you would be trouble."

He half smiled. "My redemption came when one of their females was going through a difficult labor. Although pregnancy isn't new among our people, the infant mortality rate is high. One in four cubs survives. Anyway, Dante couldn't call an ambulance or a human doctor, so they called me. I came, helped birth the baby into the world, and became indispensable ever since. They have no one else to take care of them if they get sick or injured. That's when Dante brought me here. This used to be the last healer's home. I started studying her books and notes about herbs and potions, sort of mixing some modern day medicine in where I could. She also left the name of a root-doctoring witch to help me out whenever I needed it. But that's enough talk for now. We've got other things to do."

"Wait a minute. You can't just cut me off like that."

"Yes, I can."

Now was as good a time as any. At some point, Nahla would have to go to the main house for her welcoming party. Rio hoped to bring Sinclair too, since she'd be one of the few humans with such intimate knowledge about their people. If he planned to get her past the front gate, then he had to make sure she could handle it.

"What's going on?" Worry creased Sinclair's eyebrows.

A maniacal grin bowed Rio's lips. "You'll see. There's something I have to show you."

Chapter 25

Carrying Sinclair, Rio marched out onto the deck with Nahla scampering along next to his thigh. He sat her on a teak lounger next to an outdoor, wood-burning fire pit. On the other side of the deck was a plastic play mat with giant blocks, dolls and games scattered on top, Nahla went straight for the toys.

"Where did that stuff come from?" she asked.

A smirk curled the corner of Rio's lips. "Some of the Coalition members ran a few errands for me. Seeing as you guys might be spending some time here, I thought I should make it more child-friendly. So while you were sleeping, we were out here playing."

"You're spoiling her. Next thing you know, you'll be getting her a swing set."

Rio blanched. He made a mental note to keep the swing set kit hidden in the basement until he could talk Sinclair into letting him keep it for Nahla. "Look," he said, trying to hide the shakiness in his voice, "it doesn't matter. What I have to show you, does."

He kissed her before pulling away and exiting the screened-in deck. *Come with me. I want to do this where Nahla can't see.* With each step he took, he shed a piece of clothing. His shirt went first, then his jeans. He wore nothing underneath other than olive skin shimmering in the twilight.

Discomfort flooded Sinclair. *Uh oh.* She knew what was coming, but she made it a point to stay put as long as possible. She glanced back toward Nahla, knowing she wasn't aware of what Rio was doing. Besides, she seemed more interested in stacking large blocks than her surroundings. *Thank goodness for that small favor.* A half wall coming up to meet the screen helped, too. She didn't want her niece watching a naked man strut across the lawn. Curiosity got the better of her, so she lifted her head just over the rim of the wall.

"Watch me, Sinclair." Rio crouched low to the ground, lowering himself on all fours. His dark eyes fixed on her, snaring her attention. "You need to see that not all of us are monsters."

Serrated teeth unsheathed from his upper and lower gums. Muscles slithered underneath his skin, gliding around the bones that broke in his face and back. His jaw lurched away from the rest of his head, molding itself into a feline jaw. The spotted fur thickened around his neck, spreading along the rest of his body.

Sinclair's heart thumped, her nerves urging her to run. Bones cracking his legs and arms, reforming into long limbs, she lost contact with his penetrating gaze. She glanced at Nahla who began humming to herself. *Great. Wish I had nerves of steel like that.*

A snort brought Sinclair's attention back to Rio. His spine began bending like a wobbly rope bridge. What used to be a bump on the back of his tailbone had turned into a whip. Spotted hairs sprouted to form a thick tail with six rings of black around the tip. By the time he completed his metamorphosis, he collapsed on the ground like a spotted cheetah in the African plains. Seeing him on the lawn was like an Eskimo on a beach. It was out of place.

Pain shot through Sinclair's hands. She had grasped the chair so tight that her knuckles were about to break through the skin. Though she had never been one for liking animals of any sort, Sinclair couldn't help marveling a tad at the gorgeous beast panting on the grass. When Rio staggered to his feet, he stood completely still except for his beating chest. Despite the fear tickling the back of her brain, she had to admit that Rio's wild edge was beautiful.

Nahla leapt to feet and padded to her aunt's chair. When she caught sight of the large cheetah in the backyard, she squealed at the top of her lungs.

"Kitty, Auntie Sin! Kitty!" She darted out the door and down the stairs.

"Nahla, wait!" she shouted, reaching for air.

Too late.

The little girl padded straight for Rio with her arms open wide. He was so beautiful. She slammed straight into Rio's front and hugged him something fierce, burying her face into his lush fur. He was so warm and soft, softer even than her blanket.

Okay. If her little niece could accept him without any reservations, then perhaps she could do the same. *Take a deep breath, and walk down those stairs.*

She did. Not once did she take her eyes off the enormous "kitty" her niece clung to. If a three year old could do this, then so could she. For Nahla's sake, she had to.

Rio kept his human eyes on the beautiful woman he wanted as his mate. Lowering his feline head, he slurped his tongue across his ward's cheek. He loved the little girl for her innocence and being so accepting of him. Now if he could only get Sinclair to do the same. Watching her make the effort to come to him was a large step in the grand scheme of things. He couldn't ask for more.

Lifting his head high above Nahla's and keeping his eyes on Sinclair, Rio mentally willed her to continue closing the distance. Between the stink of perspiration, the hammering pulse in her neck, and the dilated eyes, he understood her fear. That was why he tried not to move even an inch, knowing that it would intimidate her.

"Ain't he pretty, Auntie?" Nahla rubbed her nose against Rio and kissed his chest.

"Yeah," she breathed. "Pretty." When she came within petting distance, she drilled her gaze into his, eyes narrowing a bit. "Are you really in there, Rio? I mean...is it still you? The same Rio I know?"

A purr rumbled from his throat. He couldn't talk in his feline form, but he understood everything she said. If anything, his senses opened up more in this form. He could read her body language as though she had told him herself.

Sinclair lowered her trembling hand a few inches from in front of his nose. She wanted to pet him, but wasn't sure how he would react to that. Suppose he wasn't the same guy she grew fond of? After all, he looked just like the wild animals that chased down their prey, gripped their powerful jaws around their neck, and strangled them to limpness.

Stepping forward, careful not to push Nahla down, Rio bumped into Sinclair and slicked his tongue out to taste her fingertips. A stab of lust sank low to his stomach. Hot damn, she tasted good. Had he not been a cheetah, he would've jumped her on the lawn and buried himself inside her. He would give anything to see her womb filled with his babies, beautiful and sweet just like Nahla.

Sinclair reached forward and brushed a hand along his muzzle, thumb sliding down the black tear stain of his inner eye, tracing it down to his jaw. "Good lord, you're soft! It's enough that you're a full grown man with baby-soft skin. But this fur? It's like a freaking mink coat, it's so fine."

Trudging forward, he bumped Nahla aside and pushed Sinclair onto her butt. Screaming, she threw her arms in front of her to keep him at bay. Rio kept stepping until he had her entire body underneath him. Dropping down, he landed on her front and pinned her to the lawn.

"Get off me!" she shouted, pushing on his coat. "Dammit, Rio, you're heavy!"

He moved slightly to the left, covering her thigh and part of her side. A huge tongue slurped across her mouth. When her face contorted in disgust, he slurped again. Oh, he was going to love torturing her like this. Hearing her curse him out and shoving her hand up under his muzzle, he knew at least one button to push.

"Me play too," Nahla shouted. She fell against both her aunt and Rio, giggling herself into hysterics. "Wee-oh a kitty, Auntie Sin. Ain't he pretty?"

"Beautiful," she sniped. "But if he doesn't get off me, I'm going to skin his behind."

Another juicy tongue slurped across her mouth, getting her teeth this time.

Sinclair screamed.

"Rio, if you don't get the hell off me, your butt will be sleeping alone tonight!"

That did it. He wasn't about to jeopardize their sleeping arrangements. Pushing up on all fours, he stepped to the side and slumped down next to her.

Giggling Nahla decided to step on top of her aunt's thigh and pounce on his back.

Not even turned yet and already she had learned some of the finer arts of roughhousing. Good. She'd need it to establish her place in the Coalition. If he had his way about it, he'd make sure she went all the way to the top.

Sinclair couldn't help noticing how much her niece loved him: fur, tail, claws and all. Though she wouldn't say it, she knew that Nahla would be more than happy to call him "daddy".

"Rio...we need to talk," she said. "How long are you going to stay like this?" The way he cocked his head at her, she should have known that he couldn't answer her. "Never mind. Just find me when you're ready to change back to your fun-loving self."

"Goodie!" Nahla shouted, clapping her hands together. "I get play with Wee-oh all day."

Sinclair grinned. Eventually that poor man would regret turning her niece into a were-cheetah. Like when she got old enough to trample him into the ground. It would serve him right.

Chapter 26

Sinclair spent the rest of the night watching Rio. He noticed it too. Nonetheless, he went about his nightly routine without any inhibitions. When he made dinner, he made enough to feed at least five people. Nahla, being so picky about food, ate everything on her plate with an appetite that almost matched her aunt's. Wherever Sinclair went, Rio wasn't far behind. She couldn't sit, stand, or lounge without him touching her. Even worse, Nahla kept getting underfoot too, making sure that they included her in everything.

When Rio volunteered to give Nahla her bath, Sinclair wholeheartedly agreed because it would give her a break. The three year old accepted that with arms wide open and eyes gleaming. Of course, Rio wanted to make it a family affair, so he dragged "Auntie" into the bathroom with them. Their family affair continued all the way into the master bedroom where he finished a bedtime story with Nahla cuddled in the nook of his arm.

Lifting his arm, he repositioned Nahla in the bed and slid out on the other side. A soft hum made him turn back. Nahla lay completely oblivious to her surroundings. He pulled the blanket up to her shoulders and kissed her supple cheek. Her innocence brought a smile to his face as he left the room.

Splattering water from the shower caught Rio's attention. Sinclair was in there, steaming up the room and lathering up her luscious body with soap. Rio shifted his hardened erection. He'd planned on the three of them sleeping together tonight, but if he wanted to get a little something-something, then he had better make his move now.

Opening the bathroom door, he slipped inside and noticed Sinclair standing in the shower stall. She wore a plastic shower cap that made him chuckle, but it was the rest of her golden brown body that staked his hardness. He followed the lines of water cascading down her succulent curves, tracing every crevice he yearned to lick.

He swallowed, and proceeded to take his clothes off and slip on a condom, keeping an eye on Sinclair the whole time. The sexual hunger was torture, but he knew they would both benefit from it. He knew what he wanted. Standing naked in the bathroom, he opened the door to the shower and stepped inside.

"What the—?" Sinclair choked off the words as his hands cupped her breasts from behind. There wasn't much to grip, but damn if he didn't show it. "Where's Nah—"

"Asleep in the other room." He pressed his lips to her shoulder, suckling her skin. Pulling her close he molded her body against his, pressing his manhood against her butt cheek. "I want you Sinclair. You game?"

"Game for what?" She knew what he meant, but she wanted to give him a little bit of a hard time. She gasped, excitement riding through her body.

Rio whirled her around and lifted her in the air. Her ankles immediately hooked around his waist, his hands supporting her buttocks. He wasn't in the mood for games. While attacking her mouth, he rammed himself inside her, sinking down to her core.

Sinclair gasped, startled by the carnality of his attack, but relaxed enough to welcome his tender kiss. She loved this fiery side of him. Turning around, he let the water pound against his back as he pushed her against the tiled wall.

He pumped into her slowly at first. Every time she felt him thicken inside her, Sinclair moaned. He filled her so completely. She loved the feel of his rounded butt against her ankles every time he thrust inside her. With the water glistening against his body, she slid her mouth down and began moving her tongue along his muscled shoulders and neck.

"That feels so good," he breathed.

To show his appreciation, he thrust inside her again. With one hand holding her up by the waist, his other one cupped her rounded bottom.

"You're so soft," he murmured. "So sweet."

Sinclair's stomach knotted. Pleasure swamped her to the point that she thought her head would explode.

"Good lord, Rio," she gasped. "I want you. All of you."
"You have it."

He ground his groin against her, shoving harder and faster. He wanted her in ways that only a mated pair could ever understand. He wanted to claim her for all time.

Sinclair's orgasm blasted thousands of tiny prickles throughout her womb, spreading across her entire body. Stars twinkled in her eyes while her juices ran down her legs.

When her muscles tightened around him, Rio let his climax overtake him.

Sinclair had lowered her legs, though she could barely stand. It didn't matter because Rio didn't want to let her go. He smoothed his hands down her slick back.

"We've only begun to have fun," he whispered. Stepping out of the shower, Rio grabbed the robe off the hook and slipped it onto her shoulders.

With Nahla asleep in the other room, he wanted him and Sinclair to have the freedom to play with the lovemaking he had planned for them. The backyard seemed like just the right place. The soft moonlight at their backs, a warm comforter, and enough hours in the night to make it last forever.

◆ ◆ ◆

Rio loved the feel of Sinclair's naked body snuggled in the nook of his arm. A single finger traced across the smooth suppleness of her shoulder. With the moon at just the right angle in the sky, it turned the sweat on her skin into a glistening aura. Ignoring the cold, her body was smooth and brown as milk chocolate and it tasted just as sweet. He should know because he practically licked every inch of her dry. Between his legs rested one of hers, so warm and sensual that it continued to stir him.

Despite the chill running across the night air, Rio pulled the comforter over her head and gazed as the dozens of twinkling stars. He had just finished rocking Sinclair to sleep. They didn't make love once or twice. They did it four times until she was the one who had to call it quits. She said she wanted to rest a moment, but Rio knew she was done for the night. He chuckled at the idea of her thinking she had as much stamina as him. At least he could blame his overactive libido on his feline genes. What was her excuse? Nonetheless, if she could hang almost as long as some of the females from his Coalition, then she was definitely worth keeping.

There was more to it than the sex. He asked her to marry him and she didn't even know it. One of these days, he might dig up the guts to ask her outright. He admired her for her strength and courage to take on a child that wasn't hers and to stand up to Nahla's mother for so long. In essence, Sinclair had all the qualities of a fantastic female with bite.

Things had changed. He wanted more than just her in his bed. He wanted her in his life. That was the ultimate prize.

Crack.

Rio lifted his head. The wind blew. A quick whiff and he separated two of the scents. There could've been a third, but he couldn't be sure. With him and his mate lying in the open and vulnerable to anything waiting in the shadows, a sense of urgency raced through him.

He couldn't leave her to check it out and he didn't want to scare her by urging her to get inside.

Sitting up, he glanced around the woods again. Unlike some animals, cheetahs didn't have very good night vision. The best he could do was that of an ordinary human.

"Go...sleep," Sinclair mumbled. Her hand reached for his. "Cold."

He took it, kissing the back of her smooth sweetness before placing it under the comforter. Gathering up the edges, he pulled them on top of her delicate body and covered her with the robe for extra warmth.

"We're not here for your woman," a voice said.

Rio blinked. His eyes narrowed, recognizing the voice. "Quiet, Marianne." Leaping to his feet, he hurried to the spot in the woods closest to her voice. "Who's with you?"

The gangling blond strutted out of the woods. A smile spread across her rounded face. She slunk her way up to him like a human cheetah with her shoulders moving in step with her footfalls. Grinning, she draped her arms around Rio's shoulders.

Rio's stone-cold stance should have given her a clue that he wasn't amused. He eased her aside as though she was a dead carcass. "What do you want?"

Her eyes dazzled. "What I've always wanted. You."

He remained impassive.

When Marianne didn't get her smile returned, she sighed. Another attempt at flirting down the bucket. Tilting to the right, she noticed the sleeping body in the yard. "You've got gall, Rio; I'll give you credit for that. You sure go the distance to keep our Coalition out of trouble. She a good lay?"

"I'm not sleeping with her because of that and you know it."

"Oh? What could that woman possibly have that I don't?"

"Class for starters."

Despite her momentary ire, Marianne regained her composure. Taking a single finger, she slid it down his bare chest, the tip of her nail slipping through his sparse black hairs while heading for his crotch.

Rio grabbed her wrist. This time, she pissed him off to the point that he clenched it tight enough to break it.

Marianne let out a high-pitched squeal before whipping her free hand around to smack him. He caught that one too, gripping both of them enough to leave bruises come morning.

Good.

That would teach her a lesson for trying his patience. When she tried to kick him, he dodged her boot and backed her up against a tree. Her back smacked the bark so hard that leaves snowed around them.

Sinclair stirred.

Panic ignited his senses. She wouldn't understand if she woke up and caught him manhandling another woman in his backyard. Wearing nothing would make the scene worse.

Marianne wasn't the least bit amused. How dare he choose that bitch over his own kind? She wanted to scratch his eyes. "Asshole! You didn't have to be so rough."

"You keep flapping your gums like that and it'll get a lot rougher." Again, he glanced over his shoulder. He could just barely make out Sinclair behind the rustling foliage. "What the hell do you want, Marianne? Shouldn't you be with Hazel or something? Or did you drop her off at the first door you could find so you could rush over her to harass me?"

"Theresa's hurt."

Rio went blank. Whenever one of the younglings—they still considered teenagers kids—got hurt, that was a cause for alarm among his people. Choking back his panic, he asked, "What happened?"

"A trap. The teens were out running in a group and Theresa fell into a nicely disguised hole. Whoever dug it filled it with broken glass and rocks at the bottom. The fall didn't kill her, but the bleeding will."

Anger surged through Rio so fast that he snatched her by the shoulders and slammed her against the tree again. "Dammit, why didn't you tell me? You stand there slutting around while Theresa loses time. What the hell is wrong with you?"

A growl rumbled from the woods just to his left. Someone, the second presence he whiffed earlier, stalked them not too far away. That growl was a warning.

Rio agreed this was not the time or the place for this, so he released Marianne. "Who's with you?"

A smirk curled the corner of her lips. "Walt."

It figures. If you want someone to do as he was told without question, then Walt was your robot. Rio didn't like him, but he didn't hate the man either. When it came to a good fight, Walt was one person you wanted in your corner...assuming he picked one.

His eyes narrowed. "In cat form, I take it?"

Before she could answer his question, a large cheetah stalked out of the shadows, planting his front paws on the remains of a rotten stump. After a quick survey of his companions, Walt stepped off the base, narrow shoulders jostling with every step. When Marianne went to stroke his spotted head, he ducked, allowing her fingers to brush his ear.

Rio snorted. The one person Walt trusted without question was Dante. Billie was nothing more than an afterthought even though she was his queen. Marianne was nothing more than a whore trying to make her mark at the risk of anyone else's hide. Even Walt knew that.

"Where's Theresa?" Rio asked.

"She's at Dante's. He sent us to bring you back."

Crossing his arms, he glanced over his shoulder. "What about Sinclair and Nahla? I won't leave them unguarded."

"I'll stay."

"Like hell you will. The last thing I need is you sabotaging me."

Her eyes perked at the sound of that. A slow smirk worked its way into her cheeks. "So, you're her mate, are you? Does she know that?"

"None of your business."

"It is if she's going to be a part of our Coalition. She's not a shapeshifter unless..." Her eyes beamed at the realization. "*Oh-my-god*. You're going to bite her too, aren't you?"

"Hell no!"

Rousing from the other side of the trees and copses silenced them all. Rio stepped aside and grasped one of the branches, pulling it out of his way so that he could get a better look at his beauty.

The mass of blankets stirred. An arm stretched over the top of the mass and her croaky voice called his name. He gave it another thirty seconds before she completely woke.

Rio let go of the bush. "I'll go with you, but on one condition. Walt stays and watches over the house. I'll get Sinclair inside and explain to her that there's been an accident. She'll understand."

"Rio—"

He shot her a glare that sealed her lips. "This isn't negotiable. If you have a problem with it, take it up with Billie, your Queen. Now get out of here before Theresa isn't the only one hurt."

Without another word, he tore through the brushes and entered the backyard.

He hated having to be away from Sinclair and Nahla knowing the kind of danger that lurked around his people.

Chapter 27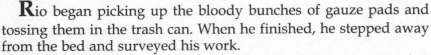

Rio began picking up the bloody bunches of gauze pads and tossing them in the trash can. When he finished, he stepped away from the bed and surveyed his work.

Theresa lay unconscious with a huge bandage covering her forehead. Not only that, she had bandages that mummified her arms and legs, with the addition of a splint around her left ankle and a stabilization device for her right femur.

It killed him to see her in so much pain and screaming at the top of her lungs when he arrived. He heard her cries from the moment Marianne turned off the engine on her car. Twice, he had to kick everyone out of the room so that he could do his work. The one person he had in attendance helping him spent more time running around the commune and gathering various items. He even sent Marianne back to his cottage to collect a few things from his lab. Why that crazy bitch hadn't returned, he didn't know.

The door opened.

Suzette, Theresa's mother, eased into the room. She was the only person he allowed inside after throwing everyone else out. Suzette lifted her tear-stained face to him as she approached the bed.

"How could someone do this?" she asked. Shaky fingers smoothed the back of the thick gauze on her daughter's forehead. "Why her? Why us?"

Rio sighed and laced his fingers behind his head. "*No sé.* I don't know. I doubt someone specifically set a trap for her."

"Then who? Why?" Her glassy eyes looked at him accusingly. "As if going after Hazel wasn't enough."

Rio sat next to her and pulled her close. God knows he wished he could have done more. "*Querida madre,* I don't know. If I did, I'd beat the hell out of them myself."

"Rest assured we'll all get that chance." Dante stood at the door with his complete attention drawn to the injured teen. He motioned for Rio to join him in the hall.

Rio squeezed her hand. She needed the comfort of their Coalition now and females would see to it for sure. Slipping his stethoscope from around his neck, he placed it on the dresser and closed the door behind him.

His King stood a few feet away with his arms folded across his thick chest. Beside him were a few of his right hand men and women.

"How is she?" Dante asked.

Rio jammed his hands in his back pockets. "She'll be okay, but she lost a lot of blood. It took more than half of my supplies to get things under control. I'll need to replenish and soon."

One of his were-cheetah brothers smirked. "You're looking for a reason to go hang out with your new girlfriend."

"Fuck you, George."

Dante eyed him. "Can it wait? The incident happened on my property during a female gathering. I need to make sure our females are safe from now on, so I have people scouting the entire home range."

At least once a week all the females bonded at the Martinelli property. It was nothing more than a bunch of women getting together, talking about their mates, hunting in the woods, and sharing bottles of wine between conversation.

Rio sighed. "Not really. I've got enough bandages for another change or two, but if someone else has an accident before then, we'll have to start shredding towels and sheets."

Dante began smoothing his ink-black goatee. "Either wait a few hours or start tearing the linens. I need every hand out there looking for traps."

"What do you want me to do?"

"Stay here with Theresa. At least until morning."

Rio's jaw bobbled. The man couldn't be serious. His King had to have known Sinclair and Nahla were in danger too. Granted they were with Walt, but the weigh would lift off his chest if could protect them himself.

"I can't stay," he said. "I have to—"

Dante shoved him against the wall. Rio knew not to push a man who couldn't control his change.

"You will do what I say when I say," he seethed. "Any questions?"

Rio lowered his eyes in submission. When he lifted them again, he made sure not to stare at his King for too long or it might come off like a challenge. "They're alone out there. My cub and her—"

"That cub needs to learn to fend for herself. That's the law of our world." He dropped his hand. "I warned you about this. I told you that woman doesn't belong in our world and you defied me. What does it take to make you understand they're not like us? Do you want that woman and her niece to end up dead?"

"They won't if you'd let me—"

"You're lucky I don't lock you in the basement." A growl rumbled from Dante. "You don't leave this house until I say so. Understand?"

Rio gulped. He couldn't stand up to his King because he wouldn't be much good to Sinclair and Nahla dead. Still, he had to say something. "I understand. But they're human and they're out there alone. They don't know about the Charlotte Coalition."

"Good. Then you've done something right for a change."

"Not to interrupt…" Kyle squeezed through the small crowd in the hall and stepped forward, though keeping his distance from his King and best friend. He wasn't stupid. "The Charlotte Coalition might not touch them."

Rio glared at his friend. "How do you figure?"

"All I'm saying is that they're just as adamant about keeping humans out of our world as we are. If they weren't, then there would be bodies lining Charlotte."

"That's not—"

"Enough." Dante stalked down the hall, pushing through his entourage. "The matter is closed. Call your woman if you choose, but you're not leaving this house, Rio. I have no qualms about locking you up."

Incensed, Rio watched as his King disappeared down the hall with the troops filing behind him. Everyone left except Kyle. If nothing else, at least his so-called friend had the gall to stay behind and risk a chunk out of his hide.

Kyle took careful steps toward his friend. "It was a lose-lose situation and you know it."

"Fuck you!" Rio body checked his friend as he started for Theresa's room.

"Dante could have you tied down or locked in the attic. What good would you be to Sinclair and Nahla then?"

He stopped with his hand on the brass knob. His head lifted just over his shoulder as he spied his Coalition brother. A twitch worked his jaw. "You mind telling me how my being here helps them?"

"You're not dead, are you?"

Rio grumbled under his breath. He yanked the door open. Kyle leapt forward and grabbed the handle to keep him from marching inside the room. Both men met each other's eyes: Rio with his cold stare and Kyle pleading for him to listen.

"You can't go," Kyle said. "Theresa needs you here, but she doesn't need me."

A flinch sneaked into Rio's eye. "What are you saying? That you'll watch over them?"

"Why not? I owe you that much."

"You risk Dante's wrath. At least I know that man can't afford to hurt me because I'm as close to a doctor as this Coalition has."

"Maybe." Kyle shrugged and eased off the door. "But it's a chance that Theresa can't take and you know that. Look, man, I know you're scared for them, but there's someone in that room who needs you more. You can't stand there and tell me all this doctoring means you choose your patients. It's not—"

The door pushed open on its own. Suzette stood there clutching a tissue to knuckle—whiteness, exchanging a look between both men. A fresh set of tears glued her eyelashes together. "What's going on? You're not leaving, Rio, are you? Please. I understand that you need to be with your loved ones, but... Theresa is—"

Rio pulled the woman close and kissed her on the head. Hugging her tight, he nodded to his friend. "I'm not leaving, Suzette. I just...I need to get back to my cottage so that I can get some more supplies."

She pulled out of his hug. "I don't understand. Dante wouldn't oppose that, would he?"

Ire surged inside him again, but he stifled it down. "He would if someone were hunting us. He won't—"

"Well, we'll just see about that!" She shoved him aside and stormed down the hall.

Rio caught up and blocked her path. He placed his hands on her shoulders met her angry eyes. "Suzette, it's not about your daughter; it's about all of us. Dante made his decision based on the safety of our entire Coalition. You can't argue with him about that."

"But you need medicine for Theresa. Who else is going to get them?"

He slipped his arm around her shoulder and led her back to the bedroom. The last thing he needed was her making trouble for him. "For now, I can make due with what we have. Or at least until Dante calms down. Theresa will be fine."

"But—"

"Uh uh. *Madre dulce*, when have I ever misled you, eh?"

A timid smile curved Suzette's lips. She placed her hand on top of his and lowered her head. "Never."

"That's right. I make it a point to take care of our esteemed Coalition mothers and I won't stop now. So no more worries, okay? Let me worry about Theresa."

His clan sister nodded.

Before closing the door behind him, Rio exchanged a look with Kyle, telling him to go to his mate and her niece.

With a little luck, perhaps Dante wouldn't notice him gone. Then again, the last time Kyle disappeared, he helped Rio bring both Nahla and Sinclair into this mess.

Chapter 30

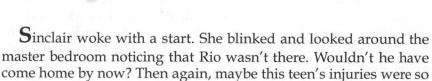

Sinclair woke with a start. She blinked and looked around the master bedroom noticing that Rio wasn't there. Wouldn't he have come home by now? Then again, maybe this teen's injuries were so severe that he couldn't leave. Perhaps he might have left a message.

She tossed back the covers, careful not to wake Nahla, and hurried into the living room to check messages. How or when the little bugger had gotten into the room, she couldn't say. No, actually, she could. Nahla fell asleep there right before Rio sneaked into the bathroom.

Boy, did they have fun. Even better, they took their escapades outside under the moonlight. Now, that's what she called an enchanted moment. In fact, she had several of them before passing out for good. When Rio came back, she'd have to talk him into a repeat performance.

Never in her life had she had so much fun with a man. It wasn't just his lovemaking, it was everything about him. He was patient and kind and so attentive to hers and Nahla's needs. After her parents died Sinclair forgot what a real family was. She felt as though the three of them were meant to be together. It was bliss.

Enough daydreaming.

Sinclair turned her attention to the phone. Zero messages. Surely, he would've called by now?

"Auntie?" Nahla shuffled out of the bedroom with a hand balled in her eye and her hair in a lopsided afro. "Head hurt."

Smiling, Sinclair slipped her hands under her niece's arms and hoisted her onto her hip. She couldn't resist kissing her soft afro and smoothing her cheek along Nahla's.

Her skin was baby soft before, but since the bite, it was more like silk. The same went for her hair. Gnarled or not, her hair was like goose down.

The changes that took place with her niece were incredible...and scary. It worried her to no end, thinking about what kind of childhood Nahla would have. Even though Rio meant well, she couldn't shake the feeling that he had made their lives worse.

"You do feel a little warm," she said. Again, she rubbed her cheek against her niece. "You hurt anywhere else?"

The little girl shook her head.

"Let's see if Rio has something in his magical medicine cabinet that might help."

Of course, he didn't have much of anything that she saw as useful in his lab. She ended up shaking her head and staring at the glass bottles labeled with words she couldn't pronounce. Without him there, Sinclair didn't dare chance something with her baby girl.

She kissed her moaning niece. "We're going to have to take a trip to the drug store."

"Don't wanna go," she mumbled.

"I know, baby. But with you..." *turning into a cheetah and all...*

She stared at Nahla, unable to say the words. Sure, she saw Rio change, in some ways, she had accepted it. However, she had a hard time imagining her niece going through the same peril. Rio said she'd get used to it, as if that made everything better.

Sinclair shifted her niece again. "I promise we won't be gone long."

Getting Nahla dressed took a toll on her patience. Between the moans, groans, and whimpering, she managed to get the little girl situated. It took more time trying to get Nahla's hair into two pompom pigtails than putting her in her clothes.

Once the two of them passed her approval, she lifted Nahla to her hip and headed out the door.

Kyle leapt out of the rocking chair.

"Eeeeek!" Sinclair grabbed her chest and stumbled backward against the door. She had had enough frights to last her a lifetime.

Kyle half smiled and ran his hand through his hair. "Sorry about that. I didn't mean to scare you or anything."

"A little too late, don't you think?" Her heart continued to stomp against her chest. "What are you doing here? Where's Rio?"

"He's still taking care of our youngling. She's real bad off."

"Oh." That news made it easy for her to back down and forget her irritation with him.

Kyle smiled at Nahla, though she didn't look like she was in the mood to reciprocate his attempt at cordiality. "So," he continued. "Where you two off to?"

"We're—. Wait a minute. Are you spying on us?"

He threw his hands up in defense. "Now hold on. Rio and I agreed that someone should keep any eye on you in case those other were-cheetahs showed up during the night."

"They attacked us in daylight."

"Whatever. The point is he didn't want you guys here alone. I sent the last cat away so I could keep an eye on you myself."

She blinked. "There was another cheetah out here? From your Coalition?"

"We changed shifts. Anyway, you haven't told me where you guys were headed."

"Why?" Her eyebrow arched. "Do we need a bodyguard for the evil drivers on the road?" She hoped the answer would be no, because if this was how Nahla would live, then it would be one heck of a problem.

"Listen. I don't mean any disrespect or anything. In fact, I like you guys and you're good for Rio. The point is, I owe that man my life. Now is there something I can do for you?"

Again, Sinclair had to back down. Just like Rio spending the night with one of his charges, it was Kyle's duty to watch them. She couldn't fault the man for doing his job.

Her hand slid up and down Nahla's back. "She's not feeling well. It's just a headache right now. I was about to go to the store and pick something up."

He smoothed the back of his hand across the little girl's forehead. "She doesn't feel warm. Rio will have my butt if I don't do anything, but I don't want to leave you guys alone out here either."

"Actually, it would help a lot because Nahla doesn't want to go. Given the choice, I'd rather keep her inside if she's not feeling well."

Kyle nodded in agreement. "I'll go see what I can find. In the meantime, stay by the phone. Rio has me on speed dial as *3. If there's anything you guys need, call."

Chapter 31

The door opened, startling him out of sleep. Three of the female were-cheetahs strolled into the room carrying breakfast and a change of clothes for Suzette. Rio watched as they pampered and offered comfort to mother and daughter. If they didn't have their arms around Suzette, then they combed their fingers through Theresa's blond hair and pressed kisses to her pale cheeks.

It always amazed him how beautiful the women of his Coalition looked whenever they flocked together. They loved their young and hated to see even one of their "sisters" in pain.

The men were another story. They didn't like to see any of their own hurt either, but their instincts dictated they go out and eliminate the enemies before tending to the wounded. With an attitude like that, it was a wonder their people survived. At least Rio had his medical training to offset that part of the male intinct.

He shook his head. It had to be something in the genes. Still, it would be nice to see the women flock around Sinclair and Nahla like that some day. Knowing them, they'll take his cub under their wing before they gave his human mate a second glance.

Billie looked at him.

Ten years ago, she defected from the Charlotte Coalition because their demented king at the time tried to force himself on her. Since then, she never looked back. With everything going on, Rio knew this had to be especially hard for her.

"My poor kitty." Even her voice sounded angelic. Billie sat on the floor next to the recliner where Rio slept. Lifting her grass-green eyes to him, she smiled. "You could've taken one of the spare rooms instead of sitting by her bed all night."

Rio ducked his head, a tad embarrassed by her compassion. "I wanted to be here for Theresa and Suzette."

Suzette had every reason to worry about her only child. Since her husband died a few years back during a construction accident, she had no one else. If anything happened to her daughter it would drive her over the edge. It was enough that he had to force her to take a valium last night so she could rest. Once she passed out, he tucked her in beside her daughter.

Billie nodded. "I understand. But you realize you're important to us, too."

He snorted. "I'm important because I'm the only doctor the Coalition has."

"Nonsense. You're important because you care enough to protect this pack."

Uh oh. The comment had taken him aback. He knew where this was going.

Billie touched the back of his hand. "I don't blame you for what you did. To the little girl, that is. Was it the right thing? No. You could've found another way."

"Billie—"

She held up a hand. "Let me finish. It goes unsaid because we're human cheetahs, but it never hurts to give someone a reminder."

He sat up in the recliner. "I don't see how—"

She held up a single hand to stop him.

"As I've already told Dante, I would like to meet this new cub of ours. As would all of our females. She's been the talk of our people and everyone's curious about her. Although I don't condone what you've done, she's...she's one of us now. Soon she'll change. Are you sure this aunt of hers is ready for what that entails?"

Rio couldn't meet her eyes. He knew he'd have to introduce Nahla to the Coalition soon, but he feared how they might react to Sinclair. Her not being Nahla's biological mother only made the possibilities worse. Supposed they tried to take the toddler away from Sinclair? Granted they couldn't do it legally, but that wouldn't stop the females from making their presence known. If Mina ever lost custody of Nahla, then the Coalition would make their move on her. That would never sit well with his destined mate.

"What about Sinclair?" He turned his attention back to her. "She's human. She doesn't understand our ways and the last thing I want to do is scare her with them."

"The cub is rightfully ours, Rio. You saw to it when you bit her."

He hoisted himself out of the chair and did his best to keep his tone and visage neutral. "Sinclair is Nahla's aunt and as close to a good mother as she'll ever have. If we don't accept Sinclair, then Nahla won't accept us. Second, I won't bring Sinclair here to be persecuted either."

"Then why not bite her too?"

This came from one of the females sitting on the other side of Suzette. She didn't know it, but she had better be thankful that Rio had to go through the grieving mom to get his claws on her. The growl rumbling from his throat should suffice.

"Shut up, Virginia." Billie grimaced at her subordinate. "If you're smart, you'll keep that kind of advice under lock and key."

Nervous laughter fluttered from the younger woman. She stood and adjusted her glasses. "No harm. All I'm saying is if Rio loves her, then maybe he should make it official by—"

"Shut. Up." Billie's glare turned dangerous as she stalked across the room and came within inches of the neophyte. "Flap that tongue again and I'll cut it off. I won't have anyone go through the horror of ushering someone through the change with a third of a chance at survival. Do I make myself clear?"

Virginia's bottom lip trembled. Lowering her gaze, she sat beside Suzette on the bed. Instead of her comforting the grieving mother, Suzette slid her arms around Virginia and hugged her close.

Rio stretched and let out a huge yawn.

Billie whirled on him, jabbing a finger in his direction. "And as for you...Sinclair is another story all together."

He dropped his arms and stared at her. "I'm not going to bite Sinclair."

"That's not what I'm talking about. A cub like Nahla is so rare that she needs the protection that only this Coalition can give her."

"I can protect her *and* Sinclair just fine."

"You bit her; you put her in danger. Why do you think our cubs don't change until they've reached puberty? You bit a three-year-old child who's too damn young to protect herself against the dangers out there. Now that we've got Charlotte hunting us she's in more danger than ever." Glaring, Billie stalked toward him. "You find a way, but I want that child under our protection. If that means we have to take her family to court, then so be it."

Rio gnawed his bottom lip to keep from striking out at her. He loved Billie like a sister, but whenever she got this angry she had the mean streak of a charging bull. "Sinclair won't understand," he muttered.

"Then find a way to—"

The door burst open. One of Rio's brothers dashed into the room huffing. Rio took one look at the blood covering his hands and arms and knew something bad happened. He was on his feet before the man could open his mouth.

Billie eyes widened. "Dante?"

He shook his head. "William. He...something..."

Say no more. Rio hurried past him and down the hall. He continued down the stairs without having to ask the cheetah where to go. The metallic scent of ripe blood was thick in the air. He rounded the curving staircase and headed to the first floor. A momentary sniff...and he darted off toward the back of the house.

A crowd huddled around the area. The stench alone was enough to let him know that it was worse then he thought.

By the time he made his way through the throng, he noticed his friend, William, lying on the floor with Dante holding him. Burnt flesh covered William's charred body. His blackened fingers clutched the St. Christopher's pendant while his bulging eyes stared at the ceiling. The little hair left on his head matted with his oozing wounds.

Rio's breath caught. He didn't have to kneel to feel a pulse or even ask someone to bring his supplies from Theresa's room. The last gurgling breath left William's lungs, deflating his chest. Rio looked away, knowing a piece of him die with his friend.

Dante brushed his eyelids shut and lowered William's corpse to the floor. He couldn't take his eyes off him. "Jason needs you," he murmured.

"What happened?" Rio's voice came through so light and airy that he hardly noticed it was his.

Dante shook his head. "Not sure. Jason and Lita took a trip to William's house in Wake Forest. They wanted to make sure he made it back to his place okay after staying out all night with the guys."

"He was in the house." A male wrapped his arms around one of the females, smoothing his hand along her back for comfort. "Jason tried to douse the flames, but he got burned too. Just not as bad. The house is still intact, but..."

"Where is he?" Rio asked.

One of the onlookers pointed down another corridor that led to the solarium on the backside of the house. Rio followed the finger and noticed more blood droplets splotching the carpet.

His thoughts went straight to Sinclair and Nahla. If their enemies could be this vicious, then why stop with a couple of humans? Maybe at Sinclair they would because they knew it wasn't wise to get humans involved in were-cheetah affairs. Since Nahla was so close to her aunt, perhaps they wouldn't harm her either. Maybe.

Yeah right. Optimism had its place…right next to a pile of shit.

"Rio!" Dante stared at him. "Jason needs you."

Really. Unfortunately, he wanted to go his mate. Dante would lay down the law now that one of his people died and two more came close.

Instead of bringing up her name, he had to shoot for another angle. "I need my supplies. Theresa's up and she's in a lot of pain. Jason's going to be the same if he's not there already."

The King sighed. "What do you need? I'll send someone to get it for you."

Through sheer force, Rio managed to turn his snarl into an aggravated sigh. "They won't know. I do. If they make a mistake, then I'll have to send them back and in the mean time Theresa and Jason lose time."

Dante's eyes tightened to slits, glaring at his subordinate cat. "Make a list. Keep your ear to the phone in case they call for further instructions. However…you're *not* leaving this house! Understand?"

How dare he stand there and forbid him from seeing his mate. God help him, Rio tensed so tight that he thought about taking on his King in front of everyone.

Dante could do or say whatever he wanted because *his* mate remained safe behind closed doors. But his? She was out there with a child and all Dante could say was that her being human would protect her. Bullshit.

Rio started for the door. Although he respected his King, this was one time he'd take his chances and go to his woman.

He never made it out of the room.

Chapter 32

Thank goodness Kyle left the house when he did. After receiving a threatening voice mail from Social Services, Sinclair needed time to figure things out. More important, she wanted to strangle Mina for turning her in to Mr. Gallagher. Was this her way of getting back once she sobered up and realized that her sister had taken her child away? She knew that Mina wasn't a vindictive bitch by any means, but booze had a way of making her twisted.

Since Rio had yet to return her phone calls, she took matters into her own hands. Otherwise, his surrogate daughter would end up in foster care. Nobody wanted to see Nahla taken away, but imagine how it would go down if her foster parents found out that they had a were-cheetah.

Doing her best to ignore Nahla's moans, she borrowed the keys to Rio's SUV—again—and sped off down the road. It was time to pay her lawyer another visit.

Sinclair reached the city, but never reached her lawyer's office. Instead, she settled for taking Nahla home where she could rest a bit. Had her temperature not spiked, she would've chanced the traffic build-up clogging the latest stretch of highway construction.

She put the SUV in park and turned off the engine. Lifting her head, she looked into the rearview mirror at Nahla.

Oh. My. Lord.

Sinclair sighed and closed her eyes. Nahla sat in the car seat with clumps of oatmeal-colored vomit running down her chin and soaking into the front of her sweater. This was the second time she threw up in this man's SUV. If he wanted to be her surrogate papa, then he had better get used to sick little kids.

Sinclair went to the back and freed Nahla from the sopping booster seat. She couldn't stand to see her little girl sit in filth a moment longer, so she stripped her free of her clothes and shed her own jacket for Nahla to wear.

The toddler laid her feverish head on Sinclair's shoulder. "I sorry, Auntie."

She patted Nahla's head. "It's okay, baby. You're sick. Rio will understand."

The thought of him scrubbing the seat clean amused her.

After planting her niece on her hip, Sinclair fumbled with her keys for the front door. Once inside, she looked around the house hoping for a note. As expected, Sinclair found nothing. Mina never failed to disappoint when it came to her absence.

"I tired," Nahla moaned.

"I know, baby."

"Where Mommy?"

Sinclair bit back her grimace. "I don't know." She placed the little girl on the couch and tugged the throw over her. "I want you to stay on the sofa, okay? Auntie Sin has to go outside and clean Rio's car."

"Are we gonna see Wee-oh 'gain?"

She kissed her niece. "We will. I just need to get a grip on things."

"What tings?"

Sinclair stuffed one of the throw pillows behind Nahla. She ran a hand through her soft hair. "Things that you don't need to worry about."

Sinclair's bottom lip trembled. She almost lost it. How was she going to hold it together?

One last look before she turned and made her way to the front door. When she opened it, her heart tripped.

Two police officers stood on the other side of the screened storm door. The taller one stared at her. Hopefully, they weren't the real deal this time.

"Are you Ms. Duval?" he asked.

Okay. No matter how many times she had encountered the cops—no thanks to Mina—she could never get used to them confronting her. However, something about the way these two scrutinized her with their eyes, she couldn't help feeling as though something were up.

She nodded. "Yes. Why? Has something happened to my sister?"

The other officer careened his head over her shoulder and glanced into the house. "Is that Nahla Duval?"

They didn't answer her question. That wasn't good. "Yes. What's going on?"

"I'm Officer Hirshenson." He lifted his hat, allowing more light to enter his face. "Your sister, Mina, reported her kidnapped."

"Kidnapped?"

That revelation was a kick to the gut. What was Mina thinking? Did she finally flip off the deep end? More important, why would these idiots believe a drunken criminal before her, an upstanding citizen with two tickets to her name? Mina had a police record and enough recorded visits from Child Welfare to fill a bathtub.

"You're kidding?" *Stay calm. Acting crazy won't solve anything.*

"Wish I was." Hirshenson sighed. "I've seen your sister's history, Ms. Duval. I also know that you don't have one."

"Damn straight. I have enough trouble making sure my niece doesn't go down that same road."

"Right now, I'm more concerned with what's going on between you and your sister. Nahla will be taken care of, I promise."

Words hung on the edge of Sinclair's bobbing jaw. She nearly let her niece's feline nature slip. Swallowing, she closed her eyes to get her thoughts straight. When she opened them, she stared at the cop. "I didn't kidnap my niece. Hell, why would I come back to the scene of the crime?"

He shrugged. "I don't know. But before you say anything to me, you'll want to have your attorney present. I only say that because I have a feeling that this is more of a misunderstanding than a kidnapping."

"You're damn right it's a misunderstanding. When I get my hands on Mina, I'll throw her ass under my foot and stomp—"

Hirshenson held up a hand. "Don't say anymore, Ms. Duval. I'm only doing my job and that was to arrest you when you showed up. Like I said, I doubt the charges will stick. Given the choice, I'd like to see that little girl in your capable hands rather than those of the system."

Hirshenson's partner reached for a pair of handcuffs. "Ms. Duval, you have the right to remain silent—"

"Wait a minute!"

One cop read her Rights while the other took her by the wrist and led her out onto the porch. Two more cops waited on the front lawn, one of them a female who rushed up the steps and entered the house.

"Wait!" Sinclair tried not to fight the officers, but the more she resisted, the stronger the one binding her wrists had become. "Please don't do this. What's going to happen to my niece? She'll be scared."

Hirshenson stepped aside while his partner finished clicking the cuffs into place. "Do you understand these rights as they've been explained?"

"I can't—"

"Do you understand these rights?" he repeated.

"Yes. Now will someone please tell me—"

A scream echoed from inside the house.

Fear gripped Sinclair. *Dear God, not again.* Her little girl had seen more than her share of police cars and violence from the hoodlum boyfriends that Mina had brought home. She didn't need to see this.

Sinclair tore away from the cop to go inside. She didn't get far because the cop hauled her back and jerked her down the steps to the nearest police car. Tears and panic had taken hold and left her scrambling to get to her niece.

"Nahla!" she yelled. "Nahla!" When she saw the female cop carrying her squirming niece it made her want to break free more. It shredded her heart to see Nahla hold her arms out to her, crying her aunt's name, and she couldn't get to her. "Dammit, this isn't fair! Please, tell me where you're taking her"

The other cop opened the backdoor of the police cruiser and shoved her inside. Sinclair leaned forward and nearly got her head cut off when the officer slammed the door shut. She refused to give up without a fight. Sinclair continued to ram her shoulder into the door and shout her niece's name.

Both cops stood in front of the window. Sinclair watched as they loaded Nahla into the other police car. When the door closed, the officer stepped aside and opened her door.

Anger tore through her. She wanted to tear those jerks away from her baby, she knew it wouldn't do any good. Besides, she had seen Mina fight on occasion and it usually resulted in jail time and fines. She had to prove to these assholes that she was nothing like her boozing sister.

Hirshenson's face softened. "I know that look, Ms. Duval. I've seen it on your sister enough times after she's been arrested. My advice is to play by the rules until we get you downtown, processed, and you get your phone call."

God, help her. She had never been "processed" before. What did that mean? Would they take her picture, record her fingerprints, and throw her in jail with a bunch of gangster women and junkies? More important, where the hell was Rio when she needed him?

Chapter 33

Rio blinked until his focus centered on a cement wall. He had no idea how long he lay on the mattress in the basement. A sharp pain ran through the left side of his face, most of it settling behind his eye socket.

Did someone hit me?

"*Maldito, mis daños principales,*" he whispered.

"You say something?"

A newspaper rustled on Rio's left side. A chair scraped across the cement floor and footsteps followed.

Lincoln Brennan crouched beside the mattress. He was a huge black man packed with so much muscle throughout his body that even his baldhead looked muscled. He sported a black mustache and a diamond twinkled on his earlobe. His trademark toothpick swirled in the corner of his mouth.

Rio blinked. "How did you manage to snag guard duty?"

Lincoln helped Rio sit. "Volunteered. I figured you would rather have me than someone like Walt down here."

Smiling hurt his cheek, so he had to settle for a snort. Turing partway on his side, Rio slowly hoisted himself from the mattress and waited until the room stopped spinning before saying anything. "Let me guess. You're my watchdog."

Lincoln nodded. "Dante didn't want you leaving the property, so clobbering you was the only thing he could think of to keep you here. And as long as we're being honest"—he glanced over his shoulder—"I think it's because he's afraid."

"Afraid? Of what?"

He shook his head before sauntering back to the table where he packed up his newspaper. "We don't know what kind of game Charlotte is playing. This mess with Jason and William doesn't even make sense. I thought werecats were smarter than this."

"Unless they're rabid." Rio massaged the back of his aching neck. "Weres only creep around when they're about to mount a full-scaled attack. Burning William's body and wounding Jason, it's like they're goading us."

"I agree. Sabotaging Jungle Kingdom was a threat. I could be wrong, but Sloan doesn't come across as the type who would stage something like this."

That got Rio's attention. He hadn't thought much about the attacks because he'd spent too much time patching up his people and taking care of his loved ones than worrying about the opposition. He'd met Sloan a time or two and the Charlotte King never came off like a raging lunatic. Speaking from the were-cheetah point of view, he seemed like a normal guy.

Shoving his hands in his back pocket, Rio closed the distance. "You think Sloan has rogues who aren't playing by the rules?"

"More like trying to start a fight." Lincoln motioned Rio to follow him through a basement that looked more like a packrat's stock pile. Cluttered furniture and dusty boxes lay everywhere. "In all honesty it doesn't matter what we think. This is still Sloan's problem and one way or other, he has to own up to it. You know the Laws better than anyone."

That he did. After killing those monsters who raped his fiancée, the Charlotte Coalition wanted to exact revenge on the Triangle. Dante convinced them that it would be wise if they retreated across the county line while they still had the chance. Rio, no matter how deranged at the time, was in his right to take his frustrations out on the perpetrators. Sloan was their second in command and agreed that his people had gotten what they deserved. Two months later, a "mysterious" accident claimed the life of their leader and Sloan took his place. They'd had their usual spats every now and then, but nothing would constitute repeated hits on their people resulting in death. None of this made sense.

Rio followed his friend up the stairs and stopped when they arrived on the landing. "She's out there, Lincoln. Alone with my cub."

The big man smiled. "Your cub. Do you realize how you sound?"

"I do."

Lincoln shook his head. "She's not your cub. Not by — "

"Does it matter? I bit her; that makes her mine." Sighing, he leaned against the railing behind him. "That little girl could've died and I saved her. The short time she's been around, I've grown to love her. She's just a baby. If Sloan gets his hands on Nahla—any one of his people for that matter—God only knows if they'll use her against me."

"Mmmm hmmm. How do you feel about the rest of the family? Because you know as well as I do making good with the aunt won't win the heart of the child's mother."

Rio didn't want to think about Mina, the boozing maniac. Whether she liked it o not, he'd have his say in this family. Nahla never had a real father. He would be more than happy to fill that void.

Rio reached for the knob. "*Vamos.*"

Lincoln stepped in front of him, blocking his way. He folded his arms across his thick chest and stared at his friend. "You haven't answered my question. I might be a were-cheetah, but I know a thing or two about black women."

A baffled look crossed Rio's face. "Is that what you think this is? A race issue?"

"Is it?"

"No! Look, I've got feelings for that woman. My stomach knots up every time I think about her being alone. The last time she was there, those damn cheetahs attacked. Do you have any idea of what it would do to me if something happened to her? Dammit, Lincoln, I can't—"

"You didn't answer my question."

"I thought I just did."

Lincoln shook his head. "Uh uh. You need a plan. You can't just walk into a woman's life and tell her, I want you because I love your niece as though she were my daughter. Not only that, you've got that child's real mother to deal with. You think she's just going to hand her baby over to you?"

Again, Rio met his eyes. "Sinclair is my mate. The only reason why I haven't claimed her is because I think it'll scare her away. Even if the bite weren't the issue, I'd still love them as if they were my own."

"But that's the problem. Nahla's not Sinclair's." Lincoln placed his thick hands on Rio's shoulders and stared him down. "If you love this woman enough to want her for your mate, I'm not knocking that. All I'm saying is that you need to be careful with this. After all, you're taking on an entire human family."

Stepping away, Rio ran his hand through his hair. "I don't get it.

Everyone thinks biting Nahla made things easier, when in fact; it only made this worse."

Lincoln gripped the knob. "Don't bail out now. I have a feeling the fight just started."

When he opened the door, two were-cheetahs stopped them. It wasn't until Lincoln gave them a warning snarl that they continued on their way.

The light from the hall stung Rio's eyes. In the basement, there wasn't much light, so no need to be overly sensitive to it. It took a few seconds for his eyes to adjust to the glare so he could see the makings of the dark orange walls. A long, Persian rug lined the floor.

"Time to check on Theresa and Jason." Lincoln pointed him up the staircase.

Rio glanced over his shoulder. "I get it. You only take me out of my hiding place when you need me."

"Not my orders, man. Remember?"

"How can I forget?" Rio continued down the hall to the main staircase.

"Dante only kept you down there for your own safety. If you want my honest opinion—"

"I don't recall asking for it."

Lincoln glared at him and continued. "As long as Sinclair and Nahla stay away from here, I think they're safer than any of us."

Another were-cheetah descending the stairs stared between the two of them. He opened his mouth to say something, but closed it and hurried on his way.

Both men stared after the guy before shrugging and going about their business. Lincoln led the way to Jason's room. When he opened the door, the scent of antiseptic mixed with the acrid odor of burnt flesh slapped them in the face.

Rose pink walls and the wrought iron bed with metal vines around the posts stood out. On the other side of the bed, curtains waved from the opened French doors. There was just enough of an opening to see the full-bloom flower garden below. From the brushstroke painting on the walls to the laced runners on the dresser and chest of drawers, this room had feminine written all over it.

Guess it was a good thing that Jason was too out of it to notice.

He lay sleeping with oozing bandages covering the upper part of his body and the length of his arms. The sheet covering him below the waist hid more bandages on his upper thighs. His burns looked severe, but at least he had his fast-healing genes to help him through the crisis that would leave a human insane with pain.

Rio glanced around the room and noted more medical supplies stacked on a table near the wall. "Someone went by the hospital?"

Lincoln slipped into the room around him and picked up a box of sterile pads. "I guess so. I wouldn't know. I've been in the basement with you all this time."

"Well, if they stopped by the house, it looks like they forgot the Theridan."

"I'm sure nobody will mind making another run."

Rio wanted to throw something through the window. Instead, he gripped his hand on the back of a wood chair and slammed it on the floor closer to the bed. Jason flinched and moaned, but didn't wake up. That movement alone was enough to calm Rio down. He didn't need to take out his frustrations on an injured man. Jason had nothing to do with this.

"You through?" Lincoln sauntered to his side and folded his arms over his thick chest.

"I'm a prisoner in someone else's home." He snatched a penlight off the nightstand and began flashing it in Jason's eyes.

Sighing, the big man sat at the end of the bed. "You might want to check the bandages. Billie had to clean his wounds while you were out cold. I think she might have shot him up with some morphine too."

"How did it happen?"

"You mean how did Billie know what to do?"

Rio stared at him before sighing and closing his eyes. "I'm talking about how Jason got like this?"

"He tackled William with a blanket, but didn't notice the lighter fluid on the ground. I guess he thought that all of it had burned off or something. Anyway, when he hit the grass, Jason landed in a leftover puddle."

Damn. Here was a guy who only wanted to help his friend and he ended up nearly killing himself in the process. Rio wondered if Jason knew his efforts were in vain or even cared. Nonetheless, he would see to it that his Coalition brother would make a full recovery.

A knock came to the door. Before either man could tell the person to enter, Kyle had barged into the room. A touch of anger and bewilderment marred his face as he looked between both men. His glare rested on Rio who seemed as confounded as Lincoln did.

"Where the hell have you been?" he shouted. He closed the

distance, hands balled into fists. "They told me you were gone."

Rio stood. "What happened? Is it Sinclair? Nahla?"

His friend grumbled under his breath. "You son of a bitch. I've been calling this house and leaving messages for the past three hours. Don't you know how to check your fucking cell?"

"Kyle!" Lincoln's irritation had caught the man by surprise. He crossed the room, glowering. "Don't bring your ass in here spouting off at the mouth unless you've got something important you need to share."

Kyle snorted. "Something important. If it was so damn important to him, he would have—"

"He couldn't, dumb ass! Dante knocked him out and tossed him in the basement because he tried to leave the house. I've been down there with him all this time. So like I said...if you've got something to say then say it before I take my hand and whop your ass across this room."

A tick worked in Kyle's cheek. "She's gone."

Rio's fury had vanished. "Gone?"

He nodded. Kyle spent the next few minutes telling both Rio and Lincoln about Nahla not feeling well and Sinclair's dressing the little girl to take her out to get something to make her feel better. He told them that he'd decided to go instead, and that he'd instructed them to remain inside. Kyle held Rio's gaze. "When I returned they were gone."

"Damn," Rio muttered. Something must have sent Sinclair on the run.

Chapter 34

Unbelievable. Sinclair finally understood what the word "processed" meant. They made her empty her pockets, snapped a set of horrific mug shots, and locked her in a cell. Her only blessing was that they had caged her up by herself. Just down the hall, other women heckled and yelled, offering up various body parts for a get-out-of-jail-free card.

Never in her life had she felt so humiliated. Sinclair sat at the back of the cell on the bottom bunk. She hadn't moved since her arrival because she feared what kind of diseases and bodily fluids infested the mattress. A gray, wool blanket covered the bed and a flattened pillow rested near her thigh. She never would have sat down had it not been for her wobbly legs. When the cell door rolled back and the locks clapped into place, Sinclair's entire world caved in. She'd spent the last few hours trying to get the clanging sound out of her head.

Nobody told her where they'd taken Nahla. She fought not to "raise her own Cain" and scream profanities into the hall. It certainly didn't help those harlots down a few cages down, so why would it help her? Plus, proving she was an upstanding citizen had to account for something. Right?

A female cop stared into her cell. "Open on five."

A buzz released the lock. Sinclair watched as the door slid back on the metal track.

"Your lawyer's here." The cop motioned for Sinclair to come out.

The cop led Sinclair into another room where she noticed Mr. Torrance sitting at a table and wearing a nice beige suite. Pudginess settled around his middle and he had blond hair that went well with his tanned complexion.

He motioned her to take the seat across from him. This was the first time since this horrendous ordeal began where a touch of safety and familiarity had washed over her.

"Ten minutes," the cop said, and left the room.

Sinclair glanced at the door. "Think they have this place wired?"

"Does it matter?" He pulled a file from his briefcase and placed it on the table. "You've got nothing to hide." Torrance folded his fingers together. "You mind telling me what's going on?"

She hunched over the table. "First, I need to know where Nahla is. Jacob, I know her. She'll be scared out of her mind. I was about to take her to the doctor when the police showed up and arrested me for kidnapping. Can you believe that?"

"Based on the arrest report, they staked out the house until you returned. Where were you?"

She sighed. "I was with a friend. When Nahla got sick, I left to—"

He flipped open a manila folder. "Would that friend be Rio Velasquez?"

"How did you—"

"I got in touch with Social Services because I knew you'd ask about Nahla. She's at the hospital for now, but they're waiting on placement with foster parents."

Sinclair shook her head. She wanted to cry, but she forced the tears at bay. "Where's Mina?" she snarled.

Jacob lowered his gaze. "The police have been trying to contact her to let her know that they've found you. So far, nobody's seen her."

"Dammit, Jacob, I don't want to spend the night in this filthy pit."

"I know." He folded his fingers together again and rested them on top of the folder. "We can only do one thing at a time. My main priority is to get you out of here. I would rather have the police find Mina so we can get this straightened out before it goes to court. If the judge offers bail—"

"I can afford it."

He patted the air. "I know you can, so that's not the issue. All I'm saying is that it'll look extremely bad if we have to go to court with this. It'll look especially bad for Mina because you have an untarnished track record and the judge will see this as nothing more than one of her drunken rages."

"But we're talking kidnapping here. This won't be a cakewalk."

"No, it won't." He leaned back in his chair. "If you go to jail,

Mina will lose Nahla. She's spent time behind bars for drunk and disorderly conduct, possession of marijuana and crack. You're the only one who keeps them from taking Nahla away or they would've done it by now. If you go to jail" — he raised his hand to calm her outburst — "that's not what I'm aiming for. I'm just saying *if* it happens. Nahla will go to foster care. Mina still won't have her daughter."

Sinclair rubbed her aching head. The longer this went on, the more it irritated her. She just wanted to go home and pretend like this day had never happened.

For that matter, she just wanted to wake up from this nightmare called reality. Mina put everyone in jeopardy with her stupid arrest charges. Even worse, if they found out about Nahla, her niece would either become a guinea pig in someone's lab or make the cover of a rag magazine right next to the Bat Boy.

"I need my baby girl back," she said.

"It'll happen. Just give me time to get the paperwork together and I'll have you out of here before nightfall." He closed his folder and began packing up. "Before I forget, are you and Mr. Velasquez...an item?"

Good question. The jerk ignored all of the messages she left for him. At this point, she wasn't sure.

Swallowing, she lowered her head and nodded.

"Do you want me to call him?"

"What good will it do? I've been trying to reach him all day. Before I called you."

"He might have called while you've been sitting in that cell. Give me the number and let me see if I can reach him."

Sinclair knew of a better way to put the fright in his behind. "How about you mention you're my lawyer and that you'll be acting on my behalf in all affairs concerning Nahla. And I mean all of them. That'll put the fright in his behind."

Torrance's eyebrow knitted. Shaking his head, he finished packing and stood. "No worries, Sinclair. We'll figure this mess out."

Better not be. Not while her niece's life was at stake.

◆ ◆ ◆

Words couldn't begin to explain the worry and fear that chipped away at his sanity. He and Kyle searched the grounds around his house just to make sure someone hadn't dragged Sinclair and Nahla away. From what they could tell, no foul play was involved. After leaving the cottage, the guys jumped into Kyle's SUV and headed to Mina's house.

When Rio's cell rang he breathed a sigh of relief as Sinclair's lawyer relayed what had happened to her and Nahla. Rio snapped his phone shut. "Someone had better be at that house when we get there."

Rio fought through his fury to piece together coherent thoughts. He growled low in his throat before giving Kyle the information.

"You sure you don't want to go to the police station?" Kyle hit a corner so fast that the tires squealed.

Rio massaged his forehead. "It's like I told Torrance. The bail money is covered. Right now, I need to help Sinclair a different way."

"Getting Nahla out of County won't? I'm sure her doctor's probably scratching his head over her latest blood tests."

"I know," Rio mumbled. "But as long as we don't have a heavy hitter to get custody of Nahla, then we're in for an uphill battle. Finding Nahla's stupid mother and forcing her to straighten this whole mess out is the best shot we've got."

Kyle shook his head. "This is unbelievable. Never in a million years would I have thought something like this would happen. I'm still having a hard time with Dante letting you out of the house."

Rio didn't. The man didn't have a choice once Nahla fell into the wrong hands. Even though he didn't want to acknowledge her as one of their own, he couldn't afford to ignore her either. Not if the Coalition wanted to maintain their anonymity.

The moment Dante heard about Sinclair's false arrest and Social Services taking custody of Nahla, he knew he needed to act. A thorough check of Jacob Torrance proved how far Sinclair would go to keep her niece out of foster care. The man was one of the best lawyers in Chapel Hill. To Rio's shock, Dante didn't stop there. Although he refused to let all twenty-two of his cheetahs scout around the city for information on Mina's whereabouts, he appointed a small group to comb the streets for her. Rio led the operation.

Bouncing into the driveway, Kyle skidded to a stop just as Rio jumped out of the passenger's side. He planned to break down the door to get inside, but the cracked wood and the hanging lock made him stop.

Kyle hurried onto the porch by his side. "Someone's been here."

"That someone wasn't Mina." Rio pushed the door open without stepping inside.

Kyle's nose wrinkled with a whiff. "Were-cheetah."

Nodding, Rio stepped inside. He flipped the main switch on the wall — good thing he remembered where it was from his last visit — and doused the living room and dining room with golden light from a single lamp.

"Think they're still here?" Kyle followed behind him.

Rio lifted his head to the hollow sounds of the house. He could hear the hum of the refrigerator motor and the ticking from the small Swiss clock on the far wall, but nothing else. He sniffed his surroundings again. A were-cheetah had been here, but his scent mixed with that of the unlit floral-scented candles on the mantle. It was the same scent from his last visit.

"No," he replied. "They broke in hours ago."

Kyle's gaze panned around the room.

Rio noticed the laptop on the dining room table. Although he had just met Sinclair, she didn't seem like the type who would leave something like this lying around. Not when thugs used this place as a revolving door. He recalled she had cordoned off a section of her bedroom as a workspace with a desk, a lamp, and her laptop.

Springing the lock, he flipped up the screen.

It was black, but the leftover scent startled him. A were-cheetah had his hands all over her laptop, meaning he probably left a ransom note.

Rio tapped the mouse button.

Sinclair didn't have a password, so the screen brightened and a note materialized.

A growl resonated from Rio. "We're going to Bogelman's Bakery."

"Why?"

He pointed at the screen when Kyle arrived to look over his shoulder. "Because I'm betting that's where Mina is."

"A bakery?" He combed his fingers though his hair. "It doesn't make sense. I thought she was a drunk."

"Drunks will hangout anywhere where they can get a drink. I'm guessing she does a little bit more than drink. My money's on that she's also doing crack. If that's true the same thing applies. An addict will go where he can to get a fix." Rio shrugged his shoulders. "This is only my take on it."

"You know it's a trap, right?"

That was the first thing that crossed Rio's mind. With everything Charlotte had done, this didn't surprise him. It was only a matter of time before they brought the Duvals into the middle of their battle.

"Yes." Sighing, Rio unhooked his phone and placed a call to Dante. "But we've got nothing else to go on."

Chapter 35

Why in the world would a were-cheetah tell them where to go? Everything pointed to the Charlotte Coalition, which Dante reiterated between tirades. Unfortunately, with so much to lose, Rio couldn't afford to let the clue slip. If Sloan wanted a meeting, then he would give him one he'd never forget.

The only Bogelman's Bakery in the entire area lay on the cusp of the ghetto that bordered on downtown Durham. Kyle pulled the SUV beside the curb, but Rio was out the door before he could turn the engine off.

He started for the front door of the brightly lit bakery, but something in the alley to the left caught his attention. There were homeless people back there. He lifted his head to the towering brick buildings, following the fire escape up to jostling clotheslines, trash infested balconies, and two junkies huddled together while trying to light a crack pipe.

The message wasn't for Rio to go inside the bakery, but rather, gave him a general idea of where he could find Mina. Watching the two skeletal guys punch each other until one handed over the glass pipe, he knew this had to be the place.

"Any idea where?" Kyle shoved his hands in his pockets.

"None." Rio stalked into the alley looking up. "You take the left and I'll take the right. She has to be somewhere up there."

"No front door?"

"No. I have a feeling nobody will open it unless we're offering something from the other side. I've got nothing except a bone to pick with Mina." He leapt up and grabbed the bottom rung on the fire escape. "If you get in trouble, yell."

"We're not waiting for the cavalry?"

His friend didn't look the least bit scared, but Rio wouldn't know that by his line of questioning. "You can wait for Lincoln and the others if you want, but I know Mina's up there, and dammit, I intend to find her."

Kyle offered up a smirk. "The Rio I knew was more sensible than this. Sinclair must be one hell of a catch for you to lose your sanity."

"She is."

Chuckling, Kyle shook his head. Without another word, he went to the opposite building and grabbed the rung of the fire escape.

Both men scaled the wrought iron stairs with the stealth of a cat creeping across the Serengeti. Although it was a different kind of wilderness, both environments held the same danger in Rio's eyes. He didn't know if someone might shoot him from one of the dirty windows or reach out and stab him with a butcher knife. Different worlds, same dangers.

"Rio!" Kyle stood on the opposite balcony two flights up from him and was pointing at a mildew-stained window.

He must have found Mina.

Rio grabbed the railing and tried to judge the distance. Although cheetahs were fantastic jumpers even in human form, he didn't relish the idea of missing his mark and crashing into the wall. Three stories down, those Dumpsters looked like they would hurt.

He had to chance it.

As if reading his Coalition brother's thoughts, Kyle raced down one level and held his hands over the railing. He motioned for his friend to jump.

There wasn't much running room, so Rio prayed his reflexes would be enough. He climbed on top of the railing and balanced himself before leaping across the alley.

He hit the rail hard enough to rattle it. Not only did he have a feeling he might have cracked a rib, but if it hadn't been for Kyle catching one of arms, he might have fallen to his death. Cats could land on their feet, but he might have landed on his back and done untold amounts of damage.

Huffing, he let Kyle help him the rest of the way. Rio sat on the steps a moment to catch his breath.

"What did you see?" he asked.

"I think we found our missing person." Kyle inclined his head at window above them. "She looks strung out!"

"Is she moving?"

"Not from what I can tell."

Damn.

Clutching his side, Rio pulled himself to his feet and gripped the metal rail. From one step to the next, he said a silent prayer that the bitch wasn't dead. If she was, then they might as well look into breaking both Sinclair and Nahla out. He doubted she would want to spend the rest of her life on the run or in hiding, but it was a chance he'd take when it came to his family.

When he reached the window, Rio pressed his face close and squinted through the darkness. Just like Kyle said, Mina lay sprawled out on her back. The light from the moon beamed on an empty bottle of Hennessey on the floor. He couldn't tell if she was alive.

He didn't have time for pleasantries. When he tried the window and found that it wouldn't budge, he kicked it.

"Are you nuts?" Kyle shouted in a loud whisper. "Someone could come running with a gun and start shooting."

His eyes narrowed. "I've got nothing to lose."

Kyle refused to argue with the man. The last time he saw that look, his friend went after the monsters who had raped his fiancée. If anything, he thought about calling Dante to come here personally to calm his friend down.

Rio reached inside and unlocked the window.

A dark shadow waltzed into the room. "Son of a bitch, Mina. What that hell did you break now?"

Although he never met the man, Rio knew his scent. Some of it was leftover in Mina's bedroom from the hordes of savages who had traipsed through her door.

"Who are you?" the man asked. "Why you gonna break my window like that, punk? I oughta knock you on your ass, you stupid Mexican. Comin' up in here and—"

Rio punched him. The man smashed into the wall behind him and landed on the floor face down. He didn't move.

Kyle hurried across the room and glanced into the hallway. "You better hope nobody else is here, man."

"Correction." He kicked the empty bottle aside and scooped Mina into a fireman's carry. "They had better hope they don't run into *me* while I'm here."

"Front door?"

Rio nodded.

When they entered the living room, sobbing caught his ear. He turned and his stomach heaved. In fact, he had to readjust Mina before he dropped her.

A baby that appeared to be little more than a year old stood in a playpen wearing nothing except a soiled T-shirt. Fear mixed with a hint of curiosity, the little boy couldn't take his wide, tear-filled eyes off Rio.

Every expletive that he could think of, rifled through Rio's brain. The monster called compassion had dropped a two-ton weigh on his conscience in the form of a neglected child.

"What are you doing?" Kyle yelled. "We can't take the kid with us."

Rio had no idea he had stepped toward the playpen until his friend had opened his mouth. He laid Mina on the couch while keeping his attention on the child.

"We can't leave him," he said.

"Like hell we can't. Man, this isn't our problem."

He shot his friend a glare. "Like hell it isn't. We just broke in here, knocked out this kid's father — I'm guessing — and now we're about to kidnap...?" He hoped to God Mina wasn't his mother. If she was, then that would complicate matters on an immeasurable scale.

Slipping his hands under the child's arms, he lifted him from the crib. Not only did the baby need a diaper, but he also needed a bath. Urine scented the corner of the mattress and it looked like the baby had torn off his shitty diaper.

"We've got to go," Kyle insisted. "Take the little guy with us and it's called kidnapping."

"Leave him here and it's called abandonment."

"Dammit, Rio, what do you think you're doing?"

By the time Rio made it to the other side of the room where he found a pack of diapers, the baby's sobs had tapered into hiccupped sniffles. "I'm changing him. Either you can help or you can take your ass down to the car."

Kyle let out a sigh and relaxed his shoulders. "Fine. What do you want me to do?"

"Go in the bathroom and see if you can find a washcloth for starters. Wet it and bring it to me." Cooing the baby to calmness, he laid him on his back and smiled. "Do you have your camera phone?"

"Yeah. Why?"

"Take some pictures of this place and the baby. Keep me out of the photos though. I need to know if this baby is Mina's or not. In fact, take some pictures of her wasted ass and her boyfriend too."

Shaking his head, Kyle turned and started for the bathroom.

Rio found it hard to tear his gaze away from the child. With Mina and her boyfriend still out, there was no one left to care for the little guy. He fought the urge to take him with them and perhaps hand him over to a Coalition member for safekeeping. However, Kyle had a point. The father had seen both their faces. He would have them up on kidnapping charges and the police beating down Dante's door.

Before Rio closed the front door, he glanced back at the smiling baby. Although they could only do so much, at least he'd made that kid's life a little better for the next few minutes. By then, the police would arrive. Once he and Kyle reached the street, Rio planned to use the phone at the corner to dial 911.

With Mina in his custody, he had formulated a plan to get both Sinclair *and* Nahla back. The sooner the better because Nahla was on the cusp of her first change.

Chapter 36

It took three cups of coffee, a cold shower, and a half a bottle of hot sauce to get Mina back into the world of the living. Rio would've preferred to hang her upside down out of a bedroom window, but Kyle stopped him. It took some doing, but they got her cleaned, dressed, and back in the SUV. Once again, Kyle played chauffer while Rio sat close enough to choke Mina'a personal space.

Lethargy hung in her drunken eyes. "Where are we going?" she asked.

"To jail. Then to Capital Med." Rio's eyes stayed on her like a cat on a fish truck.

"Jail?" She scooted closer to the window. "Hold on, man. You need to back up a bit."

"Let's get something straight. You made Sinclair's life a living hell. Don't think for one minute that I'm going to let you get off easy."

"Whatcha talkin' 'bout?"

His eyes narrowed. He fisted his fingers to keep from grabbing her by the hair. This so-called innocence crap only pissed him off more. "You called the cops and reported Nahla kidnapped when you knew damn well that Sinclair and I had her all this time."

Mina's glassy eyes widened. "No, I didn't. I mean…I reported her missing, yeah. But I didn't know—"

"Bullshit!" Before he could help himself, he snatched her neck in his grip. He never imagined himself getting this crazy with a woman. But if meant getting a better woman back, then so be it.

Kyle glanced into the rearview mirror. "Rio, man, you need to take it easy."

"Don't tell me to take it easy. Nahla's life is in danger the longer she stays in that hospital. Sinclair's locked up like a criminal, while Mina was out getting boozed and more than likely shoving a line of coke up her nose."

Mina clawed at his hand, but it remained locked in place. She locked her eyes on him, nostrils flared. "Don't you tell me how to raise my baby!"

"Raise her? Is that what you call passed out drunk in that apartment with a bottle of Hennessey on the floor? Speaking of which, is the other baby yours?"

When she didn't answer, he tightened his grip. He'd had enough of this. He shoved her away from him so hard that she smacked into the passenger door.

Mina started kicking him.

This crazy junkie had no idea who she was playing with. Rio snatched both her ankles and yanked her across the back seat to him. Once he got her flailing hands under control, he threw them above her head and managed to flip her over on the backseat.

Either this foolishness would end or he would put an end to her. Since he would be doing Sinclair and Nahla a favor, he considered it a pleasure.

But…he had another way to get her under control. "You've got a choice, Mina."

"Fuck you!"

"Oh, I'm sorry, but in case you haven't noticed, you're the one who's about to get fucked." He snagged both her wrists in one hand and unclipped a cell phone from his waist. A few clicks later, he brought up the pictures of her boyfriend's apartment and held an image of the baby smiling up to her face. "Does he look familiar?"

"Screw you!"

"No?" He clicked the forward button. "How about this one? There's you passed out on the floor. I even had Kyle place the empty Hennessey bottle by your hand."

She didn't say anything.

Rio clicked to another picture. "That's the crib the baby pissed in."

"Hey man! I don't know nothin' 'bout that. That baby ain't mine either."

Rio had a hard time believing that, but at least hearing it from her made him breathe a tad easier. "Well, I know something. You see, Mina, this is evidence. Evidence that Social Services would love to get their hands on."

"I told you that kid ain't mine!"

"Perhaps not. But if that baby is reported to Social Services and he's not yours, then guess who's going to get the blame for child neglect? Guess who's going to get the next visit from Mr. Gallagher? What do you think is going to happen if he shows up with the police, which is probably what he'll do once he sees these pictures?"

"I said, I don't—"

He leaned close to her ear. "Who does the baby belong to? Because they're going to be in deep shit depending upon if you decide to cooperate or not. Now, I'm no expert in coke-snorting affairs, but I'm guessing your boy toy back there is going to be pretty pissed if you're gone and the police show up at his door ready to take that baby."

For the first time since their backseat tussle, Mina loosened up. Although the grimace remained on her face, she seemed to have lost the will to fight as realization hit.

Rio had set her up.

"What the hell do you want from me?" she spat.

Now that was more like it—minus the cursing. However, Rio wasn't about to let her up just yet. "You messed up big time, Mina. This is the chance to redeem yourself and everyone else by doing the right thing."

"I asked you what you want."

Oh yeah. Rio could definitely smile now. "When we get to the police station, you tell them it was a mistake. Sinclair is innocent, and you damn well know that."

Mina scowled at Rio. "Why do you care? My family is my concern. Not yours."

"Wrong. You see, as long as I'm in love with your sister and I love your daughter that makes it my business."

A half smirk bit into her cheek. "I get it. You don't have a family so you're trying to steal mine."

"Given how you like to treat 'em, I wouldn't call it stealing. I'd call it a relief."

Mina looked away. "You don't get my child. If I wouldn't hand her over to Sinclair, then I sure as hell ain't handing her over to you."

Rio loosened his clawed fingers from her wrists, but kept her hands panned behind her back. "Would letting her fall into Child

Welfare's hands make you feel better?"

"They ain't takin' my child!"

He laughed. "Where have you been? You think Gallagher comes to the house for afternoon tea? Whether you like it or not, that man will take your child and there won't be a damn thing that you or Sinclair can do about it."

"You don't—"

"You think I'm lying? Go ahead with this stupid plan of yours. Because if Sinclair ends up in front of a judge, she's going to jail. She's the only thing that keeps Nahla out of the system."

"You don't know that."

He shrugged as if she could see it. "Maybe I'm wrong, but I know one thing. Instead of calling the police to ask for an update, you spent the day snorting coke up your nose and passed out drunk. How do you think that's going to look in the eyes of the police and Child Welfare?"

"We're here." Kyle pulled into a parking lot across from the police station. He turned the engine off and looked to Rio for the next move.

Rio released Mina and sat back in the seat. "So what's it going to be, little sister? Come clean or go to jail."

◆ ◆ ◆

Sinclair's legs ached and her nerves remained on edge. She still had a hard time believing this place had been her home for the last few hours. Heck, she'd never get used to the idea. The harlots down the way had nothing to fear because this was probably their home away from home on a daily basis. Not Sinclair. She had more dignity than that. More pride. Unfortunately, all it had done was to leave her quaking every time someone shouted, or something clanged against the bars.

The same female cop showed up at Sinclair's cell again.

Sinclair didn't know what to make of it until the cop signaled for her to step forward. When she walked out of the cell, the cop turned her to the left and pointed her down the hall. At the end, the female stepped up to the guard's station and began talking into the speaker. Looking at the wire enmeshed in the thick glass, Sinclair guessed it had to be bulletproof.

A box opened up from the counter and a clipboard slid out on the panel. The cop scratched a signature on the line and hit the lever to pass it back to the guard.

"What's going on?" she asked.

The cop motioned toward the door. "You're free to go. Your

sister dropped the charges."

Numb. Too many emotions bombarded Sinclair. She couldn't decide whether to hug her sister or slug her. Given they were in a police station, she decided to wait until she got home where there weren't any witnesses.

Even more mysterious...what made Mina give a damn now when she hadn't given a damn when both she and Nahla lay in the hospital on their deathbeds?

The commotion of the police station seemed foreign to Sinclair. From bringing her in to signing her out, this place was a blur. The ringing phones, voices yelling over other voices, paper shuffling, drawers snapping shut. She couldn't remember any of it and didn't want to.

"Sinclair!"

She glanced through a couple of moving heads and noticed the olive skin with the dark hair and rugged shadow sprinkling his cheeks.

Rio.

Just as relieved as she was to see him, a moment of indignation seeped inside her. How dare he come here now? She tried to reach him all damn day and now he showed up to save her. Where was he when she needed him earlier?

He cut through the clogged aisles of the station until he reached her. With a huge smile plastering his face, he embraced her with all his might.

She didn't hug him back.

As if he sensed her foul mood, he pulled back and stared at her. "What's wrong?"

She shoved him away from her. "You've got some nerve, coming in here acting like nothing happened. Where have you been? You left me in there to rot with those freaking whores and junkies."

"Hon—"

"Don't you 'hon' me." Her eyes turned to slits.

Laughing, Mina slithered through the influx of moving cops until she reached the couple. "You better have a lot more than an 'I love you' to win that hell cat over. She looks like she's about to scratch your eyes out."

Sinclair's rage went from fire to volcanic. Since she wasn't much of a screamer, she shot her sister a look that would melt steel. This wasn't over.

Chapter 37

Getting Nahla out of the hospital lacked the same emotional drama. It had the potential once Sinclair, Rio, Mina, and Kyle showed up demanding to see the toddler. However, Mr. Torrance met the social worker face-to-face and headed him off. With the charges dropped due to a "misunderstanding" and Sinclair ready to help assume responsibility for her niece, Gallagher didn't have a case anymore. Not to mention, Mr. Torrance threatened to have an inquest on possible harassment charges and illegal practices by Child Welfare. Nevertheless, Gallagher had the last word by reminding them about the court date.

Against doctor's orders—he wanted more tests due to her "unusual" rabies infection—Mina checked Nahla out of the hospital. It was a good thing that Rio kept his medical credentials up to date. Backed by Dr. Youst, who remained on the Coalition's payroll, made it easier to convince everyone Nahla had professional care available.

The little girl laid sleeping with her body curled into a tight ball and wearing an ugly white gown with the blue polka dots. She needed a comb through her afro and perhaps a bath to get the antiseptic smell off her.

Sleep or not, Sinclair pulled her baby girl into her arms. Tears swarmed her eyes until they slipped down her cheeks. She pressed so many kisses on Nahla's soft cheeks that her niece's eyes opened. Nahla's annoyed frown turned into a huge smile.

"Auntie!" she screamed.

Her arms wrapped so tight around her aunt's neck that Sinclair could barely breathe. Her baby was back in her arms and she dared anyone to challenge that ever again.

The door opened behind them. Sinclair peered over her shoulder to see Rio standing there. While admiring the two of them, he smiled. One hand rested on the door above his head while the other was on his hip.

"Wee-ohhhhh!" Nahla yelled.

"*Hi bebé.*" He swooped into the room and lifted the little girl onto arms. Just like his mate had done, he kissed her cheek.

Sinclair didn't miss his jumbled frown. She wiped the tears clean and stood. "What's wrong? And don't act like it's nothing because I saw that look on your face."

He smacked another kiss on Nahla's cheek before handing her back. "Someone's been here. Another cheetah."

"Excuse me?"

He began walking the perimeter of the room, sniffing all the corners and nooks with each step. "Nahla, sweetheart? Has anyone else been here?"

She mumbled an "I don't know."

"Think, honey." He opened the door to an empty closet. "I know doctors and nurses have to visit once in a while."

"Dat all," she said, and scratched her little afro.

"I don't understand," Sinclair said. "Why should it matter? Didn't you say one of your cheetah friends was keeping an eye on her?"

"Yeah." Rio stepped into the bathroom and turned on the light. "But the only one who should have made actual contact with her is Kyle. He's been with me all this time. I'm pretty sure one of our females was instructed to watch her, but not make contact."

"So maybe she came into the room."

He turned the light off and stepped out. "She wouldn't. Nahla's new to all this, so I'm trying to keep her contact with us at a minimum for now. I don't want to scare her."

Rio hurried to the other side of the room and began yanking Nahla's clothes out of the closet. "We need to get her out of here."

As much as she enjoyed his zeal, there was a problem. "Did you forget that social worker is still trying to stop us from taking her tonight?"

"It's late, so I doubt he'll succeed." He placed the small bundle on the bed and began untying the gown from Nahla. "Gallagher needs a court order. Without it, he can't do squat. Show me one judge who's going to help him this late at night. Especially with a court date already on the calendar."

Sinclair smiled. "You've been talking to Jacob, haven't you?"

He grinned. "Anything can happen between now and then and you know Gallagher will be hovering like a vulture after this. That makes his timing especially sucky."

"Why?"

Rio slipped Nahla's shirt over her head. "She'll change any time now."

Sinclair's heart went from fireworks to slush. She just got her niece back...only to lose her to some horrific transformation. Closing her eyes, she prayed Rio was wrong.

◆ ◆ ◆

They retreated to Mina's house.

Rio knew that vehement look in Sinclair's eyes as she watched her sister carry her sleeping niece up the stairs. It stung her so bad that even his supportive touches couldn't drag her out of her resentment. Even he knew she had every right to it. However, if Mina needed to start acting like a mother to her daughter, then the time was now. Sinclair must have realized that, too, or she would have done more than scowl at her sister.

Rio wanted out of this house. More than anything, he wanted to take Sinclair and Nahla back to his place where they could live without worry. She could go to work and not have to think about Nahla's safety. Her niece—his daughter—could grow up in a loving family. There were drawbacks, but that didn't mean the odds were impossible.

"Were you serious?"

Rio stopped just as he had passed the main bathroom on his way to Sinclair's room. He wanted to make sure she was okay when Mina posed the question at his back.

He turned. "Serious about what? About calling the cops on your boyfriend?"

She grimaced before returning to the bathroom.

Deciding to take the bait, he followed.

Nahla sat in the bathtub splashing water with a ball. The moment her eyes set on him, she whimpered and held her arms out to him. Had it not been for Mina swooping in first with a towel, he would've scooped her out of the tub and snuggled her small body to keep her away from the cold. Even when Mina lifted her in her arms, she struggled to get to Rio. To keep her from crying—and possibly changing—he pulled her into a hug.

Mina snorted and shook her head. "She sure loves Sinclair...and you."

He smoothed his hand along her back. "Of course she does. Sinclair's her flesh and blood."

"Uh huh. You can't tell me that my child doesn't have feelings for you too."

He couldn't argue with the woman seeing as Nahla calmed down. "She's a sweet little girl who loves everybody."

"Mmmm hmmm." Mina yanked another towel off the floor and tossed it into the open hamper. "Did you mean what you said about my sister? About loving her?"

Rio paused to think. He didn't doubt his feelings toward Sinclair, but he questioned when he had admitted something like that to her? Resolved, he said, "Yeah. I love her."

"Does she know that?"

"What do you care?"

"I care because if you're going to be a part of this family, then I need to know what your intensions are. She deserves someone who's gonna be good to her. Not those hardheaded fools I bring home. My baby girl doesn't need that kind of uncle figure."

Rio narrowed his eyes on the woman. "Look at me, Mina. Do I look like one of the *tontos* you date? And don't bring race into this. When it comes to knuckleheads, it's colorblind."

She snorted. Leaning over the tub, she unstopped the water. "Sinclair's been watching out for me and Nahla for a while now. If it hadn't been for her, we wouldn't have this house. I owe my sister. Big time. If the least I can do is make sure her man does right by her."

"What makes you think I haven't done right by her?"

Mina placed her hand on her hip. "Because you're sweating bullets, walking around the issue. What good is it to love someone if you don't tell them? Why don't you step up and be a man for a change? Stop licking the frosting when you can have the whole damn cake."

Did he hear this woman right? Did some alien take over her body in the last few hours? Although he could have done without the vulgarity, and in the presence of a minor, he couldn't ignore what she said. Pussyfooting around Sinclair was far from his intentions, but he didn't want to move in too fast and have her see it as a ploy to get closer to Nahla. Rio knew in his heart what he wanted. It was her. If necessary, he'd take her with all the baggage, strings, and nooses attached. Love blinded him so bad that he couldn't recall the last time he felt like this about anyone.

Nahla entered into a whimpering protest when he tried to hand her back to her mother. One look from him and she stopped with her large eyes begging for pity.

Mina was a bitch. Nothing could change his mind about that. However, that was as close to a blessing as he could ever expect from her.

A quick kiss to Nahla and he hurried down the hall to Sinclair's bedroom. When he threw open the door, he expected her to still be in the shower. Not sitting on the bed in a robe and staring at the floor.

Rio closed the door and hurried across the room, dropping to his knees in front of her. He took her hands in his. Smoothing some stray hairs from her tired face forced a half smile on him. "Do you love me?"

She lifted her head and stared. "Excuse me?"

"You heard me. I want to know if you love me. Because I certainly love you."

She nibbled her bottom lip. Shaking her head, she stood and tried to get away from him, but he snagged hold of her arm.

"What do you want from me?" she asked.

He pulled her back to the bed and sat her down. "I want you. Not because of Nahla, but you. I've been around many beautiful women in my time. It's rare to see a woman who's not only beautiful on the outside, but on the inside, too. The sweet thing is you don't even realize it. That's why I love you."

Sinclair swallowed. To hear something so sweet like that come from a person's mouth left her stunned. She wanted love, but the person she wanted it from was her sister. Somehow, hearing it from Rio had fulfilled her in a way she never thought possible. She refused to cry.

Rio cupped her cheeks. "You're my mate, Sinclair. If I have to spend the rest of my life proving it, then I will. But if you don't love me, then tell me now because I'm not out to force you to do anything you don't want to."

She rolled her eyes. "You couldn't force me to do anything."

It took him a minute to understand what she'd just said. When he did, a smile splayed across his lips. Chuckling, he fell back on the bed. "After everything we've been through, I should've known that."

Sinclair fell back on the bed beside him. "You don't know me and you're willing to put your heart into a statement like that. I don't know if I'm ready to live up to the same."

Rio propped himself up on his elbow and smoothed his hand

under the fold of her robe. When he outlined the lower part of her breast, her body jerked with his touch. His penis began rubbing against the zipper of his pants. "Are you planning to date someone else?"

She giggled. "No."

"Then consider it a commitment. I don't want anyone else. I want you. I can settle for being Nahla's uncle, but I can't settle when it comes to you."

He rolled over so that half his body covered hers. He wanted to tear that robe off and make sweet love to her. Taking his time, he slid the robe over her shoulder, exposing her Hershey Kiss nipples. His mouth watered before sliding his tongue across her sweet skin.

She smelled of fresh lavender. That scent made him think about planting a flower garden on the side of the house so that he could make love to her in it. In his mind he could see her surrounded by the flowers. *Such a beautiful sight.*

A moan brought him back to his senses.

Sinclair cupped his cheeks and brought his lips up to hers. She wanted to taste him so bad it hurt her insides.

Sensing her passion, he undid the belt on the robe and slid her up further on the bed. The ache in his crotch hurt so that he thought it would radiate up to his head.

Sinclair reached down and began undoing his pants. Clawing at his waistband, she shoved his pants down his thighs. She moaned her pleasure as her eyes fell on his tented underwear. Palming his manhood, she began stroking his length from tip to balls. He grunted in the middle of their kiss. She smiled. She had the reaction she wanted.

Rio continued kissing her, his tongue exploring her delicious mouth. He climbed on top and snuggled his legs between hers with his penis slicking along the side of her inner thigh.

Using her toes, she shoved his jeans down his calves and ankles until they dropped to the floor. The anticipation alone made her weep below.

He smelled her sweetness readying itself for him. A grin splayed his face as he reached down and directed his manhood inside her.

Sinclair threw her head back as he poked through her entrance. "Oh God!"

"He's not here," Rio replied.

Every inch of her body cried out in pleasure. More moans escaped as he began plunging deep. His erection radiated with wondrous heat, engulfing her as he rode her.

Rio loved her deep, tight womb. He couldn't stand hovering above her, so while he worked her from below, he lowered his mouth and captured hers. Next, he took both of her hands in his hand and clutched them above her head. He wanted to dominate her.

Suckling filled the room. His hips pumped faster and Sinclair squeezed her internal muscles, stroke for stroke. Her juices flowed. Neither cared. They wanted their passion sated and they wouldn't stop until it happened. He slicked his hardness out, leaving just the mushroom tip inside her, before reentering her and burying his manhood balls deep.

"*Te quiero,*" he breathed. "I love you sooooo much."

"Oh man." She hated she couldn't come up with something better than that.

She bit her bottom lip as her climax began. Her back arched to help drive him deeper inside. When he answered her need, she thought her head might pop off.

"I love you," she breathed. "Oh, how I love you."

A huge smile burst onto his face. He lowered his mouth to her and began pushing himself inside faster and harder.

Pompeii had nothing on her when her climax exploded. Rio followed only a second or two behind, spurting his juice inside her. Both of them screamed with an orgasm that threatened to devour their souls. The aftershocks shimmering through Sinclair had topped it off like a delicious cherry on a sundae.

Rio collapsed on top of her with a smirk on his face that read "Sex of a Lifetime." And why not? He planned to make sure that their love lasted just as long.

Chapter 38

Rio woke Sinclair the next morning in a hateful mood. Mina had slipped out during the night. She left the front door unlocked and didn't leave a word of her whereabouts. Sinclair rolled over, nodded, and went back to sleep. That was a typical morning. When he called Mina's job, he found out her boss had fired her two weeks ago. Once again, Sinclair nodded and fell into a deep slumber. Mina lasted two weeks longer than she had thought. That was a good thing.

The door opened a third time. Sinclair punched the pillow and turned to scowl at Rio. That man kept her up all night. Now, he wanted her awake and out of bed? For what? She'd been on disability since all hell broke loose, so it wasn't like she had to be anywhere.

Rio stood at the door with Nahla on his hip and a duffle bag in hand. Okay, so he didn't have breakfast on his mind.

She clutched the blanket up to her boobs and squinted at him. "Have you lost your mind? Where are going with my niece?"

He lowered the toddler to the bed and went to her drawers for clothes. "I'm taking her out of here. You're coming with us."

"Excuse me?" She kissed Nahla on the head and fluffed her afro. "You haven't answered my question."

"Nahla's going to change. When she does, I'd rather she not be in this neighborhood when it happens." He slammed one drawer shut and tore open another.

Again with those words. *Change.* She always feared coming home to find Mina had sold her daughter for a vial of crack. Not anymore. The thought of Nahla's little body cracking and shifting to become something else scared her more.

◆ ◆ ◆

Another day had passed without a word from Mina. Years ago, Sinclair stopped worrying about her sister's habit of going missing for days on end. This was her routine. However, with Nahla's court date looming over their heads she needed to make sure that Mina remained sober enough to make it pass the judge. If not, then they could kiss Nahla good-bye.

Sinclair never expected help from Dante. Although he had worked from behind the scenes, he had a few of his people scouring the streets for Mina. Once they found her, they would throw her in the back of a car and bring her to Rio's. Apparently, she wasn't the only one who wanted her sister clear-headed. She appreciated his efforts, but that didn't make her any more beholden to him.

Rio became a master at relaxing her. By the time he finished taking her body to orgasmic bliss, he collapsed just to the side of her, dragging his arm across her flat stomach. His hand smoothed just below her navel, sending him into daydreaming mode.

"Damn, woman. I'd give just about anything to see your belly rounded with my baby."

"Whoa, Jungle Jim." Panting, she stared at him. "You're moving way too fast."

He popped his head up one hand and pulled her close. "Don't you want children?"

"I do," she answered honestly. "But raising one that wasn't mine was a lot of work. I can't imagine what it would be like for one that is."

He pressed a kiss to the side of her head. "How many times do we have to go through this? Nahla is my blood. Given the sweet little morsel that she is, I love her as if she were mine all along. You of all people know that I could've walked away any time. I want to be here. With both of you. Mina, baggage and all. It doesn't matter."

"It doesn't, huh."

He kissed her temple. "No." Another kiss. "It doesn't. I love you."

Sinclair propped herself on both her elbows and stared him. For the past three years she had lived with her sister, Mina's boyfriends seemed to think that she was a part of the menu. Many times, she's had to fight them off and sometimes call the cops to cart them away. Her sister's thugs went from slapping her on the ass to trying to overpower her in the living room. She hated them for it, but she hated her sister more. Mina would just laugh it off. "Relax" she'd say, or "you need to get laid anyway."

That was only part of the reason why she had trouble giving her heart to this man.

"What is it?" Rio raised his head and probed her with his eyes.

Sinclair shifted her focus to an invisible point on the other side of the room. "Will said he loved me. When he realized I couldn't leave my niece in the hands of my inept sister, I found out just how much he *really* loved me." She turned her attention back to Rio, giving him an honest stare. "Don't say things like that. Not unless you really mean it. I can't take another disappointment right now."

Sighing, he ran a hand through his ink-black hair. "If you think I'm kidding, let's take this to the Justice of the Peace tomorrow. We've already got our little flower girl sleeping in the other room." Nuzzling her, he slipped a leg between hers and began pressing kisses against her cheek and neck. His semi-erection leaned against her thigh. "I may not know much, but I know I want you as my mate."

Sinclair sat up leaving the rest of her lower body snuggled against his. "Nahla doesn't know what it feels like to have an uncle."

"Father."

She rolled her eyes. "Whatever. You think I can just infuse you into our lives and not think about her feelings too?"

"Then let's ask her. Wake her up right now and ask her what she thinks about me being her new *padre*. Because I already know what the answer is. We have an innate bond that goes beyond human understanding."

"Auntieeeee!"

Both Rio and Sinclair jumped to their feet, grabbed at the doorknob. Heart racing, Rio nearly ripped it off the hinges to get to Nahla's bedroom.

Grass-snake muscles rippled under Nahla's tear-stricken skin, slithering throughout her body. Bones cracked and popped into place, reshaping themselves into a feline frame. Black-spots and amber colored hairs sprouted across her skin, thickening with each hysterical breath.

As Rio raced to the bed Sinclair remained solid, fingers clawing at the door knob. Neither words nor thoughts could come to mind as she stared in terror at her niece. Even worse, her baby's blistering eyes pleaded with her, begging for her aunt's comfort.

That wasn't her baby. Some monster had taken over her niece's body. In her eyes, Nahla was gone.

"Sinclair," Rio shouted. She had no idea he had been screaming her name for more than a minute. Holding one hand out to her while nestling a mutating Nahla in his lap, he said, "Sweetie, it's okay. Come. Sit with us."

"I can't," she breathed. Turning her attention away from him and her niece, she tightened the belt on her robe and headed for the door leading to the deck. "I...I need some air. That's it. Some air." Unshed tears blurred her vision.

"Sinclair," he warned, eyes deadpanning on her. "Where are you going? Your niece needs you."

"Just give me minute, okay?" Her breath caught, unwilling to look toward the bed. "I...I need to wrap my brain around this. I'll be back."

With that, she yanked open the door and ran across the backyard, leaving Rio screaming at her back.

◆ ◆ ◆

Shoving bushes and twigs out of her way, she tore through the underbrush at such a feverish pace that she hadn't noticed the rocks digging into the souls of her feet. Darkness blanketed every inch of the dense woods. With the crescent moon above her head, she still had a hard time seeing more than a few feet in front of her.

That wasn't her dear, sweet Nahla. She wanted her niece back.

So much had changed. How could they sit there talking about babies and marriage as though Nahla were a human child? She'd noticed the changes in her niece: increased appetite, acute sense of smell, her baby scent gone. These were clues that her little girl would never be the same. How could she ignore them? Nahla was gone.

Sinclair stopped. Her chest and lungs heaved to suck in the cool night air.

This was all her fault. If she had never let Nahla talk her into going in the 3-D jungle gym, none of this would've happened. Her aching stomach told her it wasn't a good idea. Why, in God's name, didn't she listen? Now she was blaming Nahla for something that wasn't her fault. Her niece never asked to be a were-cheetah. She never asked to get hurt. Nahla was her flesh and blood. How dare she leave that child in someone else's care? She was no better than Mina; always running away when the going got tough.

Sinclair turned back. She was stronger than that, dammit.

Her foot came down and springs snapped. A metal vice bit into her leg just above the ankle. Thunderbolt pain sliced through her skin, digging to the bone. Sinclair screamed. Pain surged all the way from her calf to the ends of her hair. When she toppled to the ground, chains jerked and pulled, latching her in place.

Wallowing in agony like an anguished animal, Sinclair saw through her blurred tears the animal trap clamped around her ankle. The cold metal dug so deep into her skin that the slightest movement hurt.

Sinclair fell back on the cold ground. "I deserve this," she cried to herself. "I don't blame you, God, for punishing me. I'm a weak-ass bitch who never deserved a child."

A silhouette loped out of the darkness. A large German Shepard kept his head low to the ground, nose snuffling along the undergrowth while making his way toward her. When he got to the animal trap cinched tight on Sinclair's ankle, he growled.

Fear had dug a new path inside her thumping heart. It choked off any screams that might have otherwise ripped through the woods.

A wet rag clamped over her mouth. Despite the pain inflicted on her leg, she kicked and screamed through the cloth, clawing at the hand and arm that held her. A new slice of pain stopped her injured leg from flailing, but she reached back and dug her nails into skin.

Her assailant grunted.

The more she struggled, the limper her body became. It was like someone had tied heavy weighs on the end of her limbs.

The son of a bitch. He…he…drugged her.

Everything went black.

Chapter 39

Rio couldn't believe it. How could Sinclair abandon her niece like this? Was she insane? More important, was that the same woman he'd just proposed to? He knew she was stronger than that. Was he wrong?

Whimpering brought Rio back to his senses.

He glanced at Nahla and stroked a hand across her pulsing cheetah-like head. "It's okay, baby. Just let it happen. I'm here for you and that's all that matters." Another whimper made him pull her close. "Don't fight it, Nahla. If you fight, it'll only hurt worse. I promise you, the discomfort will go away after a few changes."

The little cub had completed most of the frightening transformation during her sleep. That wasn't a bad thing, considering.

Rio was an adult when he was bitten, so he knew how awkward the first change was. One minute his skin burned, then it itched. When the bones started snapping, the noise scared him more than the actual act.

But Sinclair…

His thoughts went back to her. She ran off, knowing damn well it wasn't safe out there. Not with the Charlotte Coalition still lurking around.

Nahla already had two family members run out on her. He prayed Sinclair wasn't the third. For the first time since they met, Rio was actually pissed at his mate. Until now, he thought that was impossible. To see the pain in Nahla's eyes as she chirped for her aunt to come home… After everything Sinclair had seen and been through, why get scared now and run away like that? He understood her needing some air, but her disappearance made no sense. This wasn't like the woman he had come to love.

Rio picked up the cell phone he left on the nightstand and called Kyle. "Something's happened to Sinclair." Rio was certain of that or she would've returned by now.

"What's going on?" Kyle's voice went from a mumbled greeting to alertness.

"There's no time. I need to find her, but with Nahla being in cub form, she'll slow me down. The longer Sinclair stays gone..."

"Say no more. I'm on my way."

Rio breathed a thank-you in Spanish. "I'm going to get a jumpstart on her scent. Nahla will be with me, so track us when you get here."

He hung up.

Moving the exhausted cheetah cub from his thigh Rio went outside to change. He learned the hard way that changing indoors wasn't a good idea.

Concentrating on his transformation, his bones began cracking, muscles shifting. A nudge in his back and legs forced him to the ground on all fours. The change didn't hurt anymore. Years of snapping and pulling on his shifting body made it seem like any other day.

By the time he finished, he lifted his cheetah head to the air and sniffed. Why didn't he smell it before? Dammit, how could he have missed it?

Blood was on the breeze.

◆ ◆ ◆

"From what we can tell, they carried her off." Kyle kicked up dust from a tire track in the dirt. "What little I've found, Sinclair's scent stops here."

"Damn." Rio fought not to clutch Nahla too tight.

He spent the last hour combing the woods around his place. The only thing he found was dried blood and some torn underbrush. His mate fought, but the blood and her missing implied she lost the battle. That alone clenched his gut. He buried his tears and headed back to the cottage to call in the reinforcements.

Someone took his precious loved one away from him. He'll be damned before they get their hands on the other. "I've got to go—"

"You'll go nowhere." Dante slapped his cell phone closed and joined the other men. "Both Lincoln and Marianne have assembled their teams. Unless they find more to go on, they're chasing nothing more than a ghost."

"But she's my…"

He let it go. As much as he loved Sinclair, he needed a mate brave enough to stand up to the rigors of their world.

No matter how angry he was with her, he relented to the worry flooding his thoughts. Her scent and the sticky blood trail he found brought him back to his senses. Although it upset him that she had left the house, Sinclair never asked to be attacked. This was the second time it had happened in his woods when he should've been on his guard. What was he thinking when he bought Sinclair and his cub here?

Rio fought to bring his mind back to the problem at hand. "Any ideas on who set the traps? I encountered one in the woods near Donna's place."

Growling, Dante smoothed a hand across his baldhead. "I'll give you one guess."

"Charlotte," Kyle seethed.

"Shit." Rio growled. To calm himself, he scratched Nahla's fluffy Mohawk.

Dante stared at the cheetah cub. "Maybe you should take her home. One so young needs a close guard and constant supervision. Of course, the females would be more than happy to take her off your hands."

Don't think he hadn't thought of that. However, if he turned Nahla over to them, Sinclair would have a hard time getting her back. Human laws or not, Coalition Law would find a way to override her parental rights. "No. She's my responsibility until Sinclair comes back. She's all I have now."

"Which reminds me…" Dante stepped closer to his friend. "Why in the world did Sinclair go into the woods in the first place?"

Rio's animosity flipped to anxiety. "She needed some air," he lied. "I thought she'd pass out if she stuck around for Nahla's change, so I sent her outside."

"Trekking through the woods is one hell of a fresh breath."

"What do you care?" Rio reeled in his anger before it got him into trouble. As it was, Dante's eyebrow arched with a questionable stare. He could feel the crush of his King's dominance weighing him down. Rio planted a kiss on Nahla's head, calming him for the moment. "For all we know, she might have led someone away from the house."

Dante stared at his beta cat before getting back to the problem at hand. "Kyle, I want you to stay with Rio and Nahla. Don't let them out of your sight."

"Where are you going?"

Dante flipped his cell phone open again. "I'm going to pay Sloan a visit. If he harms a hair on Ms. Duval's head, I'll bring hell to his front door...personally."

Rio handed his cub to Kyle and approached his King. "I'm coming with you. If Sinclair's hurt, then she's going to need my help."

"That child needs you more. You said it yourself." Dante jerked around as someone greeted him on the other end of the phone.

Nahla did a sort of stutter bark. She pushed and clawed in Kyle's arms, her whippy tail held high. She didn't know him that well and wanted her "daddy" to hold her.

"She wants her papa." Kyle chuckled, handing her wiggling body to his friend. He patted the top of her head. "She's a sweet little thing. Prettiest cub I've ever seen."

Rio pulled his face back, ducking away from Nahla's sloppy kisses without much success. "I'd prefer not to go through something like this again."

Kyle laughed. "Then don't bring her around the home range. Those women are hungry to claim her. Sinclair's going to have a heap of fun trying to fend them off, so get your boxing gloves on."

Rio snuggled his nose into Nahla's mantle again and engulfed her sweet scent. "She's my baby, Kyle. I love her. So help me if anyone touches her, I'll..."

Kyle threw his hands up in defense. "Whoa, buddy. Time out. I'm on your side, remember? I guess Sinclair's kidnapping really has you knotted up. Not that I blame you."

If he so much as parted his lips one millimeter, it would open up the floodgates. Instead, Rio kept his face nuzzled in Nahla's silky fur.

Dante snapped his cell phone closed and clipped it to his side. "I've arranged a meeting with Sloan."

"About Sinclair?" Granted he should have sounded a tad more enthused, but he couldn't help it.

"He won't say."

"That's bullshit. First they say they're not responsible for the accident at Jungle Kingdom, now they're saying they don't have Sinclair. What are they going to come up with next? They've been in Mina's house twice and they know about Nahla."

"If they wanted to hurt her, then why leave a note to help us find her sister?"

For that, Rio had no answer. Everyone was sure it was a trap.

When nothing came of it except their best interests, taking back his finger pointing hadn't crossed his mind. Obviously, Dante must have thought about it if he brought it up.

"They're up to something," Dante seethed, eyes narrowing on asphalt. "A meeting with Sloan and his mate is set for tomorrow night. I suggest you get some rest, Rio. After all, we agreed to three additional Coalition members from each side. I plan on you being one of mine."

Chapter 40

Stabbing pain tore through Sinclair's leg. She bolted up so fast that it took a moment for her eyes to adjust to the dim light. Every time she moved, the metal cot creaked under her body. Salty sweat trickled into her eyes. One swipe of her hand across her heated forehead and she knew the pain assaulting her leg wasn't the only thing that wore her down.

On the other side of the open cabin, a man sat with his back to room. With the exception of a crackling fire in the fireplace, several oil lamps helped lighten things up. Dark, rough wood adorned all four walls. Curtains remained closed. Whoever this mercenary was, Sinclair could tell he took his solitude serious. No pictures on the wall, a small television next to what looked like a CB radio. The small kitchenette had nothing more than a half size stove with two burners, a bathroom-size sink, and a refrigerator that barely came to her waist. Good thing she didn't have to use the toilet. There had to be a reason why he had curtained off the corner of the room.

"I wanna know one thing," the man seethed. "Why the hell are you layin' around with their kind?"

Sinclair blinked. "Is that why you didn't kill me? So you could get answers?"

"Something like that."

The man turned sideways in his seat. His beard was dark oak like his medium length hair. Despite the bags and hollow look in his dark eyes, he seemed a tad on the loony side. Thick shoulders filled out a plaid shirt and his jeans needed a good cleaning.

Sinclair clenched her jaw, putting up her own front. "You can't keep me here."

He snorted. "Does the name Cavanaugh ring a bell?" When she didn't answer, he continued. "I guess Rio hasn't told you the story about my sister, Ashley."

Sinclair's stomach clenched so tight that she thought she would puke.

"I see he told you after all. Did he tell you that she had a brother who took great lengths at enhancing his looks over the years? Probably not. It's amazing what a plastic surgeon and a box of hair dye can do."

She wanted to call him an insane bastard, but now was not the time to volley insults. Not if she expected to get away with her life intact. "You met Rio?"

"A few times. But after Ashley was committed, she told me some wild stories about him. Like him being a cheetah and living with a group of them in the woods. I didn't believe it. All it took was one visit to his place and I knew Ashley was right. They're all a bunch of freaks."

Another pot and kettle reference. "This is about revenge, isn't it? Use me to get back at them." Disgusted, she shook her head. "All Rio wanted to do was help your sister."

Cavanaugh jetted out of the chair so fast that it crashed onto the floor. Rage filled his psychotic eyes. "I know what that bastard did! He bit Ashley. It wasn't enough that some bastard raped her and destroyed any chance of her ever having children. But then he had to finish the job."

Bit her? But Rio said… Sinclair raised her hands in surrender. Until she knew otherwise, she might as well indulge this nut's insanity.

"In case you haven't kept score, he bit my niece too."

He snorted. "Don't play me, lady. I've seen you fucking him like some whore."

"Then you missed the part where I couldn't handle my niece changing into a monster. Why don't you ask me why I was running away? You lost your sister, but I've lost my three-year-old niece to these maniacs. How the hell do you think I feel?"

Whether she believed that or not didn't matter. Cavanaugh believing it was. If she could get on his side, she might stand a better chance at getting away from the madman.

He snorted before stalking to the stove and lifting the kettle off the burner. "I want this to end so I can get on with my life. Thank God in less than twenty-four hours it will."

"Oh? You plan to slit your wrists and save all of us from your whining?" Oops. That sort of slipped.

"You're a real bitch, you know that?" He placed a spoonful of sugar in his black coffee and began stirring.

"And you're a real jackass if you think I don't know that you kept me alive for a reason. Tell me, Cavanaugh. You gonna rape me to get back at Rio?" Sinclair had finished playing with this man. If he planned to kill her, then she refused to make it easy for him.

"Would you like some coffee?" he asked, a crooked smirk twisting his lips. "No? Let's talk then." He grabbed the back of another chair, dragged it to the side of her cot, and plopped himself in the seat. "I thought about rape. Fortunately for you, Rio's people didn't rape Ashley. Raping you would hardly affect Sloan's people either. Unless…one group assumed the other did it."

A thought crossed Sinclair mind so fast that she blinked twice to make sure she understood her internal voice. "You're responsible for all this, aren't you? For the war between the Coalitions. You're the one who sabotaged the maze at Jungle Kingdom."

A chuckle shook his shoulders. "That idiot Sloan wanted to call a truce. Now I can't let something like that happen. Since I know I'm no match for cheetahs, it made sense to let them kill each other off. Trust me, honey, that jungle gym wasn't my first piece of sabotage. Neither was setting those traps in the woods. Did you know the cops found some booze at Jungle Kingdom? Too bad some jerk set fire to it and ratted them out."

"You're a real bastard, you know that?" Sinclair gripped the sides of her cot until her knuckles ached. "The only thing your behind cares about is your stupid revenge."

For the first time since their meeting, a mark of sorrow broke into Cavanaugh's stern face. "Look, lady…I'm sorry about your kid."

"You're no better than the rest of them. They hurt your sister, so you hurt them. At least they didn't set out to drag my family into the middle of this. I would've gone through life being happy not knowing were-cheetahs existed. All because of you and your damn revenge my niece is one of them."

Cavanaugh said nothing. He stormed out of the small cabin, slamming the door so hard that a metal horseshoe clanged to the floor from the opposite wall.

So much for trying to get on his good side. Even worse, she wasn't any closer to finding out how she fit into the rest of his plan.

None of that mattered now. All she wanted was Nahla and Rio. Her family. She didn't care what they were.

◆ ◆ ◆

"Why did Auntie Sin leave?" Nahla wiped her runny nose with the sleeve of her nightgown. "She comin' back, wight?"

Rio pulled the little girl onto his lap and blew into the spoonful of chicken noodle soup. "I'm sorry pumpkin. I never should've kept you out so late. I forgot that cubs tend to catch colds like normal children. At least they don't last as long."

He meant to answer her question, but in the last few hours Nahla's well-being had become his single priority. Taking care of her was both a blessing and a curse. He enjoyed getting to know her. On the other hand, he couldn't help seeing Sinclair in her almond eyes, shapely smile, and beautiful brown skin.

He wanted to hate her for leaving, but he couldn't. Sinclair was scared just as anyone would be. If he had only taken more time to prepare her for the inevitable, maybe she wouldn't have run off like that. To shift in front of her was one thing. To see it happen to a beloved child was another.

Nonetheless, if Sinclair wanted nothing to do with Nahla, then he prepared himself to take full guardianship of her. Though he never had children of his own, there was a first time for everything. Not even Mina would stand in his way.

Feeding her another spoonful of soup, he lowered his nose into her lopsided afro. A deep inhale and he filled his lungs with her sweet, childlike scent. If he could describe her smell in one word, honeysuckle would be it. Rio puckered his lips and placed a small kiss on the top of her head. She couldn't be more precious to him than what she was now.

A knock at the door jarred him from his thoughts.

Lifting Nahla from his lap, he sat her in the chair so that he could answer it. He didn't plan on any visitors until tonight. He and the others would drive over to the Grapevine Inn for their meeting with Sloan and his people.

Pulling back the curtain, Rio cursed under his breath. Alice, a female from his Coalition, waited on the front porch with three plastic sacks in her hands. A gust of wind blew a strand of her curly black hair across her nose. A toothy smile had crept into her dark eyes.

Sighing, he held the door open. "To what do I owe the pleasure?"

She smacked him with a kiss before stepping into the hall. "Silly jerk, aren't you glad to see me?"

"You want the truth?" He closed the door and took the bags.

"Ha. Ha." Scanning the small cottage, her eyes rested on Nahla who sat on the opposite side of the table in the kitchen. "Is that her? Oh my god, Rio, she's such a cutie. Hi, honey. I'm your Aunt Alice."

Rio rolled his eyes. Good thing Sinclair wasn't here to hear that or a real catfight would ensue. He stepped in front of her to block her from his charge. "Did Dante send you?"

Beaming, she lifted her head over Rio's muscled shoulder and transfixed her attention on Nahla. "He wanted me to check on you two. Thought maybe you could use a hand with the cub while her aunt was gone."

Nahla dropped her spoon in the bowl. "Auntie Sin not gone. She be back."

Alice pushed around Rio and approached the table. An aberrant smirk splayed her lips. "Of course, she'll be back, sweetheart. But in the mean time since she's not here—"

"Don't want you. Want my auntie!" Nahla eyebrows knitted together in a scowl.

"I know, baby." The chicken and noodles floating around in the bowl caught her eye. Alice pulled back and stared at Rio. "What's wrong with you? It's morning and you're feeding her soup? She should be having pancakes and bacon and eggs. Good lord—what kind of babysitter are you?"

"Alice, if you came here to—"

"I came here because Dante wanted me to check on you. So you're feeding our little cub soup, then she must be sick. How could you let—"

"You need to go."

"Rio, I'm just trying to help. The cub needs guidance and a strong female presence to help her through the transition."

"She has that!" He knew her mind games too well. That's all this was to her. Nothing more than an elaborate sport. "If you come here thinking that you can take Sinclair's place, you've got another thing coming. There's no way in hell, she'd give her niece up, let alone want you to be her guardian. And if you try to coax Nahla away, you're in for one hell of a fight."

"She needs—"

"I know what she needs and you're not it." Taking her by the arm, he dragged her to the door, cursing in Spanish the whole time. Throwing it open, he pushed her outside. "Thanks for the groceries and the clothes. But if you ever come back with anything less than respect for my family, I'll skip your ass across the driveway like a rock skips on water."

Her jaw dropped for a rebuttal.

He slammed the door. Leaning his back against the cool surface, he lifted his head to the ceiling in silent prayer.

Please God. Let me be right about Sinclair. And no more challenges to her position. Not while she isn't here to defend it.

Chapter 41

Sinclair jerked awake. The last vestiges of a nightmare about her niece shifting into Big Foot had washed away. Waking up as some lunatic's hostage reawakened her anxiety.

Though she couldn't tell how long she slept, blue skies had turned darker. Her captor would most likely exact his revenge soon and take her life in the process. The longer she slept, the easier it would make his task.

Rolling onto her side, she pushed off the mattress and brought her feet down. The squeaking of the cot grated her nerves. Swiping a hand at the sweat beading her forehead, she searched the one-room cabin.

Cavanaugh was nowhere in sight.

Pain licked through the wound on her leg. Gritting her teeth, she glanced at the bloodstained bandage just above her ankle. It hurt like a son of a bitch. She wiggled her toes just to make sure they still worked. If her wound wasn't infected before, it was now.

Still, she had to get to Nahla and Rio. Whatever this psycho had in mind, it didn't bode well for anyone regardless of Coalition loyalties.

Grinding her teeth, she pushed off the bed, keeping as little weight on her sore leg as possible. It took some doing, and fighting down a bout of nausea before she made it to the small window next to the door. The German Shepard that approached her in the woods lay on the front porch. That crazy bastard had his pet guarding the door.

Great.

She needed a weapon.

Sinclair hobbled to the kitchenette area and began yanking out drawers. The best she had come across was a spoon. Some good that'll do. She needed something more lethal.

Pulling open the cabinet, a couple of mugs caught her attention. She needed something; anything sharper than a butter knife would do.

Snatching one of the mugs, she hobbled across the floor to the cot and smashed it against the metal frame. The small pieces wouldn't help but the larger triangular piece might come in handy. Carefully sweeping the other pieces underneath the bed, she prayed Cavanaugh wouldn't find them.

A bark beyond the door sent her heart into overdrive. Cavanaugh was back.

Adrenaline pumping, Sinclair shoved the triangular piece under the pillow and got back in bed. She pulled the blanket over her body and turned her back from the door, feigning sleep.

The door creaked opened. Heavy footsteps thumped across the floor and stopped. There was a huff and they started up again, moving further away from her.

Sinclair turned onto her back. Faking sleep or not, she didn't trust the maniac where she couldn't see him. Rubbing her eyes, she caught the stoic look on his face.

"Good," he said, turning away from the coffee maker. "You're awake."

"I'm finding it hard to sleep thanks to your bear trap."

Stepping over to the table, he lifted a pair of sweats and a button-front shirt from the seat and tossed them on the bed. "Put 'em on. I've got a pair of sneakers too, though they might be too big for your feet."

Suspicion crept into Sinclair's visage. "Where are we going?"

"To meet your mate."

◆ ◆ ◆

Refusing help from Cavanaugh, she climbed into his pickup and the two took off down the road. He said nothing most of the way. That worked for Sinclair because she wasn't in the mood to talk to a murderer.

She thought about grabbing the steering wheel and running them off the road. Why not? At this point, she had nothing to lose. However, she wanted to make sure they were close to their destination, saving her a torturous journey through the woods.

"You mind telling me where we're going?" Sinclair asked, breaking the silence.

"A place called the Grapevine Inn," he replied keeping his eyes on the road. He watched as Sinclair reached down between her legs, massaging her calf. "Hey! Keep both hands where I can see them."

She shot him a glare. "Look, buddy. My leg is itching. Since you didn't give me anything that I could use to change the bandages with, it's probably infected. So forgive me if I have to scratch."

He tapped the dashboard. "If your leg hurts, then you put it up here where I can see you scratching it."

What a paranoid idiot. Then again, he had good reason not to trust her.

Sinclair lifted her foot onto the dashboard and pulled back her pant leg. The bloody bandage was soaked through. Just looking at it she felt as though her fever had hiked up a notch.

Slipping her fingers under the inside of the bandage, she pulled out the triangular shard and shoved it under her sleeve.

"How much farther?" she asked.

He nodded his head at the windshield. "Right around the bend up here."

Now was the time.

Sinclair dropped her leg, letting the ceramic shard slip down to her hand. Gripping it tight, she whipped her hand around and stabbed him in the cheek.

Rats. She meant to get his eye.

Cavanaugh howled and grabbed his face. Sinclair yanked the steering wheel toward her. Growling, Cavanaugh grabbed it back, but his slick fingers couldn't get a good grip.

The pickup twisted and fishtailed, skidding across the double-yellow line. One second headlights lit up the railing, and the next, they panned across a line of trees.

Sinclair gave it one good jerk and steered them off the road and down a small ravine. Throwing her hands up, she screamed as they plowed into a tree. Airbags deployed across the front, binding them in place along with their strangling seatbelts.

Stabbing at the airbag, Sinclair pushed it out of her way, undid her seatbelt, and scrambled out of the pickup. Hurt or not, she needed to get to the Inn and warn the others. Staying alive was the only way to tell them about Cavanaugh's treachery.

Sinclair stumbled through the woods. Every time she reached a less dense area, running turned into a throbbing nightmare. Pain sliced up her leg nearly paralyzing her. Sweat cascaded down her forehead, neck, and back. When the terrain turned to another small incline and a bubbling brook at the bottom, she rolled her eyes. What next?

"Bitch!" Cavanaugh shouted. "I'll find you!"

She had to ask.

Sinclair tripped and stumbled her way down the hill, splashing into the brook. The water was cold enough to numb her leg. At least that bit back some of the agony from her injury. After splashing through the water, she made her way to the other side and climbed out of the ravine.

A blur slammed into her side and tackled her into the dirt and dead foliage. By the time Sinclair got her bearings, a snarling muzzle hung inches away from her face. Rank breath assaulted her. The German Shepard snarled. She had forgotten the dog was in the trunk bed.

Fight, girl! Fight!

Sinclair clawed at the beast's snout, tearing anything she could. Thick fur and skin collected under her fingernails, but it didn't stop her from assaulting the beast. She even went so far as to unleash her own barbaric yell.

The dog's jaws caught hold of her forearm, but her fingers raked across the animal's eye before it could lock his jaws tight. Even when the animal let out a yelp, she kept pounding at his face, driving him away from her. The dog backpedaled and recuperated from his attack. That only made him madder.

Remaining seated with her back against a tree, Sinclair grabbed a rock.

The animal lunged for her. Claws scraped across her front, tearing her shirt and leaving deep furrows in her skin.

Her rock slammed across the side of the beast's head.

Yelp!

Sinclair kept pounding at the animal's head. Fury burned through her. She didn't care if she had become a savage beast by her own right.

Even when the dog stumbled to the side, Sinclair whipped the rock at him. It smacked between his ears. The dog yelped again before scampering into the shadows.

The attack left her shaken. A heavy wind wormed through the trees and leaves, cooling every pore on her glistening skin. The scratches burned her chest. Warm blood slicked down her front, turning cold against another heavy breeze.

"Where are you, you bitch!"

Didn't that man know when to quit?

Forcing the pain from her mind, Sinclair got to her feet and continued through the woods.

Twigs cracked and snapped with each step. It didn't take a genius to know both monsters would stalk her to her death. She smelled of blood and the animal wanted it. The other one wanted her to sate his vengeance.

That wasn't what kept her going. She needed to get back to her niece and Rio.

If she died out here, the Triangle Coalition would swear up and down Charlotte had something to do with it. With her dead and her niece left as an orphan, Rio would tear them apart just like he did when his enemies raped his fiancée. She doubted Charlotte would stand for being falsely accused for something like this. A full-blown war would ensue and Cavanaugh would have his revenge.

They were being played. She needed to stay alive for everyone's sake.

Sinclair broke through a line of trees and stumbled into the parking lot of the Grapevine Inn. The white building was no more than two stories high.

A Pathfinder caught her attention. Yeah, it belonged to Rio all right. The small booster seat made her gasp.

Why would Rio bring Nahla to a Coalition meeting where danger lay in wait? Could he be that dumb? He claimed how much he loved Nahla, so why not leave her with a babysitter? Then again, even she had trouble trusting just anybody with her niece. Perhaps Rio was the same way. If so, then that scored a couple of points with her.

Nevertheless, she wanted to hold Nahla. Her being a cheetah cub would take some getting used to, but it didn't matter anymore. She loved her little girl no matter what. And Rio, too.

Growling caught her attention. She jerked around.

Cavanaugh's dog readied for an attack more than a dozen feet away. Tension coursed through his hunched shoulders. With his ears flat on his head, a snarl revealed deadly teeth. That animal wanted blood.

Chapter 42

She grew tired and agitated by the animal's harassment. "Where's your master? He leave you to take the fall?"

The dog lunged.

Sinclair dropped and rolled under the carriage.

The beast hit the side of the SUV so hard that it set off the alarm. A whooping noise sliced throughout the parking lot, lights flashing in tune with the blaring horn. Despite the noise, the dog scuffed around the vehicle, nose snuffling along the ground. He wedged his head underneath the frame and began barking at Sinclair.

Silently, she dared the animal to come after here. She'd simply crawl out the other side and stomp his head into the ground the moment he stuck it out.

That was what the dog did. Clawing up the pavement, he lowered his rump and began easing under the carriage. The growling and snapping jaws continued edging toward her.

Sinclair kept her eyes on the beast. *Come on, you bastard. Come and get me.* She inched away from the dog, keeping her face so close to his jowls that she could smell his putrid breath every time he growled.

Hands snagged her ankle. Sinclair screamed and thumped her head on the metal undercarriage. That certainly shut her up, but it didn't make her any less grumpy about Cavanaugh catching up to her.

The dog jerked is head around too. A fierce growl rumbled throughout his chest. Before Sinclair could blink, the dog slid backwards. Claws scraped the asphalt before he lifted off the ground. Two pairs of legs stood on either side of a waggling tail.

Bones crunched and a final yelp left Sinclair trembling. The tail went limp and the dog's body crumpled to the ground.

Uh oh. Suppose the person holding her ankle wasn't Cavanaugh. Suppose it was something worse like the Charlotte Coalition.

Just as she reached for a metal rod, another hand grabbed her other ankle and yanked her backwards across the pavement. Rough asphalt scratched her clawed skin. Screw the pain. She'd beat the hell out of the jerk who—

Rio crouched next to her with a timid smile curving his lips. "You could've called."

"Why you son of a…"

There weren't enough words in the world to explain the delight that went through her. Relief and simple joy were a good place to start. Those gorgeous eyes and his wavy, black hair. She missed his woodsy smell and the way his day-old shadow scratched her face when she kissed him. His exotic skin was as smooth as the accent rolling off his tongue.

She threw her arms around his neck and pulled him into her lips. Her tongue roved back and forth, feeling every inch of him. For her own piece of mind, she needed to make sure he was real.

Rio could have eaten her alive. He wanted to throw her over his shoulder, carry her home like a caveman, and molest her beautiful body until she cried for him to stop. The more he thought about it, the more his manhood pulsed with excruciating pain. If he stood now, he'd embarrass himself for sure. He did what he could not to lay his body between her legs and make love to her right in the parking lot. Never in his life had someone ignited him like that.

"Auntie Sin!"

Sinclair's eyes bulged. She shoved Rio away and sought out her niece. She'd apologize later. Right now, she wanted her baby.

Nahla squirmed and whimpered to get out of Dante's arms. The bald man set her down on the pavement and watched as she scampered into her aunt's waiting arms.

The tears Sinclair held back had finally broken free. She clutched her niece's tiny body so tight that only God himself could pry her away. Her hands smoothed over her niece's clothes to make sure she was real and whole. Rio did a wonderful job taking care of her precious cargo. She couldn't have asked for more.

"As heartwarming as this is," Dante said, stepping forward, "you mind telling us how you got here?"

Sinclair's wet eyes went wide again. "Shit! Someone take her.

Take her!" She pushed Nahla in the first awaiting hands she could find. Those happened to be Lincoln's who stood by as a part of Dante's entourage and an excellent show of force.

"What's going on?" Rio asked, helping her to her feet. He gave her a quick once over and knew she had been through hell and back and hell again. The blood covering her over-sized raggedy clothes said as much. While he propped her against his SUV, he knelt down and began lifting her pant leg. "Who did this to you?"

"There's no time," she insisted, yanking his sweater to right him up again. "We have to get out of here. All of us."

"Are you sure you mean 'all of us'?"

This came from Sloan. He stepped around from the backend of the SUV.

He looked much better without the police uniform. Though he was slimmer than Rio, he still had the toned muscles curving his ribbed, short-sleeve shirt. Short brown hair waved against a light breeze. How he managed a smile while standing among his enemies had her at a loss.

A brunette sauntered around him, snaking her hand along his forearm until she grasped his hand. Her free hand rubbed her swollen belly. She grinned with a set of cranberry lips and slightly plump cheekbones. She couldn't have been any taller than Sinclair and yet, she seemed lethal.

"All of us," Sinclair repeated, meeting Sloan's gaze. Turning to Dante and the others, she continued. "It's not them. They're not the ones who've been sabotaging your business or setting traps on your property."

Dante advanced on her. "How do you know about that? Who've you been taking to?"

"The same guy who planted booze in Jungle Kingdom and tried to set the place on fire." She couldn't recall Cavanaugh's exact words, but it must have hit a nerve with Dante. His lips stretched to a thin line and a glare poured on Rio.

"Don't look at me," Rio said, throwing his hands up in defense. "I never told her a thing."

"I take it dinner is over." Billie sauntered over to them. "You must be Sinclair. My name is Billie. I'm Dante's mate and Queen of the Triangle Coalition."

Sinclair nodded to her. If nothing else, the woman had great poise and a sense for fashion.

Dante's gaze shifted from one person to another, finally resting on Sloan. Turning his back, he broke eye contact. He looped his hand around his mate's arm and headed for a black BMW. "We're out of here, my love. I'll fill you in when we're in the car."

"But what about our meeting?" Sloan asked.

"It's called off until you hear from me again." He pointed his trigger at the car.

"Wait a sec." Sloan pulled away from his wife. "If this human has information that concerns both our Coalitions, then I have a right to hear it too."

A heavy sigh smoldered through Dante's flaring nostrils. He threw another quick glance at Sinclair before eyeballing his counterpart. "Then we go somewhere safe. Preferably back to my enclave."

"Bullshit. My people and I aren't going anywhere near yours. How do we know your people won't hold us hostage when we get there?"

"Then why not Rio's place?" Sinclair suggested. "You can't hide an army inside. Plus, it's still considered Triangle Coalition property."

Why Sinclair had to be the voice of reason, she couldn't understand. Perhaps that was what these people needed seeing as they couldn't think past their distrust of each other. Pure childishness, if you asked her. Maybe she came to understand these were-cheetahs better than she thought.

She hobbled away from Rio's hands to stand between the two Kings. Their challenging stares were nothing more than a stupid test of wills. Someone needed to put a stop to it. If she didn't, then the longer they remained out in the open, the easier it would be for Cavanaugh to pick them off. That bastard was crazy enough to do it, too.

Making eye contact with both of them, she clenched her jaw to keep from screaming. "There's a traitor among you. Otherwise, Cavanaugh never would've found out where you were holding your meeting. So, are you going to waste time fighting each other or finding the traitor?" She went silent, giving the two Kings a chance to think about what she'd just said.

"Did you say 'Cavanaugh'?" Sloan asked. "As in Anthony Cavanaugh Jones?"

"She must mean Alan." Rio closed the final steps between the three of them. He placed his hand on Sinclair's shoulders and turned her to face him. "Are you sure about this?"

She shook her head. "He called himself Cavanaugh. I don't know any Anthony or Alan."

"Anthony did some work on our farm," Sloan replied. "We kept having problems with the electric fencing and the animals running loose on the property. He came into our market one day and asked if he could put his business card up on our announcement board. That's how we found out he was an electrician. So naturally, we called him out to fix the fence."

"Naturally," Lincoln muttered.

With Nahla perched on his hip, Lincoln came and stood beside her. As tall and thick as he was, Sinclair had no doubts her baby was in very safe hands. In fact, one of his dark hands along covered Nahla's little back as if to provide extra shelter. She took a moment to watch him sooth and pat her silent little girl. He must have had some experience with kids.

Sloan stared at him. His expression went from accusatory to a murmured curse when he realized what Lincoln meant.

The Charlotte King shook his head. "His background check was clean, so that's why we never suspected he might be the one responsible for sabotaging the electric fencing. Damn."

The woman—his wife—smoothed her hand around his upper back. Her sharp fingernails scrapped across his shirt, turning into a delicate massage at the nape of his neck. "It's not your fault," the woman said soflty. "The bastard had us all fooled."

Rio must have known something because a heavy sighed exited his lungs. He wrapped his arms around Sinclair and hugged her tight to his front.

"Alan Cavanaugh is one of Ashley's brothers," he confessed. "I only met him once and he came off like a really likeable guy. As for Anthony, he's been stationed in Hawaii for the past couple of years. The last time I saw him was at Ashley's funeral. He seemed like a decent enough guy, although I'm betting he used the last name Jones to pass the background check. Why would he—"

"Enough already." Sinclair pulled away from Rio and the rest of the small crowd. "It's great that you all sound like you believe me. But we need to finish this elsewhere. Cavanaugh is out there and he's crazy enough to blow up the entire inn to get to you guys. All I want to do is get my niece home. Preferably, intact."

"Agreed." Dante triggered the alarm on his BMW.

An explosion blasted them across the parking lot.

Chapter 43

Rio's SUV turned into an ambulance. He would have loaded up Dante had it not been for his King ordering him to get everyone to safety. Someone had to stay behind and talk to the police. Since Dante's car exploded, it made sense that it should be him. Of course, Billie refused to let him deal with the trouble alone, so she remained at his side.

Shrapnel hit most of them along with the searing heat from the flames. The only one who came away practically unscathed was Nahla. Lincoln shielded her from the blast, but it shocked Sinclair to see the rest of the were-cheetahs dive for her too. Even when things settled down in the aftermath, everyone checked her baby girl to make sure she was okay. She was like a prize to all of them.

When Evelyn, Sloan's mate, began experiencing sharp pains, they knew it was time to leave. If an ambulance pulled up, they would want to take her and the others to a hospital. After what they went through with Nahla, they couldn't go through that again.

Rio ran back and forth through his cottage, rifling instructions before taking off to assess someone else's injuries. All he had to worry about with Nahla was a small strawberry wound to the right of her forehead. He couldn't say the same for Evelyn because it looked like she might go into labor. Lincoln's entire left arm oozed with blood glistened with his sweaty neck. When Rio tried to evaluate his wounds, the big man pushed him away, insisting he worry about everyone else. Sinclair had the same wounds he'd found her with and a few more bruises to add to the mess. Sloan came away with broken ribs and blood dripping from a deep gash near his temple. It would need stitches.

"What do you need me to do," a deep voice seethed from behind.

Rio looped his stethoscope around his neck and began feeling around Evelyn's protruding belly. He needed all his senses of perception to get a good feel for the twins she carried.

"I need you to sit down somewhere," he said, eyes closed.

"I can't sit here while Dante's out there trying to cover for us."

"He gave you an order, Lincoln. You don't have much of a choice."

Evelyn screeched and grabbed her stomach. Rio leaned close to her face and began instructing her on how to breath through the pain. Even her taxed mate sat on the bed with her to join in the exercise.

Rio didn't want her to have those babies. It was possible that whatever damage they might have suffered, her body could heal it in twenty-four hours and she could go to full term. Then again, if the damage was bad enough he might have to deliver those babies right there. He needed help and soon.

One person came to mind. If Lincoln wanted something to do, then he had no problem putting him to work.

Rio excused himself and the big man from the guest room and closed the door behind him. Surveying his friend's wounds again, he peeled away some of bloody, shredded shirt still embedded in the wound.

He pulled his thick bicep away. "Rio, there's no time —"

"Shut the hell up and let me look at this. I can't send you to Donna's looking like a truck hit you."

Hesitant, Lincoln moved his arm toward his friend. "Donna is that weird chick in the woods, isn't she? The one you get the herbs and stuff from."

Rio nodded. He stepped across the hall and into the kitchen for a clean cloth. "She's got stuff I'm going to need. I don't want to take anything from Dante's place because I'll need it for Theresa and Jason."

"Just give me a list and some directions on how to find her."

"You might want to take someone with you."

"Who?" His face remained stolid while Rio cleaned his wound. If he had pain, he refused to show it. "Dante has most of them out following leads on Cavanaugh. There's a skeleton crew at most left here."

Rio stared at him. "There's also a maniac on the loose too and a thing known as strength in numbers. Take one of Sloan's guards from the front door."

Lincoln sighed. "Just tell me what you need. I can take care of myself."

He had no doubts about that. In fact, he did a good job with getting an unconscious Sloan and pregnant Evelyn in the back of the SUV. "Tell Donna it's an emergency. Tell her everything that's happened and if she's smart she'll get the hell out of her hovel."

"Why?"

"She was the one who clued me in about the traps in the woods."

Lincoln's eye narrowed. "How do you know she's not our traitor?"

His statement was like a softball to the chest. Rio refused to believe Donna would have something to do with this. Sure, she knew a lot about them, but she had no reason to want revenge on his people either.

"She's not." Rio went back to cleaning dirt from Lincoln's weeping injury. "Donna had the chance to do away with our people many times over."

"Who's Donna?" Sinclair hobbled into the kitchen still wearing her filthy clothes.

Rio wanted to whisk her off to the nearest emergency room, but she protested, using Evelyn's grave condition as an excuse. In truth, she knew he couldn't stay in the ER because he needed to tend to everyone else's wounds. After twenty-four hours of hell without him, she didn't want to spend another minute alone.

Rio had checked her leg about a half hour before. He needed to make sure the bone wasn't exposed to air. Otherwise, he wouldn't have a choice but to rush her to the hospital. The best he could do for the time being was tear some sheets and make due with what he had in the house. Still, she needed to be careful.

All he could manage was a sigh. "What the heck do you think you're doing? You're supposed to be resting. For heaven's sake, you might have broken a bone or something."

A scream came from the guest bedroom. Sinclair crocked her eyebrow. "Not with all that yelling."

He sighed again and shook his head.

Sinclair stared at him. "Rio, I was there when Nahla was born. I might be able to help."

"With what? How to breathe? I've got Sloan already doing that." Hurt, she folded her arms over her chest.

Rio tossed the cloth and hurried around the breakfast bar with intentions to snatch her off her feet. When he bowed to pick her up, pain squeezed his lower back. He most likely twisted a couple of muscles and had some deep bruising to go with it. Until now, he did a good job at playing off the own pain.

"Uh-huh." Sinclair pointed at him. "You see that? I knew there was something wrong with you. You moved too slow when you got out of the truck."

He cut his eyes at her. "It doesn't matter. I can still move faster than you."

"So?"

"So if you don't get back in that bedroom, I'll take my chances and carry you there."

He meant it. Even if she managed to get Nahla to sleep through all of this, she would surely wake up screaming to a nightmare or two. With everything that happened, he didn't want his charge left unattended. In fact, he didn't want either of them left by themselves.

Her being here didn't mean...? Of course, Nahla's transformation scared her, but she couldn't be scared now, could she?

Sinclair fisted the front of his shirt and pulled him to her lips for a quick kiss. "Fine. But when you're done running around, I know a place where you can hide."

When she turned her back and hobbled away, he couldn't keep his eyes off her cute rounded butt. Hell, she looked sexy even with the limp. He knew what her double meaning meant. There would come a point when he'd take full advantage of it, too.

Lincoln cleared his throat. "You're going to give me those directions, right?"

Sighing, Rio nodded and returned to the kitchen.

◆ ◆ ◆

Rio couldn't wait to set his eyes on his beautiful mate. The way she stood up to both Kings, a regular were-cheetah would've gotten his head knocked off for butting between them. Regardless of what Sinclair had to say, he wanted to scold her for overstepping her bounds. As a human, she had to understand that sticking her nose in a King's business was grounds for a backhanding.

Still, he couldn't escape the fact that she had balls enough to do it. His baby cakes strolled right up in there without a moment's thought. Hot damn, she had gall! There was no way she was the same woman who ran away from her beloved niece twenty-four hours ago.

After checking on Evelyn and waiting for the last of his Theradin to take effect, the pregnant were-cheetah finally drifted off. Rio and Sloan pushed the twin beds together so that he could be close to his wife. Once Rio had him settled, he convinced the King to trust him enough to take some medicine too.

Now that they were both resting, he wanted to tend to some other business. After checking on his sleeping charge, he opened the bathroom door and found Sinclair cleaning the last of her wounds in front of the sink. Not a shirt or a bra was in sight. Only her sweat pants. Dripping water brought his attention to the frothy bubbles in the garden tub.

What he wouldn't do to be the one bathing her. He would've had candles, a box of chocolates, and rose petals christening a bath for a goddess. One of these days, he'd make it a reality.

"You never said why you took my niece to a catfight?" She didn't look up because she knew it was him.

"I couldn't leave her with just anyone," he said, gripping the waistband on her sweats. He meant to help her out of her pants, but a different need stirred his manhood. He ground the throbbing bulge against her rump. His hands smoothed along her hourglass waist until they reached her breasts. He palmed the small globes and dropped his lips to the nape of her delicate neck. Her body temperature remained a little on the warm side, but if she didn't complain about not feeling well, why should he?

"You're going to be the death of me," she whispered.

"I'd like to be something else to you." He slid his mouth across her shoulder blade, suckling and tasting her. Rio could smell her captive's odor all over her. "Burn these clothes. I don't want that bastard's scent on you. You're mine. Not his."

Had he made the proclamation under different circumstances, Sinclair would've ripped into him. But she didn't want that lunatic's odor on her either. If Rio could smell Cavanaugh on her, then she would make sure her bath took care of it.

Sinclair wrung out her damp washcloth and began rubbing it against her wounded chest. Rio gripped her sweats again and slid them down her thighs and legs.

Again, he weakened. Sure the blood had his attention, but with her curved butt less than an inch from his face it made him falter. Closing his eyes, he smoothed his cheek against her butt cheek. Heavy, heated breathing, followed by a lick of his tongue and a single kiss. He wanted her so bad that he couldn't wait any longer.

"Make love to me in the water," he whispered. "It's big enough for two and I want to feel your body under mine. I want to cover you with my scent and reclaim you as my mate again."

Sinclair wasn't sure about the mate part, but damn if her body didn't listen. The more he smooched her ass, the more she wept between her thighs. Then it dawned on her. She wasn't wearing any underwear. With Nahla asleep, it wasn't like they couldn't take advantage of each other. Besides, she had to make up for lost time and there were guards around the house.

The bathroom dipped before her. She could feel herself falling to the right, but not quite slumping yet.

"I have to sit down," she said, clutching the rim of the sink. "My leg hurts and I'm...getting a little dizzy."

Before she could get his response, the bathroom light whirled and she fell backwards into his arms.

Damn! What was wrong with him? His mate was hurt and all he could think about was a quick fix. She needed him, though not in the sexual sense. His pounding heart ached as her eyes rolled around in the sockets. Rio cradled her body in his lap.

"I love you," she breathed. She cupped his bristled cheek and smiled. "But I think you need to bandage me up first."

Chuckling, he kissed her head and cuddled her close. "How about we get you in that bathtub first and make sure you don't drown?"

The front door slammed open. Even Nahla woke up screaming for her aunt and Uncle Rio.

After getting her to her feet, Rio helped her into the bedroom. Not saying a word, he pointed at the bed where she claimed Nahla in her arms to quiet her down. Snatching the lamp off the dresser, Rio cracked the bedroom door. It wasn't the best weapon for a fight, but it would have to do. Besides, he didn't have time to change to the better weapon inside him.

"Rio!" Lincoln shouted. "Get your ass out here! Dante needs you."

A sigh left his lungs. He set the lamp back where he found it and left the bedroom. Better to have someone he knew breaking into his house than a stranger.

Dante sat on the couch holding his arm. He had dislocated it in the explosion. Rio managed to pop it back in place before they left so that he could look less injured while talking to the cops. At least the paramedics wrapped his bleeding head and his burnt hand before he left.

Rio entered the living room and stopped. He blinked as though that might help him make sense of the newcomer on the scene.

Donna lay on the floor in front of the television, bound and gagged.

Chapter 44

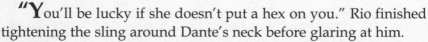

"You'll be lucky if she doesn't put a hex on you." Rio finished tightening the sling around Dante's neck before glaring at him.

"She wouldn't come, so I convinced her." Lincoln remained standing with his back to the room. Injured and probably in pain, the man still assumed his sentinel position.

"She doesn't work like that, Lincoln. Dammit, how do you think I get the supplies that keep our people in good health? You're lucky I convinced her to take a look at Evelyn."

Dante snapped his cell phone close and leaned back on the couch's cushions. He closed his eyes, although both men knew he wasn't asleep. "I've already authorized some of the women to start gathering supplies for Donna. There'll be enough to keep her happy for months. I promise."

Rio snorted. "You know as well as I do that Donna won't forget something like this. That's how she is."

"Then make amends in other ways, too."

Rio continued to stare at him. How he managed to make it back to his place without swerving off the road was a miracle. Just before showing up at his house, he dropped Billie off at the enclave as a show of solidarity. It was a good thing Lincoln returned when he did or they wouldn't have found him slumped behind the steering wheel of Sloan's Mercedes until morning.

"Are the rest of Sloan's people still around?" Lincoln asked.

Arching his eyebrow, Dante nodded. "The one who waited at the scene with me has contacted their people to give them the news. I gave him directions on how to get here. Why he hasn't shown up yet, I don't know. Maybe he got lost."

"What about our people?" Rio asked. "How are they coping?"

"Billie's doing her best, though she'd rather be here. She knows most of the Charlotte Coalition, so perhaps Sloan and Evelyn will feel more comfortable with her around."

"I'll bet," Lincoln muttered.

Dante lifted his head and glared at his subordinate. "What's that supposed to mean?"

Lincoln finally broke away from the bay window overlooking the backyard. "She used to be one of them."

Rio raised a hand to stop his train of thought. "*Mirada*, we've been through this. Sinclair said that Cavanaugh was the one we wanted. After what happened in that parking lot, I tend to agree."

"But she also said there was a traitor."

Using the couch as leverage, Dante stood, directing his scowl at his subordinate. "My wife is no traitor. Now while I appreciate your keen observation, you best point it elsewhere or there'll be more than one explosion tonight."

Although both men were a few feet apart, Rio knew he needed to step between them before things got out of hand. "This is getting us nowhere. Everyone is either sick or injured, so that makes us more vulnerable. Finger pointing is the last thing we need."

"Uncle Wee-oh?"

A tiny voice stamped out the rising tempers suffocating the room. Nahla wore a pair of animal-print training pants and a white tee with her small belly protruding. She rubbed her eye with her fist and leaned again the archway leading into the living room.

"Auntie Sin stole da covers."

Rio smiled. She looked adorable standing there with her lopsided afro and lips pouting. Ignoring his clan brothers, Rio went to the little girl and hoisted her on his hipbone. She smelled of flowers and herbs.

He stroked her small back as she laid her head against his shoulder. "What are you doing up, sweet pea? Don't you know it's past your bedtime?"

"Can't seep. I'm scared. And I don't have no covers."

He kissed her supple cheek. "Uncle—"

He stopped and thought about that for a second. This was the first time he noticed her calling him *uncle* anything. He would love to be more to her than that, but he'd take whatever he could get. Even better, she acknowledged him as a part of her family. That carried a lot of weight in his world.

A grin parted his lips. "Uncle Rio will be in as soon as he's finished in here. In the mean time…" He snatched the throw on the back of the couch and swaddled her in it. "Will this do?"

She nodded.

"Good. Now how about—"

"I can put her down." Donna strolled into the room and stared at Nahla. Still sporting her oversize overalls and a tight-white tank top, she put on a smile and glued her eyes to the little girl.

Lincoln closed the distance and held his hands out to Nahla. "Don't. She'll probably run out the door with her. I'll put her down."

Donna scowled at the large man. "You fool. You wouldn't be put in a position to protect anyone had I gotten my hands on you first."

"We needed more than just your herbs, woman. We needed you. You need to stop hiding and get out of that shack you call a house. Speaking of which, that's close to looking like a one-room shack except for the curtained off area. Kinda like the same place Sinclair described where her kidnapper lived." He hoisted Nahla from Rio's arms and stepped into the hall. Throwing a hand over his shoulder, he said, "Later," and disappeared in the master bedroom.

Rio rolled his eyes. He knew Donna could get rid of his people any time she wanted to. What kept her from it, he didn't know. However, he stuck to his guns about that. They relied on her for medicine, so the last thing he wanted to do was screw up their special arrangement. Dante must have thought along those same lines if he planned to take care of Donna without him having to suggest it.

Sighing, Dante sat in the center of the couch before throwing his legs up on the cushions. "I'm going to bed. Unless the house is burning down, don't wake me."

"What about Billie?"

"Or unless my wife comes. I don't know if she'll show or not. She's busy holding down the enclave."

Rio made a mental note to grab some more blankets from the hall closet for the makeshift infirmary he used to call a cottage.

Donna turned and started down the hall to the front door. "Walk with me cat."

Dread came over him. That was telling what Donna would say about dragging her into this. Someone had to face the female piper, so it might as well be him. However, he didn't expect her to head outside. After stopping at the hall closet to grab a coat, he hurried behind her.

Donna leaned against the railing, staring into the driveway.

"Why do you help your enemies?"

Huh? He didn't expect the conversation to go like that. Since she stood there, rubbing her arms, he slipped his coat over her shoulders. "We found out tonight that Sloan's been keeping an eye on Sinclair. They…they know what Nahla is."

"She's a cat too. The one you bit to save her life, no?"

Rio had to think back to remember if he told her that much. "Yes."

"Then why would they care?"

"Because Nahla is special to both our people. She's the youngest person to ever survive the change."

"So everyone treasures her because she is the future of your race. Perhaps her children will become were-cheetah sooner or they'll be stronger. Maybe a little of both."

Rio nodded. "*Si.* It's likely. Sloan told us where to find Sinclair's sister. He had his people watch over Nahla while she was in the hospital. They planned to steal her away and give her back to us if we didn't get to her on time."

"Why?"

"Better our kind is with us than with humans who might exploit her for their own greedy interests."

"You trust Sloan and his people?"

"No. Then again, they had the time and the opportunity. They could've done whatever they wanted and we'd never know."

"But the war between your people would continue."

"Perhaps." He leaned his back against the railing and folded his arms across his chest. "Where are you going with this?"

Donna exhaled. "I believe in a little of this and a little of that when it comes to the supernatural. One of those beliefs includes seeking the truth in matters."

"I don't—"

She narrowed her eyes on him. "I'm within my rights to take a piece of hide for what your friend did to me. But his reasoning— stupid by the way he carried it out—sought a higher purpose. Your friend wasn't only thinking of you or his King. I guess in a way, he was thinking of your enemies too. Of getting them help."

Rio snorted. "I doubt that."

"Doubt what you want, but it happened and the circumstances work in his favor. I won't take a piece of anyone's hide, but if any of you violate me or my home again, everything tonight is forfeit. I'll damn you and your Coalition to hell."

Then he'd make sure Dante got the message, too. "So we're

good?"

"For now."

That's the most he could ask. "Good. Because I could really use your help around here. Sloan's guards should've been back by now. Not to mention, everyone in there is busted up. Even I'm hurting. But I need to make sure that Evelyn is—"

She raised her hand to quiet him. "She'll be fine. You did well by giving her the Theradin. I brought some raspberry leaf and ginger for when she wakes up. They'll help with toning her uterus and relax her."

The front door opened. Lincoln stepped onto the porch and handed Rio the phone. "It's for you. The crazy bastard nearly woke up the whole house." He went back inside the cottage without another word.

Rio had no idea who'd call this late. If it were someone from the Coalition, they would've called Dante instead of him.

"How are you doing, Mr. Velasquez?"

Rio didn't know the voice, but he had a good idea of who the bastard was. "Cavanaugh?"

"I'll keep this short. Those two cheetahs never made it to warn their people. Guess what'll happen if their Coalition never gets the message?"

In other words, he had killed them. God only knows where he dumped the bodies. If he were careless, then they would probably end up on the front step of a police station. If he were good at what he did, then the front step of the Charlotte Coalition. Any way he looked at it, Rio knew his people just got screwed.

Chapter 45

Sinclair's awful day started at five in the morning when she bolted up in bed. Nightmares suck. She expected the little dumpling lightly snoring next to her would be the one screaming in bed. Nahla may have moved and whimpered a couple of times, but other than that, she slept just fine. Well...there was that one time she woke up, nudging Sinclair for the blankets.

Sinclair leaned forward when the voices from the other room grew louder. She caught bits and pieces, but it wasn't enough to put together a coherent conversation.

Rio made her promise that she would stay in the bedroom while the others discussed were-cheetah business. He explained the rules about respecting the leaders and what she did was considered insolent. He didn't want to see her backhanded for not minding her own business. Neither did she for that matter. Of course, things would only get worse from there. Unlike the rest of his Coalition, Sinclair believed in fighting back if any man ever laid a hand on her. Just ask Mina's good-for-nothing hoodlums.

A knock came to the door. Nahla lifted her attention away from the building blocks in the corner and scampered onto the bed. It didn't surprise Sinclair that her baby girl wanted protection. However, it hurt her that the little girl didn't feel safe even under Rio's roof anymore.

"Come in," she replied, tucking Nahla close to her side.

Rio entered the room. A huge smile splayed his face. He missed more than one day of shaving and it began to show. The dark circles under his eyes made her think stress. She fought not to go in there and tell those people to leave her man alone, but this was his place and she couldn't do anything of the sort. Like them, she was a guest in his house.

"You two look so cute together." He closed the door and approached the bed. Shaking his head, his smiled brightened. "I can't wait to get you two alone. Where we can be one big happy —"

Sinclair grinned. "Were you gonna say 'family'?"

Pinkness flushed his cheeks. He dipped his head like a little boy charming his elementary school sweetheart. "We'll talk about it later. Right now, I need to fill you in on what's been going on."

"You mean no more secrets?"

He shook his head. "No more, *mi amor*."

Sighing, Rio plopped down next to them and checked her bandage. For once, he was glad she listened to him by staying in bed.

Sinclair learned a lot in the next few minutes. Dante and Sloan agreed to tell everyone that they've gone into hiding. With a traitor floating among them keeping a low profile was the best option. Billie and Sloan's second-in-command were the only two people outside their group who knew where they would be at all times. To them, it would look like the group had packed up and moved on to safer pastures. In reality, they'd stay put until Evelyn was well enough for travel. Her condition had improved drastically over the last few hours, thanks to Donna's herbal remedies. Trust among their core personnel, including Sinclair, was key if they wanted to survive.

For once, it pleased her to know she mattered to them. It had little to do with Nahla being bitten or her relationship with Rio. Sinclair had saved their lives. In the eyes of the leaders, that was enough. She had become a member of the clan by her own right.

"But what about Mina?" Sinclair asked. She knew the answer to that and found a new reason to be nervous. "Oh-my-god."

Sensing her panic, Rio placed a hand on her shoulder. "*Amor*, don't worry. Dante thought about that too. In fact, Sloan volunteered to send one of his people to Mina's last night, but she wasn't there. The guard is still there, but she isn't. I'm guessing she's out somewhere enjoying a binge."

"And if she isn't? Suppose that maniac got to her?"

Nahla would be better off. He kept that to himself. Coldhearted as it sounded, he wondered if she had thought the same thing.

"There's nothing we can do," he said. "We just have to wait it out."

She knew he was right. The only way to tell if Cavanaugh had Mina was to wait until he played that card. If he didn't, then they'd have their answer.

Sinclair cuddled her niece to her side and kissed the little girl on the head. When this was over, she would spend every waking moment with her niece. A child her age shouldn't be around this kind of violence. They needed to heal.

Nahla whimpered. She placed her small hands on her aunt's thigh and pushed her way into the circle. She leaned between both Sinclair and Rio, easing her head between theirs. "Want kisses too."

Both of them chuckled.

Sinclair patted her niece's bottom. "Girl, get your narrow behind over here before we bite it off."

When Rio lunged to tickle her sides, the toddler's laughter brought Sinclair out of her funk. Man, how she loved the sound of not only Nahla's, but Rio's laughter too. This is what a real family sounded like, and she cherished every second of it.

◆ ◆ ◆

Rio stepped into the main room just as Dante got off the phone with Billie. His King had received word from her that they had found the bodies of Sloan's guard on Triangle Coalition property. Someone tipped off the police, but the were-cheetahs were lucky enough to dispose of the body before they arrived. The cops summed it up as a crank call. However, word had gotten back to the Charlotte Coalition. Sloan's people were ready to wage an assault on the Triangle for this final violation.

With Evelyn out of danger, Donna chose to leave at that point and take her chances at her hovel. Rio couldn't blame her and nobody stopped her when she walked out the front door.

"We need to keep up the charade," Dante said. He sat with one leg extended to the floor while his other leg bent to rest on the rung of a barstool. One last gulp and he finished his beer. Rio slid him another before he could ask. "Until we can fish out this damn traitor, there's not much we can do."

Sloan nodded. "True, but it's dangerous to pretend like this. We're using our people against one another."

Rio couldn't agree more.

When they'd found out about Cavanaugh's latest scheme the Kings had come up with a plan—a dangerous one—to let Charlotte think The Triangle had killed their own and held their King hostage. Rio hated it. However, he wasn't in a position to voice his opinion. At least one good thing came out of this. With Evelyn feeling better, now was the time to set up shop elsewhere. If anyone leaked information to their enemies, then it would narrow down who the traitor was.

"Tomorrow we leave," Dante said. "We can set up camp at Wild Oak Campgrounds."

"I know that place." Sloan nodded, his thoughts directed inward. "I think we should rent a camper. That way it'll be easier to stay on the move."

"Good idea. We'll still take the extra vehicles in case something happens."

"Let's hope it doesn't," Rio mumbled. Sighing, he decided to go for a third beer.

Both leaders clapped their beers together in an agreement.

It was nice to see both of them getting along, Rio marveled. However, he worried how long it would last. One more upset by Cavanaugh and not even Dante or Sloan might be able to hold their people back. The crazy bastard might get what he wanted after all.

Chapter 46

Rio busied himself in the kitchen tending to the needs of his guests. Given the choice, he would have preferred giving Sinclair and Nahla his undivided attention. He envied them sleeping soundly in the master bedroom while he spent time quelling everyone else's cabin fever. Rio never realized how small his cottage was until now.

"Your mate and her niece are very pretty." Evelyn thumbed toward the hall, indicting Sinclair who slept across the way. "You must love them very much."

Being the gentleman, he pulled out a barstool and helped the pregnant woman sit. "Thank you, but you should be resting. Not out here." Rio flipped his kitchen towel onto the counter. "I'm cooking up a huge pot roast dinner. Think you're up to sampling some?"

Stretching her arms over her head, she purred. "Will I ever? But it's good to know I won't be the only one eating for more than one."

Confusion marred Rio's face. A timid smile bowed his lips. "I don't follow you."

Evelyn tilted her head, eyebrows knitting. "Oh? You mean you don't smell it?"

"Smell what?"

Redness flooded her creamy cheeks before she could duck her head. "Oh boy. Maybe I shouldn't have—"

"What?" Whatever bothered her this much, he wanted to know. Especially if it concerned his mate.

Taking a breath, she lifted her head and met his eyes with a grin. "If you don't know, then chances are she might not know either.

Really, Rio, it takes another pregnant woman to know that smell."

"Know what—?" Studying her smiling face, the thought punched him in the gut. "You mean she's...? Sinclair's...?"

Beaming, Evelyn nodded.

He grabbed the counter to keep from swooning to the floor. His Coalition brothers would've never let him live that one down.

Grinning like a man who hit the lottery, Rio flew out of the room and headed into the bedroom where Sinclair and Nahla napped before dinner.

Now it made sense. Wanting no other scent on his mate other than his was natural. No wonder he wanted to tear her clothes off and douse her with his scent both inside and out. A change in a female's hormones will do that to a male. Had Sinclair been a were-cheetah, he might have paid better attention to the signs.

He lifted the edge of the blanket and spread Sinclair's ankles apart. The antiseptic odor leaking through the thick bandage elicited a growl. That son of a bitch, Cavanaugh, would pay for hurting his mate like that.

"What the—?" she whispered, stirring in her sleep, pushing up on her elbows.

"Shhhh," he shushed. "Go back to sleep. I want to check something."

Sinclair was awake. "Not between my legs you don't. Can't you see my niece is sleeping right next to me?"

Rio lifted his head. A smile danced on his face. Nahla lay on her side with her knees bent. He wanted to smother the little girl with loving kisses.

"I need to talk to you," he whispered. "But..." A glance at Nahla. "I don't want to leave her alone."

"Then say what you have to say."

A smile crept up his cheeks. "I've got a better idea."

Rio left. Twenty minutes later, he returned with a doublewide sleeping bag slung across his arm, two pillows tucked under his other arm, and his fingers clutched around the handle of an oil lamp. He mumbled something along the lines of "stay put" before sneaking out the backdoor and onto the deck.

The deck had two exits. One led down the wide hall that separated one side of the cottage from the other. Rio used the one leading from his bedroom.

Sinclair kissed Nahla on the head and tucked her under the blanket. Scooting to the far end of the bed, she threw her legs over the edge. With the voices just on the other side of the French doors, it would be easy for anyone to come in here while she slept.

"What are you doing?" Rio whispered, tiptoeing back into the room.

Sinclair couldn't stop salivating at his naked body. Good lord if he became anymore aroused he could use his erection as a support beam. She swallowed. How delicious it would be to get her hands on that.

Rio scooped her off the bed so fast that she let out a squeal. Good. Because if he had his way about it, he'd have her squealing a lot more. "Didn't I tell you to stay off that leg?"

"Well, it's not like I asked for it."

His smile faltered. "No, you didn't. But someone's going to pay. Mark my words."

Sinclair didn't want to think about that anymore. Her thoughts rested on the surprise he had in store for them.

Heavy wind blew through the screened in deck. Sinclair's grip tightened around his neck as a tremor worked throughout her body. Rio chuckled, letting his heated hand soothe her back.

It didn't take much for him to convince Lincoln to leave the backyard. Perhaps it was the lust in his voice that clued him in. The big man smirked and made up an excuse about seeing to dinner.

Once Lincoln disappeared, Rio set everything up starting with a log on the fire pit and a beautiful, candlelit dinner waiting on a bistro table. Impressed, Lincoln even offered to go to the store and buy them some chocolate covered strawberries and wine. Rio declined, citing the new state of his mate.

Lowering his betrothed onto the navy blue sleeping bag, he laid his body close to hers for warmth. He was right. The fire pit had warmed the lower part of the deck where the boards came up halfway. The orange-yellow glow of the fire and the oil lamp sitting on the chair added to the sex permeating the air.

"If it's too hard I can—"

Sinclair pushed her tongue into his mouth to shut him up. Chuckling, he parted her legs and snuggled his lower half between her knees. Keeping her busy with succulent kisses, he yanked the rest of the sleeping bag over the two of them. His fingers clawed at her underwear, but his eagerness got the better of him. He tore them off and saddled the tip of his manhood against her entranceway.

Sinclair swallowed and pulled out of the kiss first. "Bet I know what you want."

He grinned. "I bet you do. I guess that means dinner will have to wait."

"Don't you know it."

The two of them made such sweet love that Sinclair wanted to cry when she reflected back on how she came close to losing the man of a lifetime. Sure, the sex was terrific, but Rio offered her so much more than the physical. More important, he wanted to give her a world she never could have imagined in her wildest dreams. His loyalty and protectiveness of her made her feel more love than anyone had shown her since her parent's death. He loved Nahla too. She bet that if he had his way, he'd adopt her. What more could a woman ask for?

She loved him rocking back and forth on top of her. Keeping it slow and luxuriant, it dragged Sinclair's orgasm to an explosive conclusion. Any pain or fever she felt took a backseat. She liked it when he got a little rough with her, but Rio turned lovemaking into a fine art. No matter how she liked her sex, once she got with Rio, it didn't matter as long as he gave it to her.

Sinclair's back arched and her pelvis shot forward. She buried him so deep inside her that she swear he massaged her cervix. God, this man was good.

Rio hit his climax while she shuttered through multiple orgasms. If anything, his spurting seeds thrust her into another major orgasm.

When he finished, Rio rolled to his side to keep from squashing her. A huge smile plastered his face. Pulling her close, she snuggled in the nook of his muscled arms.

"A girl could get used to this."

"How's your leg?" he asked, the doctor side of him emerging.

"Hurts like hell, but it's a good hurt."

He started to sit up. "Maybe I should take a look—"

She caught his shoulder and shoved him down. "You leave this sleeping bag and I'll hurt something you hold dear."

Chuckling, he assumed his position again with his defensive arm around her shoulders. Tugging her close, he kissed the top of her head and slid his free hand across her smooth skin. "Our dinner is getting cold."

"Honey, it's already cold. That's why they invented microwaves."

"True. But seeing as you're pregnant, you need all the nourishment you can get."

She chuckled. "Yeah right. You'll have to come up with a better excuse than that if you want me to marry you."

Now that she thought about it, they didn't use a condom this time. Hell, they hadn't used one before either. How many times did they use one? It had to be at least seventy-five percent of the time. Sure. But all it took was that other twenty-five percent to become pregnant.

Nah. She wasn't pregnant.

"I'm serious, Sinclair. You're going to have my baby."

Now it was her time to push off the sleeping bag and stare at him. "Rio, don't play like that."

Startled, he sat up and with one knee bent. "Excuse me?"

She rolled her eyes and slid her hand up his thigh, coming within threatening distance of his manhood again. Sighing, she replied, "Don't take this the wrong way, but one of these days I'd like to have a baby. I'm just not sure if now is the right time. I just met you. We haven't even gone through the get-to-know-you phase."

"I can smell it on you. Taste it too, if necessary. Just because you don't have heightened senses to tell the difference, doesn't mean I'm wrong. You're pregnant with my baby."

"Uh huh." She crossed her arms just below her small breasts and smirked at him. Her painful claw marks made her bite her tongue. She uncrossed her arms and let them fall to her side. "I love you, but I'd believe in a pregnancy test before your sense of smell. If we're talking about bringing another life into this scary world of yours, I'd rather we wait until we got through this crisis first."

Rio tackled her to the floor, sliding his leg between hers while his length rested against her thigh. He cupped her cheeks and kissed her. When he pulled out, his eyes dazzled at the sight of her.

"You love me?" he asked, his eyes penetrating hers. "Are you serious?"

Was she? For once, that was an easy question to answer. "I do. I didn't know how much until I almost lost you. It hurt like hell knowing I might not see you or Nahla again. Pretty crazy, huh?"

"No. A little slow, perhaps—" A slap to the back of the head cut him off. He chuckled. "But still precious to my ears. So, I'm asking you. Will you marry me?"

She sighed. "God, Rio, that's just such a loaded question."

"But we love each other and you're carrying my baby. That's all the reason I need."

"Being pregnant isn't a good enough reason and you know it."

"What are you scared of?"

She paused to think about that. "Commitment, if you must

know. It scares the hell out of me. How do I know what we have is even real?"

He stared at her. "If you have to ask the question, Sinclair, then maybe it's not."

Damn. She didn't want to see the hurt in his eyes. When he turned his head away from her, she pulled his chin back. "I didn't mean it that way. I love you, Rio. There's no doubt in my mind. But I can't help being scared of…"

He blinked. Looking out into the woods, he understood her fears. She wasn't afraid of committing to him. She was afraid of committing to this life. That, he could understand. Given the choice, he never would've committed to it himself. Too many people died because of it.

This was the first time he regretted ever getting involved with Sinclair. How could he let himself fall head over heels, knowing damn well it wasn't fair to subject anyone to this dangerous lifestyle? All it would take was another were-cheetah skirmish to reawaken her fears.

Maybe that's why his love ran off into the woods, he thought. Not because of Nahla's change, but because of the changes in hers and her niece's lives. She didn't want any parts of it. She blamed herself for running away when Nahla needed her most. Whether she realized it or not, that was a crock. After everything she had gone through with Mina, he knew Sinclair wasn't a wimp. Those things she had some control over. The supernatural world didn't allow for any control. Most of all, not by a human.

Rio folded his fingers with hers. He wanted to pull her close, but he needed to look her square in the face for what he needed to tell her next.

"Sweetheart, I can't make any promises outside my house. I don't know what this world holds for you or Nahla. It terrifies the hell out of me when I think about Ashley and how I might be opening the door for it to happen again."

"Rio, I—"

"Let me finish." He pressed two fingers to her plump lips. "Knowing what I know now, I can't live without you two. If it means selling my home because you would feel safer in the city, then so be it. I'd give my life to protect you guys. Yes, it's a chance and my world is dangerous…but damn if you two aren't worth it."

What does a woman say after a confession like that? God knows he hit the nail on the proverbial head. This supernatural world of his was a scary place, though something in her gut told her to believe him. More than anything, she wanted to take a chance with him. Not jump into marriage so fast, but perhaps work toward that end.

"I..." Her jaw trembled, head lowered. "I believe you. I want to see where this goes. But I also want us to take our time. Can you understand that?"

Smiling, Rio repositioned the pillow closest to him, laid on his back, and pulled her against his chest. "I do. I don't mind taking it slow, if that's what you want. But we can't ignore this baby thing either. My proposal still stands, waiting for you to make a decision. No pressure. Not even about the pregnancy."

"Good." Sinclair snuggled her nose just to the left of his nipple. "Now shut up so we can both get dressed and go to bed. Nahla will be out here come morning."

He did just that.

Chapter 47

As Sinclair predicted, sometime during the night, Nahla had slipped outside and crawled into their sleeping bag. She was used to having her own bed, but every once in a while, she got the urge to snuggle with Auntie Sin. Now with Rio around, she found that urge more enticing. It was as though she wanted both of them in her sights from now on and even brought her own blanket in case they stole the covers from her.

Half asleep, Sinclair could feel a cold draft on her foot. It was freezing just like the night she had caught it in that trap. Heat rushed from the wound, spreading across her skin, but the pain brought her close to passing out.

Sinclair pulled her ankle under the blanket, but a hand kept dragging it back in place. It reminded her of the chain that held the bear trap in place. A moan slipped out of her. She gave it another tug, still unable to recover it.

What the hell? Someone must have caught hold of her again.

She jerked awake, throwing the blanket off her and Nahla.

Rio was at her side. "It's okay. It's okay. You were having a bad dream. I was trying to change your bandages."

Sinclair shook loose the confusion dusting her brain. "No, Rio. He was here. I saw him. He was coming out of the shadows because the bear trap caught me and…and…" The more she spoke, the crazier it sounded. Taking a deep breath, she pulled the blanket over her whimpering niece. "What's wrong with me? It's like that son of a bitch stole the last of my marbles."

Rio finished fastening the bandages and pulled the blanket down on her legs. Before tucking himself underneath the covers, he tossed another piece of wood into the fire pit. "Don't worry," he soothed, repositioning Nahla between the two of them. "I'm surprised you slept as long as you did. The rest of the house quieted down not long ago. Dante said something about getting a lead on Cavanaugh, so Sloan and Lincoln went with them."

"Is it legit?"

"Very possible. When Billie pulled everyone back to the enclave for the night, one person was unaccounted for. Two of Sloan's people searched the guy's apartment and found used bear traps caked in mud."

"Sounds like someone was where they shouldn't be."

Rio nodded. "Looks like their plan paid off. While one clan sleeps, the other keeps watch. Everyone's out now hunting for the guy."

Sinclair rubbed her niece's small back and sighed. "I just want this to be over."

"Cross your fingers we're closer. There's been too much blood spilled over this." He smoothed a finger along Nahla's plump cheek. "Innocent blood, at that."

Something gnawed Sinclair's mental gut. She didn't have any fancy intuition or psychic impulses, but she knew enough to pay attention to her feelings whenever they screamed at her. In this case, her instincts wouldn't let her sleep until she figured it out. What Rio said about Nahla's importance to both coalitions seized her.

Staring into her puzzled face, Rio smoothed a strand of hair from her milk chocolate cheek. "You're in deep thought. What is it?"

"How much does my niece mean to Dante, if anything at all?"

"*Mi amor*, he's gone out of his way to accommodate her. He thought sending another female to help...bond with her...might lessen the blow of your absence. When that didn't work, he came here himself. He talked to her, played with her, even took her for a walk in the woods to help her get accustomed to some of the plant and animal life. She likes him and he's grown fond of her. In all honesty, I think it was there all the time, but he acted on it in a stupid way."

Her snort turned into a smile. "How so?"

Rio half smiled. "He wanted me to send you guys away to protect both of you, but more so Nahla. She's going to be one of the most important shape-shifting cheetahs of all time. She's the future of our race."

"My little sugar-bear leading your crazy behind?" She fluffed her niece's afro. "For some reason I have a hard time seeing it."

He chuckled. "Women play more of a role in our society than you think. If Billie didn't have Dante, she could easily lead our people. We treat our females like goddesses."

"So Nahla's important to everyone then."

"Um…I thought I just said that."

"So, if she's this all-important person to your species and there are traitors among us, then Cavanaugh knows too, right? He could use her to bring your entire race down."

A gust of wind carried a foreign scent. Rio's head jerked into the breeze, the sleeping animal behind his predatory eyes had awakened. In one swift movement he gathered Nahla in his arms to protect her from whatever or whoever was out there.

Nervousness sliced through Sinclair as she caught his gaze. It occurred to her to snatch her sleeping niece out of Rio's hands, but she remained put. He would never hurt Nahla.

"Here," he snapped, practically dumping the little girl in her hands.

Fumbling at first, Sinclair had a firm grip on the groggy three year old, rocking her back to sleep. She didn't want Nahla scared. Not yet anyway. "Rio," she whispered. "What's wrong with you?"

"We've got intruders."

Grabbing a pail of water, he doused out the flames in the fire pit and turned out the wick in the oil lamp. Complete darkness enveloped the backyard. Rio encircled his arms around Sinclair—supporting Nahla too—and eased them to the side of the deck.

Sinclair watched him grab the sleeping bag and tuck it in around them. Grasping his arm, she got his frenzied attention. "What do you think you're doing?"

"I'm hiding you and Nahla."

"But—"

"No buts." He finished tucking them inside the bag, leaving a flap open for her head. "I want you two to stay here. If you hear anything, take Nahla and run into the woods. When you reach the creek, turn right and follow it up to the main road. When you get to the bridge, go right, but stay along the road. You'll come to a huge mansion sitting off in the distance on the right. That's where my enclave is."

"Rio," she whispered, grabbing his arm again. This time her fingernails sunk into his skin. "I'm not leaving you."

He forced a half-smile to his lips and plucked her hand free. "Sweetie, you have to think of Nahla. She's our cub."

"I don't give a damn if she's—"

"All right then, how about her being your niece and you being pregnant?" He arched an eyebrow to this. "Sinclair, if anything happens to me, I want you two to get to safety. Understand?"

"But—"

"What did I just say about the buts?"

Damn him. She wanted to go to watch his backside, but with Nahla in tow, she wasn't going anywhere. That little girl meant the world to her. The same went for this "pretend" baby growing in her womb.

"Fine," she snapped.

Cupping her face, he planted a huge kiss on her lips. When he noticed Nahla's tiny eyes had opened, he put on a happy face and kissed her too. "Take care of your aunt for me, okay?"

She nodded.

It shredded his heart to know that he had to leave them. Given the choice, he would've herded both of them to the enclave himself. Unfortunately, there was this innate territorial programming in his genes that wouldn't let anyone run him off his land. Not without a fight, anyway.

Chapter 48

There as also Evelyn to consider. Granted she wasn't Rio's mate or a member of his Coalition, but she, like Sinclair, carried the future in her womb. He had to make sure she was safe too. He couldn't do that from the deck. Whether or not Sinclair understood all of that was irrelevant. She would just have to learn their ways one battle at a time.

After covering up their heads with the flap of the sleeping bag, Rio pushed one of the wooden deck chairs in front of them. He unfolded the legs on a matching table and righted it up, making everything look as normal as possible. With a little luck, it was so dark that human eyes wouldn't see them.

Turning his back, he headed into the cottage and closed the door.

"I scared," Nahla whispered.

"Shhh, baby. Be quiet. When I tell you to run into the woods, I want you to run. You understand?"

"But Auntie—"

"I'm serious. I don't care what Rio said. I'm not leaving him alone to fend off whoever's out there. Now be quiet before someone hears us."

It was a good ten minutes before Sinclair heard something stirring in the backyard. Despite the trees rustling on the wind, something moved with a rhythm of its own. Blades of grass shuffled under the weight of a person inching across the lawn.

When the screen door opened, Sinclair's grip on Nahla tensed. She didn't want to scare her little girl, but it was too late to put on a brave front.

Through a vertical slit in the sleeping bag and the horizontal slits in the chair, they watched two figures creep onto the porch.

"Wait," a female voice whispered. A sniffle. "They've been here. Not that long ago either."

"Well, they're not here now," Cavanaugh replied.

"We need to make sure they're in there before we torch the place," another male voice said. Sinclair surmised that he waited in the backyard somewhere.

Spotted fur crashed through the backdoor, knocking both Cavanaugh and the female back the way they came.

Rio had changed to his cheetah form, spouting venomous roars to warn them off.

A second—smaller—cheetah charged out of the cottage behind him and went after the other guy. They'd spent the last couple of minutes changing forms and readying themselves to attack anyone who dared to trespass on their territory. Too bad their attackers didn't think that far ahead.

Sinclair pushed the chair out of the way and jumped to her feet, letting the sleeping bag spill on top of her niece. A red gas container by Cavanaugh's feet caught her attention.

She couldn't just stand there. At the same time, she didn't want to get clawed anymore than she had. Still, she had to do something about Cavanaugh. He was the only person who was somewhat her match.

Before he could get his hands on the container, she hurried down the steps and tackled him to the ground. Being the thick man that he was, he kicked her up and over his head, tossing her onto her back.

Cavanaugh clawed through the grass until he had the gas can in his hand. Unscrewing the yellow top, he splashed the gas on the porch. A pungent stench lit up the backyard. Everyone stopped tussling and stared at Cavanugh raking his thumb across a lighter switch.

An insane grin splayed his face as he scanned the yard and found Rio. "This is for Ashley, you bastard."

"Nahla!" Evelyn shouted from the backdoor, terror glazed over her eyes. "No!"

Cavanaugh shrieked.

The little girl had turned into a cheetah cub and bitten the man on the ankle.

Anger tore through Cavanugh. Lifting his foot, he kicked her aside.

That son of a bitch. He might as well have kicked her in the gut.

Pure, unadulterated rage swept through her so fast that it turned into a second skin. How dare that bastard lash out at her child?

Growling through her clenched teeth, Sinclair leapt on the man so fast that she couldn't see straight, let alone recall he had about a hundred pounds on her. Given the force with which he fell, nobody would have known. Straddling his back, she yanked his head backwards and slammed it into the ground.

She wished she had the strength of a were-cheetah so that she could tear his sorry ass apart. She would've gladly taken a bite herself if it meant she could make this poor excuse for a rat suffer.

When she lifted his head to slam it into the ground again, Rio swooped in and grabbed his throat between his powerful jaws.

Cavanaugh screamed while blood spurted out of an artery in his neck. Frantic, he tossed Sinclair off and clawed at Rio's feline face.

Sinclair recouped and pounded her fists in the back of the man's head. Hurt or not, she refused to let that animal live after what he did to her baby.

Savage yowls radiated from Rio's mouth. He meant to kill the bastard, too.

Together, Sinclair and Rio tore Cavanaugh apart. She punched savagely at his back while Rio tore the man's throat out.

Spasm's racked Cavanaugh's body before it went limp between Rio's jaws. The cheetah whipped his head from side to side to make sure. He wasn't taking any chances where their lives were concerned.

By the time he let Cavanaugh go, the silence throughout the rest of the backyard caught their attention. Billie, the smaller cheetah, had the other male trapped with his back against a tree and unable to run with a huge gash down his thigh.

Sinclair had no idea Billie was inside. However, it made sense to have someone in power watch over them while Dante and Sloan hunted down the "Cavanaugh" lead. How she knew it was Billie, she couldn't say. Perhaps she had hung around the cheetahs for so long that she began paying more attention to her instincts.

The female—Rio stared on in shock at the sight of her—lay dead at Evelyn's feet. Marianne, one of Dante's most trusted people had her head twisted to face her ass. Although Hazel could've been in on the whole thing too, he doubted it. Only a power-hungry maniac would use their own flesh and blood to divert the attention away from them. That was right down Marianne's alley.

Once the shock wore off, it made sense. How else would Cavanaugh have gotten such privileged information about both sides? Since he didn't recognize the male, he knew it had to be a part of the Charlotte Coalition.

He got his answer seconds later.

Grimacing, Evelyn stalked across the backyard to where Billie watched over the last survivor. "Brandon."

"D-d-don't," he stuttered. "Please. I'll tell you anything you want to know. P-please."

Fisting his hair, she yanked his head back and glared at him. "You'll do more than talk. You'll die a slow, painful death."

A whimper caught Sinclair's attention.

"Nahla," she gasped. Scrambling off Cavanaugh's back, she found the toddler huddled underneath the deck. The horrendous stench of gasoline defiled her nostrils, but that didn't stop Sinclair from wanting her little girl in her arms. "Come on," she coaxed, reaching a hand toward the cheetah cub. "Come on, baby. It's Auntie Sin. No one will hurt you ever again. I swear."

Hesitant because of the fight, Nahla crept from her hiding spot on her belly, one tender paw at a time. When she went to stand on all fours, her front leg gave way and she stumbled.

Tears blistered Sinclair's eyes. She scooped the cub from the ground and nestled her in her arms.

There was a time when Sinclair thought she'd never get used to having a cheetah for a niece. No more doubts after tonight. Nahla was, and would always be, her heart. After all, she helped save their lives. That was the mark of a true cheetah princess.

Epilogue

Sinclair wanted to tear Rio a new one when she found out he had bought her niece one of the most expensive swing sets Toys R Us had to offer. Was the man insane? Even worse, he bought it for her too late in the year. Nahla had to sit around for months before she could really enjoy it.

The insanity hadn't stopped there. Or perhaps, for once, she needed to think of Mina consulting Mr. Torrance as a blessing in disguise. She granted Sinclair full custody of Nahla. That was the best Christmas gift her sister could've given her.

Though she wouldn't outright admit it, Sinclair's heart broke for her Mina. Somewhere either her wayward sister lay in the streets with a needle stuck in her arm or so drunk that she couldn't even walk. It scared her that someday the police might call and ask her to identify her sister's body. For all the bad treatment she bestowed upon her, Mina finally managed to think clear enough to do the right thing. Although she loved the little girl, Sinclair wished for a resolution where Nahla could have two mothers and not just one. Perhaps Mina thought this was the best way possible.

Standing behind the screen door with a glass of orange juice in one hand, Sinclair smoothed her hand along her swollen belly. Tomorrow would mark eight months. Hallelujah. Though she adored the little wonder growing inside her, she couldn't wait to see what he looked like. Would he have silky hair like his father or kinky like mom's? If he had the sweet temperament like his big "sister" than what more could she ask?

Rio nearly hit the roof when she experienced her first bout of morning sickness. He preferred Donna's hand to some OB/GYN who might want to suck all the amniotic fluid from his baby. Still, they wanted to know the sex. However, they had to switch doctors every couple of appointments because they found anomalies in Sinclair's blood. Seeing as his mate's scent's changed to that of a were-cheetah—she still wasn't one—he could only imagine what her blood work would look like.

Nahla's constant giggles warmed Rio. She loved her new "dad" and never hesitated to call him Daddy. The way he laughed and pushed her on the swing with the wind blowing her two pigtails, he adored his baby girl. As far as he was concerned, she was his as much as the baby growing inside Sinclair.

Nahla let go of the swing at the high end of the arc.

"Girl!" Sinclair shouted. "What have I said about—?"

The little girl leapt into her "father's" arms and hugged him tight.

Sinclair rolled her eyes while the knot loosened up her nerves.

Those two... They had no sense of danger. Nahla had more bumps and scratches on her legs ever since he had turned her. Whenever the little girl fell down, she'd brush herself off and go about playtime as usual. Rough and tough. Because of that, Rio became the main disciplinarian while Sinclair backed him up.

This whole incident had changed their lives, but only for the better. Sinclair went back to work for a few months, but now she was on maternity leave. She couldn't thank Billie enough for watching over her baby girl while both she and Rio went to work. Rio gave up his job at Jungle Kingdom so that he could work at a private practice for more money and better hours. He even taught at the university on occasion. As for Nahla, preschool was out of the question until she had better control over her changes. With Billie being her secondary guardian, that wasn't a problem. She had taken such a liking to the little girl, that she treated her like a *real* little princess.

"Umph!" Sinclair's hand touched the side of her distended belly.

Rio's eyes widened as he rushed to the deck. Placing Nahla on the floor, he reached for Sinclair and guided her to a chair. He gave her the once-over, doctor-type scrutiny. "You okay?" he asked, placing a hand on her stomach. "Is it the baby?"

She guided his hand to where she had hers. "Your son is kicking the daylights out of me. Are you sure he'll be half and half? Because I've seen how much your furry butt can lift. He's got—"

Another thump cut her off.

Rio's eyes went wide again. He pressed a kiss to her stomach and grinned. "He's a fighter, that's for sure."

"I wanna feel!" Nahla scampered to her aunt's side. "I wanna feel!"

"Okay." Chuckling, she took her niece's small hand and held it up to her belly. A light thump came on cue.

"Wowwwwww! He gonna be a chee-ah like me, huh?"

Rio picked her up and placed her on his knee. "Not quite, baby. He'll be half our strength, but stronger than your aunt. He'll probably have some of our heightened senses, but not all. At this point, I'm hoping he's got at least speed on his side."

Nahla frowned. "What good is he then?"

Laughter burst out of both Rio and Sinclair. Leave it to a child to get to the root of the matter.

"He'll be part of your aunt," Rio said, finishing off the last of his chuckles. "Plus, he'll guard your throne, Princess. You have to remember to treat him well if you want him to do a good job. Treat him with the same respect and love that Aunt Sin and I show you and he'll be one of your biggest advocates."

Nahla's eyebrows knitted in puzzlement. "What's uh ave-cat?"

"Never mind," Sinclair said, pushing up off the chair. "Right now, I've got to get dinner started."

Rio placed Nahla on the deck and pointed her towards her toys. When he rose next to Sinclair, he hugged her from behind just under her milk-filled breasts. Leaning close to her ear, he licked the lobe and whispered, "Since we have to pick up your engagement ring anyway, how about we go out for dinner, *mi amor*? That way I can have some time to snack beforehand." A finger flicked her tender nipple.

Shit. Cream had saturated her oversized bloomers. That man was going to be the delicious death of her.

"Mmmmm," he moaned. "That smells like a deal to me." He rubbed his hardness against her backside. "Guess who's happy to see you too?"

"Aw hell!"

Sinclair couldn't wait until tonight.

Author Bio

Marcia Colette is a part-time writer and a full-time Quality Assurance Engineer. She has a bachelor's degree in biomedical engineering and a Masters in Information Technology. Writers such as J.K. Rowling, Laurell K. Hamilton and John Saul inspired her to become a writer. Marcia resides in North Carolina, and you may visit her website at http://www.marciacolette.com